DRIFTER'S END

***Other Five Star Titles
by Ray Hogan:***

Soldier in Buckskin (1996)
Legend of a Badman (1997)
Guns of Freedom (1999)
Stonebreaker's Ridge (2000)
The Red Eagle: A Western Trio (2001)

LA CROSSE COUNTY LIBRARY

DRIFTER'S END

A Western Duo

RAY HOGAN

c.1

Five Star • Waterville, Maine

Copyright © 2002 by Gwynn Hogan Henline

An earlier version of "Hell's Corners" appeared under the title "The Night Hell's Corners Died" by Clay Ringold, first published in a paperback double novel by Ace Books. Copyright © 1972 by Ace Books, Inc. Copyright © renewed 2000 by Gwynn Hogan Henline. Copyright © 2002 by Gwynn Hogan Henline for restored material.

All rights reserved.

Five Star First Edition Western Series.

Published in 2002 in conjunction with Golden West Literary Agency.

Set in 11 pt. Plantin by Christina S. Huff.

Printed in the United States on permanent paper.

Library of Congress Cataloging-in-Publication Data

Hogan, Ray, 1908–
   [Hell's Corners]
   Drifter's end : a western duo / by Ray Hogan.—1st ed.
     p. cm.
   "A Five Star western"—T.p. verso.
   Contents: Hell's Corners—Drifter's end.
   ISBN 0-7862-3253-6 (hc : alk. paper)
   1. Western stories. I. Hogan, Ray, 1908– Drifter's end.
   II. Title.
PS3558.O3473 H45 2002
  813'.54—dc21   2001055577

Table of Contents

Hell's Corners

I

Cord Munger stirred lazily on his chair and glanced across the table. The craggy, beet-red face of the old cowhand sitting opposite was slack, and his eyes were closed. Elsewhere in the Crossroads Saloon only two card games were still in progress, four men participating sleepily in one, five in the other.

Munger leaned forward, laid a hand on the older man's shoulder, and shook him gently. "Time we was heading back, partner. Getting on towards the middle of the morning."

They had been at the table all night, and, when the men who had been sitting in on the game had dropped out shortly after daylight, both had settled down to catching a few winks of sleep. It was regular procedure for the cold-eyed gunman turned cowhand and his leathery old friend—this coming into town each Saturday evening when work was slack at the Flying A and devoting the night to playing poker.

Jed Zumwalt roused, drew himself up, and glanced about absently. Smacking his lips, he brushed at his stringy mustache. "Yeah, reckon we'd best," he murmured.

Munger got to his feet. From his place behind the counter the dozing bartender came to abrupt attention. His eyebrows arched questioningly.

Munger touched the older man with his eyes. "Need another drink?"

Zumwalt, stretching stiffly, shook his head. "Had enough,"

Ray Hogan

he replied, and, circling the table, angled for the doorway.

The bartender eased back, resuming his slump. "See you next week."

Munger nodded. Zumwalt said—"The good Lord willing."—and, pushing the screen door aside, led the way out onto the wide porch that fronted the saloon.

Rubbing at his jaw, the older man scanned the sun-swept street. "Right pretty Sunday morning," he said as Cord paused beside him. "Was we the right kind of fellows that folks around here are hoping for, we'd take ourselves to church."

"No doubt," Munger conceded. He was a dark-faced, quiet man, as spare in build as he was with words.

"Was a time when I went right regular . . . or earned a hiding from my pa. Sure was a long time ago."

"Expect every man has his taste of religion in one way or another," Munger said. His luck with cards had not been good that night, and such left much to be desired insofar as his state of mind was concerned. But the sun felt good, and his ill humor was already beginning to slip away. Yawning, he allowed his gaze to run the deserted street. **Territorial Hotel— Wilcox's Barber Shop—P. Lalicker, Gen'l. Mchdse—Carter's Grocery & Meat Market—Skull Saloon—Davidson's Dry Goods Store**—and a dozen or so other business firms standing shoulder to shoulder along Hell's Corners' main avenue. All were closed, or appeared to be, in deference to the Sabbath, but he could see Button Hays, the youngster who worked for Lalicker, moving about inside the establishment. He needed tobacco and a box of .45 cartridges, Cord reminded himself. He'd pick them up before they rode out.

"How you reckon these counter-jumpers are coming with their idea of cleaning up the town?"

Munger shrugged. "Big job. Can't turn a trail town into a

8

Bible class like they're trying to do overnight. Expect they started realizing that when they found Charlie Shortridge dead."

"New marshal that's to take his place is due in today, I hear tell."

"He better be a good man. Stringer and his bunch are about as tough a bunch of hardcases as I've ever run across."

Jed Zumwalt settled his watery blue eyes on the Skull Saloon. "You figure for sure it was them that bushwhacked Charlie?"

"Who else? Pete Grinnell wants things left like they are . . . wide open, and Stringer's backing his hand. If it goes the way Lalicker and the others want, Grinnell might as well lock up the Skull and move on. Might say he's only protecting his investment."

"Yeah, reckon so. Folks around here sure did get pure all of a sudden, howsomever. Was a time when they wanted trail-hand business."

"Way it goes. Made their pile, now they're looking to get respectable. Let's go."

Munger took a step toward the edge of the porch, then paused as four men pushed through the swinging doors of the Skull and came out into the open.

"Speaking of the devil," Jed Zumwalt murmured, "there's the boss man hisself."

Cord made no answer, his glance resting on Ben Stringer, leader of the gang who made Grinnell's place, and Hell's Corners, their headquarters, his younger brother Virg, and the two who usually sided them, Cal Misak and Fritz Thornburg. The remaining eight or ten that made up the bunch were likely still inside. Stringer and his followers were suspected of many things but mostly of being active in stealing horses that were later sold to the Army, and of being

involved in the occasional stagecoach robberies that oc-
curred. However, no one had ever been able to prove any of
these suspicions. An attempt to do so was probably the
reason Town Marshal Charlie Shortridge had been found
dead on a lonely stretch of road north of town with several
bullets in his back.

"More guts than a Army mule," Zumwalt muttered. "I'd
say they was plumb sure of themselves."

"Can afford to be. Got this town by the short hair. Rooting
them out's going to be a chore for somebody."

"For a fact . . . and I'm a mite surprised that Lalicker and
the rest of the town ramrods didn't come propositioning you
to take on the job." The old 'puncher hesitated, glancing
meaningfully at the low slung, well-worn gun on Munger's
hip. "It's a cinch they know about you and how things was in
the past."

"Just the way it is . . . in the past," Cord said quietly. "Had
my day of gunfighting. Anyway, I'm the last man Lalicker and
the town bosses would want packing their star. Way they see
it, I'm no different from the kind they're trying to run out."

He moved off of the gallery of the Crossroads and stepped
down into the powdery dust of the street. Up at the far end of
town the bell of the Christian Church began to toll, summoning the faithful to services. Idly he listened to the clean,
clear sound, the memory of days—years long ago reviving a
memory within him. There had been a small chapel at the or-
phanage. . . .

"Well, howdy-do and rope me for a cross-eyed horny toad
if it ain't them two high-toned cow-nurses from the Flying
A!"

10

II

Munger shifted his narrow attention back to the porch of the Skull Saloon. The men were ranged along its edge, Ben Stringer leaning indolently against a corner roof support. It was his brother, Virg, doing the talking.

"They's too good to associate with us poor boys in Pete's. They do their drinking and card playing in the Crossroads. You figure they're better'n we are, Ben?"

Stringer smiled, shook his head.

Misak raised his arm and flipped a dead cigarette at Zumwalt. "Hey, Whiskers, I'll bet you're about half as old as Santy Claus. They have to tie you on a horse to keep you from falling off."

Jed moved slightly to avoid the cigarette butt. "Sometimes," he said mildly.

Virg immediately took it up. "You reckon this here's one of them times?" he asked, glancing around at the others and grinning broadly.

"Nope."

At Zumwalt's laconic response the outlaw frowned, pursed his lips. "Now, I ain't so sure about that. You're looking mighty peaked to me . . . you and that there partner of yours, both. Say, don't he know how to talk?"

"You better hope that talking's all you ever have to do with him," the old 'puncher warned softly.

Virg Stringer's eyes spread. "Whooo-eee! He must be one

11

of them there mean ones we hear tell about! You reckon we ought to see just how mean he is?"

Cord Munger's jaw tightened. His shoulders came back slowly as his cold eyes fixed on Stringer. "You're drunk. Go on inside before you get in trouble."

"Me . . . drunk? Why, I ain't so! I'm as sober as them Holy Joes a-marching off to church . . . ain't that right, Ben?"

The older Stringer grinned, nodded. "It's the truth."

Cord's glance swung to Ben. "He's your boy. Better look after him."

A pained expression crossed Virg's face. "You hear what he called me . . . *boy?* I wonder how big the men grow down where he comes from!"

Fritz Thornburg hawked, spat. "Jackass big, I reckon."

Zumwalt reached out, caught Munger by the arm, pressed hard with his bony fingers. "Don't go letting them rile you."

The rigid line of Cord Munger's shoulders softened. "Sure," he conceded, turning to move on. "Got to stop by, see Button. Needing to pick me up some. . . ."

"You ain't a-leaving, are you?" Virg shouted, beckoning to the men beside him and coming down into the street. "Like I was saying, we're aiming to give you some help getting on your horses and fixing it so's you won't fall off. We plain don't want no Flying A cowboys doing that."

Munger halted again. A paleness showed in his eyes, and there was an impatience threading his voice. He glanced at Zumwalt. "That fool's going to keep on. . . ."

At once the old 'puncher wheeled to face Virg Stringer, approaching with the others on a course designed to intercept. "Why don't you all get back to your drinking or whatever you was doing in Pete's? We don't want no trouble with you."

"Ain't no trouble . . . not a-tall!" Virg declared. "Why, it's

12

a sort of a duty, us seeing that you Flying A fellows get home without hurting yourselves. Get their horses, Cal, and bring them over here . . . and shake out them ropes hanging off the saddles. Be needing them to tie them on with."

Munger came fully around. "Gone far enough, mister," he drawled. "Telling you now and for the last time . . . forget it."

Virg wagged his head. "You hear that? They just ain't appreciating what we're aiming to do for them."

Ben Stringer, his features sober, thoughtful, as he considered Munger, dropped a hand on his brother's shoulder. "Let's go back inside, kid. I'll stand for another bottle."

"And pass up helping these boys?" Virg said. "No, sir, we got to do right by them." He moved up to Munger, arms extended. "Here, I'll just hold this mean one tight while you grab old Santy Claus, Fritz, and soon's Cal gets them horses over here, we'll. . . ."

Cord Munger's open hand lashed out, slapped the younger Stringer sharply across the face, rocked him off balance.

"Hey! God damn you, I'll. . . ."

"Move on," Munger rasped.

"Like hell!" Virg yelled, and lunged.

Cord stepped back and swung a hard right to the outlaw's head. The blow missed, grazing Stringer's jaw, only slowing him. From the tail of his eye Munger saw Ben and Thornburg moving in. Their features were set, strained. A few strides away at the hitch rack, Cal Misak had wheeled, was watching with interest.

"I'm telling you," Jed Zumwalt's voice lifted above the scuffing of boots in the dry dust, "you'd best go on your way . . . leave us be!"

Virg Stringer, once again on balance, rushed in. Munger caught him with a quick left, following with a right that

13

landed squarely. The outlaw sagged to one knee. In that same moment Ben Stringer closed—and halted as Munger pivoted to meet him. Misak yelled something unintelligible.

Zumwalt repeated his warning. "You all are asking for trouble . . . big trouble!"

"Ain't never seen none we couldn't handle," Ben declared grimly.

Abruptly he began to stumble backwards as Munger drove a rock hard fist into his belly. He caught himself, dropped into a crouch.

"He's mine, Ben!"

Munger spun again, getting a fleeting glimpse of the younger Stringer reaching for the pistol on his hip. He buckled forward, arm moving swift and smooth. The gun in his hand blasted, sending up a chain of echoes along the street. Virg Stringer, weapon only about half clear of its leather, jolted and went over backwards as the heavy bullet slammed into him, driving life from his body.

Before the outlaw was completely down, Munger, face a dark, frozen mask, had pivoted. His gun, smoke still trickling from the muzzle, covered Ben and Thornburg. Off to the right Misak was motionless under the drawn weapon of Jed Zumwalt.

"Anybody else?" Munger asked softly. "If so, I'll holster and we'll start over."

Voices were sounding at the upper end of the street where several men had come into the open in response to the gunshot. Across the way others were coming out onto the porch of the Skull Saloon, including Pete Grinnell, the gold watch chain with its bear-tooth fob, looped across his paunch and shining in the bright sunlight.

In the stiff, hushed tension Ben Stringer hung motionless, eyes locked with those of Munger. Finally he straightened,

14

doing it slowly, allowing his hands to drift away from his sides. "Not now," he said in a barely audible voice. "Be another time . . . my pick."

Thornburg relaxed. Cal Misak looked questioningly at Zumwalt. The old 'puncher nodded, and the outlaw crossed to where Virg lay. He bent over the man, examined him briefly, and looked up. "Dead," he said, glancing at Ben. "Drilled him clean."

Stringer said nothing, motioning Thornburg to Misak's side. He waited until they had lifted the body between them and, then turning, led the way back to the Skull Saloon.

III

Poised, a steel spring yet coiled and ready to release at the slightest notice, Cord Munger watched the small procession cross the street. Beyond them, on the saloon's porch, Grinnell and others of the gang waited in sullen silence. Stringer and the pair carrying the body of his brother reached the gallery and stepped onto it. The outlaw chief shook his head slightly, and Grinnell and the others fell back, allowing the party to pass between them and enter the building. Then, one by one, they followed, disappearing behind the batwings.

"Jeez!" Zumwalt murmured in a long breath. "For a couple of minutes there I figured we'd be taking on the whole kit and caboodle!"

"Not the way Ben Stringer'll play it," Munger replied, eyes still on the saloon's doors. "Be out to get me himself . . . any way he can."

"Which'll be from the back," the old 'puncher said, and then added: "Let's get the hell out of the middle of this street. Standing here is sure inviting a couple of pot shots."

Munger nodded, dropped his pistol back into its holster, and with Zumwalt at his shoulder cut back to the board sidewalk and out of line with the front of Grinnell's place.

"Guess we ain't done yet," said Zumwalt dryly, and jerked his head in the direction of the general store.

Munger swore softly. Approaching determinedly were

Price Lalicker, Rufe Ackerman, owner of the Crossroads, Abe Florsheim, the hotel man, barber Newt Wilcox, along with several other of the town's lesser lights. Lalicker, who served in the capacity of mayor, was angry. It showed in the firmness of his stride, the set of his jaw. A tall man, somewhere in his forties, he had the arrogant air of a small mind deemed successful by his fellow merchants.

"You know the law on gunfighting in the streets of this town!" he snapped as the delegation came to a stop in front of the two men.

Jed Zumwalt bristled, taking a step forward. "You expecting him to just stand there flatfooted and get hisself killed?"

Munger smiled thinly. "You're wasting your wind on me. Go tell that to Ben Stringer."

Lalicker frowned and looked away.

Florsheim scrubbed nervously at his chin. "Guess maybe he's right, Price. Man has to protect himself."

"Just what he was doing," Zumwalt said hotly. "Was them that started the ruckus . . . we was heading for home."

"No matter," Lalicker declared, recovering quickly. "If he hadn't been carrying a gun, it wouldn't have happened. That's a law that's going to be observed in this town soon as the new marshal takes over."

"Place is going to get cleaned up and made a decent place for folks to live," Wilcox added fervently, bobbing his round head. "We ain't putting up with no more hell-raising and killings."

"Tell it to Stringer and Grinnell," Munger said again.

"Aim to . . . as soon as he gets here which ought to be right about now," the barber said, consulting a thick, nickeled watch dug out of the vest pocket of his rumpled gray suit. "Stage is due 'most any minute."

Florsheim cleared his throat. "Was . . . was Virg dead?"
Munger nodded.

The men facing him had been attending church and were dressed for the occasion—wool suits complete with buttoned vests, stiff-collared shirts and neckties, and the heat was doing little for their comfort. Price Lalicker stirred impatiently, brushing at the sweat beading his forehead.

"Things are as bad here as in some of the worst towns. . . ," Lalicker stated, "Wichita, Abilene, Miles City . . . all the others! Killers walking the streets, making a mockery of the law. . . ."

"Did you have to kill him?" Florsheim asked Munger, breaking in on the distracted merchant. "Couldn't you've just wounded him . . . stopped him?"

A humorless grin cracked Munger's lips. "Man don't have much spare time when another's going for his gun."

"What's the difference?" Lalicker demanded. "A shooting is a shooting . . . and we aim to put a stop to it around here. Want you to understand that, Munger. It's going to stop . . . it's got to! If you can't keep out of trouble, then you're not welcome here. That clear?"

Cord's expression did not change. "Not looking for trouble," he said, and turned his attention to Rufe Ackerman. "I ever start anything in your place?"

"No, can't say as you have."

"I pay my bills in good money?"

"Yes, always do."

"You got some other reason for not wanting my business?"

"Yes, he has," Lalicker said before the saloon owner could reply. "Just the plain fact that you're trouble . . . you draw it."

Cord shrugged, stared off toward the smoky hills to the east. The grass on the flats intervening, green only a month ago, was now a crisp brown under the late summer sun. It wouldn't be long before the leaves of the cottonwoods turned—and he'd planned to move on before then. Now he was not so certain he wished to. Pulling stakes of his own accord was one thing, being forced was something else. "Not that I draw it," he said slowly. "It's that there's always somebody looking to. . . ."

"All the same!" Lalicker shouted angrily. "It's your kind that gives a town a bad name . . . and we plain don't want you around!"

Munger studied Ackerman thoughtfully. "He speaking for you?"

"I'm speaking for the whole town!"

Cord ignored the merchant and continued to look at Rufe Ackerman as he awaited the saloon man's reply.

"Well, it's not that I don't want your business, it's just that if we're going to make this a decent town for folks to come and live. . . ."

"You tell me flat out you don't want me in the Crossroads any more, and I'll find another place to spend my money. I want to hear you say it."

Ackerman squirmed. "Can't very well tell a man not to come, long as he don't start trouble, but. . . ."

"Then I'll be back Saturday, same as usual . . . my partner and me."

Lalicker's face darkened. "Now, see here! That's not the way it's to be. I said. . . ."

Munger's patience was coming to an end. "I know what you said," he snapped. "It don't mean a damned thing to me. Happens I mind my own knitting, cause no trouble for anybody . . . but anytime a man picks a fight with me and goes for his gun, I'm not backing off. Rule's the same in this town for me as it is in any other."

There was a long silence, broken, finally, by one of the men in the crowd unknown to Cord. "He's talking sense, Price. Can't blame him for looking after himself. And we can't be expected to turn down cash business."

"The kind he brings we can," Lalicker retorted.

"Ain't so sure some of us can afford it. Maybe you can. You've done made yours, but there's aplenty of us that need all we can get."

"You want a decent town, don't you? One where your wife and kids can walk the streets without getting hurt . . . or maybe killed . . . don't you?"

"Sure, only. . . ."

"Then you've got to figure on making a few sacrifices to get it. You won't miss his business, anyway . . . his kind. Be plenty of new folks moving in, bringing new money when the word gets out that this is a fine place to live. We'll all be better off."

"Could be, but I just can't see turning a man away because he stood up and defended himself against an outlaw. Seems to me we're flogging the wrong horse."

"Meaning the Stringer gang?"

"Just who I mean."

"They'll be taken care of. The new marshal will see to that. Meanwhile, it's up to us to do what we can to help. We turn our backs on the kind that's made this town what it is . . . like Munger, here . . . we'll be taking a long step in the right direction."

"And there's a chance it'll all backfire and end up wrong," another voice spoke up. "Maybe it's the kind like him that're really keeping Stringer and the others from running wild and taking over. So far he's been the only one they haven't been able to scare off. You stop to think of that?"

"Man we've got coming in. . . ."

"Reckon that'll be him now," Wilcox said, again glancing at his watch and pointing to the far end of the street. The lead horses of the stagecoach were just swinging around the corner of the Walsh place.

"Man we've got coming in," Lalicker continued, frowning with annoyance at being interrupted, "will be able to handle them . . . and in the proper, lawful manner."

Most of the men were not listening but had turned instead to watch the oncoming stage. It rolled to a stop in front of the Territorial Hotel, dust boiling up from the horses' hoofs in powdery clouds. The driver anchored his leathers, swung down from the box, and opened the door. After a moment's delay a slightly built man stepped out, paused beside the wheel, and glanced about.

He was neatly dressed in gray cord pants and white shirt with a black string tie. He wore no coat, but his vest, open down the front, was of silver brocade with the edges of the pockets trimmed with black piping. His flat-heeled boots were highly polished, and the flat crowned hat placed squarely on his head was a creamy white and looked new. The hair showing beneath it was gray, matching his cropped mustache and goatee.

The driver moved up from the rear of the coach and set a metal suitcase at his feet. The newcomer nodded his thanks, squatted beside the container, and opened it. Reaching in he procured a belt and holster, strapped it about his waist, and added a long-barreled ivory-handled pistol. Then, closing the case, he took it by the handle and crossed to the cluster of silent, watching men.

"Name's Sim Bledsoe," he said, nodding to all. "I'm looking for a Price Lalicker."

"That's me," the merchant replied, extending his hand.

Bledsoe shook it gravely, his lean, seamy face expressionless. "My pleasure. This a private meeting? If so, point me to my office and we'll talk later."

"Nothing private," Lalicker said. "There's been some trouble . . . a killing."

The lawman's eyes narrowed, drifted slowly over the crowd, flared when they came to Cord Munger. The corners of his thin mouth pulled down as he shook his head. "No need telling me who did the killing," he said in a low voice.

IV

Munger smiled crookedly. "I see nothing's changed, Sim."

"Not where you're concerned," Bledsoe replied in a cold voice.

Price Lalicker considered the lawman frowningly. "You know him?" he asked, jerking his thumb at Cord.

"From Dodge, Fort Worth, Lordsburg . . . maybe a dozen more towns. Know him pretty well."

"As a . . . a gunfighter?" the merchant pressed, stammering over the question.

Sim Bledsoe studied Lalicker quietly and nodded.

"Then why hasn't he been jailed . . . sent to the pen before now? What's the matter with the laws of this country?"

"Never broken any of them far as I know."

"Shooting . . . killing another man . . . that's not a crime?"

"Not when it's self-defense, which is how it's always been when he's mixed up in it."

"Self-defense!" Lalicker groaned in disgust. "Only a dodge, a way to beat. . . ."

"You find somebody faster with an iron than he is and you'll solve the problem," Bledsoe said dryly. "Only thing I . . . or any lawman's . . . got against him is that where he is there's usually trouble."

"Exactly what I've been saying . . . we keep him out of our town and things'll level off and settle down."

The lawman shrugged. "Could be some truth in that, but

23

there's always the other side of the coin." He turned his attention back to Cord. "What happened here?"

"Man by the name of Virg Stringer started a fuss with me, then pulled his gun. I dropped him."

"Was Stringer that drew first," Jed Zumwalt put in hastily.

"Figured that. This Stringer . . . I know him?"

"Could be. Got a brother named Ben. Ran with a gang that hangs out in that saloon over there . . . the Skull."

"That all they do?"

Munger shrugged, ducking his head at Lalicker. "Ask him. He's running this town."

"Asking you. . . ."

"Don't know anything for sure about them," Munger said.

"Not for sure, Marshal," Wilcox spoke up, "but folks around here'll give you ten to one odds they're stealing horses, selling them to the Army. . . ."

"And taking a hand in the hold-ups that go on," another voice added.

Bledsoe pulled off his hat, running long fingers through his thick hair. "Odds . . . that means you figure that's the way of it, but you ain't got no proof."

"No, sir."

"One reason we hired you," Price Lalicker said, again taking charge of the conversation. "We want them run out of town, and kept out . . . along with all the others of their kind."

Bledsoe shifted his glance to the front of the Skull Saloon. A half a dozen of Stringer's bunch had appeared and were lounging in the shade on the porch, watching intently.

"You sure that's what you want?"

"Of course! We're going to make Hell's Corners into a decent town. Why else would we send . . . ?"

"Only mean I've worked in a few places that had the same idea. Was fine at first, then when things got tough and the squeeze began to hurt their pocketbooks, they all were for changing their minds."

"Won't be the way of it here! We want a good, clean, law-abiding place, one where folks can go about their business without being afraid of getting held up or hurt or maybe hit by a stray bullet."

Bledsoe listened thoughtfully, then shrugged. "Well, you're doing the hiring, so you're calling the shots. I aim to do what you tell me."

"Good. Guess we understand each other . . . and you'll have my . . . our support a hundred percent."

A wintry smile crossed the lawman's face. "Yeah, I know . . . right up to the time when there's shooting to be done. Always the same . . . but never mind, it's what I expect."

Lalicker frowned. "If there's any doubt. . . ."

"No doubt, just talking facts. You got a deputy?"

"No. Never figured there was a need."

"Man who had this job ahead of me is dead. Appears that ought to answer that, but let it ride. We'll hash it out later." He turned to Munger. "Reckon first thing I'm to do is to tell you to hang up that gun . . . or stay out of town. Nobody but me'll be wearing iron around here from now on."

Cord wagged his head slowly. "When I see that includes the Stringer bunch, I'll think about doing it, not before."

"You'll do it starting now, or don't show up on the street again. You living in town?"

"Working on a ranch north of here. Usually come in once a week, on Saturday."

"Fine . . . gives you a whole week to get used to the idea. Next time I see you I'll expect to see that gun missing."

"We're all agreed we'd as soon he'd not come to town at all," Lalicker said. "We can do without his business."

"Don't see how you can keep him out long as he's not

breaking the law. Free country and a man can go anywhere he pleases long as he don't bother nobody."

"Munger's the exception," the merchant snapped. "Wasn't for him and his kind, there'd never be no trouble."

Bledsoe's thin shoulders stirred. "I start keeping people out on that kind of say-so, your town'll die mighty quick. Want you to realize that."

"We don't think so." Lalicker paused, looking closely at the lawman. "You upholding him?"

"Not a bit, and I ain't denying his kind brings trouble. Only saying you can't draw the line the way you're wanting to and make it work."

"I . . . we think you can," the merchant said flatly. "And that's what we're expecting from you."

A fleeting expression of indecision crossed Sim Bledsoe's weathered face, and then, as if prompted by some inner realization, he nodded. "Be however you say, Mister Mayor." Raising his glance, he touched the men gathered on the porch of the Skull Saloon once again with narrowed, speculating eyes, and came back to Cord. "You heard what's been said. You ain't welcome here. I'm beholden to you for that night in Silver City, but that don't stack no hay here now. I've got a job to do, and I'm asking you straight out to make it easy for both of us and stay clear of this town."

Munger smiled bleakly. "You know me better'n that, Sim."

"Ain't no sense you bowing your neck just because you've been told you ain't welcome. Expect there's a plenty more towns close by you can do your drinking and card playing in."

"Reckon there is."

"Merchants here will refuse your trade," Lalicker said. "That'll change your mind."

"Maybe, but they'll have to do it first. I won't take it on your word."

"That mean you aim to ride in Saturday, same as always?" Wilcox asked.

"I'll be here."

"Then you can figure on getting yourself locked up," Bledsoe stated.

Cord Munger shrugged. "Reckon it'll be a chore for you, Sim. No man's ever jugged me yet without a reason."

"You've heard mine."

Munger's lips pulled into a scornful smile. "That's no reason, and you know it. Only the gabbling of a bunch of counter-jumpers turned holy and trying to cover up how they made all the money they've got piled up in their safes."

"Maybe so, but it's their town, and it's what they want," Bledsoe replied evenly. "I'd as soon have no trouble with you, but I've got a job to do, and I aim to do it."

"Then start somewheres else, not with me," Cord snarled, and, pivoting on his heel, strode to where his horse waited at the hitch rack.

V

"Dog-gone, ain't he a humdinger!" Jed Zumwalt said in a marveling voice as they rode away from the crowd gathered around Bledsoe. "All gussied up like a circus horse."

"Good lawman . . . once," Munger said, pointing for the general store. "Past his day now."

"Does seem a mite old for the job. You figure he can handle it?"

Cord shifted on his saddle. "Hard telling. Ben Stringer and his bunch are pretty tough, and they don't much care how they get to a man. Unless Sim's as fast with that gun he's carrying as he used to be, he's in for a bad time of it. Think maybe he is, anyway."

The old 'puncher looked up. "How so?"

"His eyes. He's been knowing me eight, ten years, but he never spotted me until he got up close. I don't think he's seeing so good."

"Then he's sure in the wrong calling. You doing what you said, riding in next Saturday same as always?"

"Same as always. If Rufe Ackerman don't want my business, he'll have to tell me personally . . . not Price Lalicker."

"What about the marshal?"

"He knows the law, that it can't keep me out unless I break it. Won't be doing that."

Zumwalt was silent for a brief time. Then: "Reckon we

28

could go up to Oakville. Ain't but about ten miles farther off."

"Like this place."

"Figured you'd say that," Jed murmured with a sigh. "Pride sure gets stuck slanchwise in a man's gullet sometimes."

"Call it what you want but a man's got the right to go where he pleases."

"Yeah, heard the marshal say that, only it don't jibe with what Lalicker wants."

"Lalicker's just a man with big ideas about himself floating around in his head. He'll learn."

"Likely, only he'll probably get your friend Bledsoe killed doing it. What was that he said about your doing him a favor?"

"Sim's no special friend of mine. He knows me, and I know him. Ends there."

"But you done him a good turn. . . ."

"Same as I would any other man caught in the fix he was. Happened in Silver City . . . he was town marshal. Half a dozen hardcases had him backed into a corner. Didn't like the odds so I stepped in. First time since I've run into him."

"Well, he ain't forgot it, and I reckon it's paining him some to. . . ." Zumwalt's words trailed off. A note of incredulity entered his tone as they drew to a halt in front of Lalicker's General Store. "You ain't a-stopping *here!*"

"Where I buy my needs . . . from Button," Munger said, swinging off his horse.

Jed swore softly. "This sure beats all," he said, glancing over his shoulder. The cluster of men was moving toward the marshal's office. "You and that younker've got a mighty big thing going between you."

"He's an orphan, same as me. Sort of makes us kin."

The old 'puncher wagged his head and came off his saddle stiffly. Hawking, he spat into the dust, following Munger up the two steps to the landing and across it into the cluttered interior of the structure where the boy, grinning broadly, awaited them.

"Sure is good to see you, Cord!"

"Same here, Button. Everybody treating you right?"

"Yes, sir. Was that the new marshal I seen climbing out of the stage?"

"That's him. Name's Bledsoe."

"You know him?"

Munger nodded, then leaned against a counter. "From a time back. Was a good lawman."

The boy nodded his head. "I reckon he'll straighten this here town out plenty quick."

"You can figure on him giving it a try," Cord said. "I'm needing a box of Forty-Five cartridges and a couple of sacks of Bull."

Button turned at once to get the items desired. Zumwalt threw a second glance down the street. The front of the Skull Saloon was now deserted, and the crowd that had trailed Bledsoe and the town's elders into the marshal's office was now filing out, returning to their businesses or homes. Evidently the formal swearing in of Bledsoe by the mayor had been completed, and he was now the official lawman of the town. A single figure broke away from the others and began to bear directly toward the store.

"Better get your buying done," Jed murmured. "Lalicker's a-heading this way."

Munger wheeled lazily, stared off into the street. "Do my business with Button, not him."

"His place, I reckon. . . ."

Cord said—"Do tell."—and reached into his pocket as the

boy returned. "How much, partner?"

"Be a dollar and a half altogether."

Munger counted out the money from the coins in his hand, gathering his purchases. "How you coming along with your savings?"

"Fine. Got almost ten dollars put away."

"Willie still holding that horse you're aiming to buy?"

"Sure is. Says he'll wait. . . ."

"Well, here's an extra dollar I ain't got no use for. You can add it to the ten. How much more have you got to go?"

Eyes glowing, the boy accepted the coin. "Need thirty-five dollars in all. I . . . I can't just take your money, Cord. Wouldn't be right."

"Why wouldn't it? Nothing wrong with one friend helping out another, is there?"

"No . . . only seems I ought to earn it."

"Once you get that horse you can. I'll find a chore for you to do, and you can pay me back that way. Meantime, I'll be watching out for a saddle and the rest of the gear you'll be needing, scout us up a bargain."

Price Lalicker's boot heels rapped against the board floor of the store. Button looked up quickly, his face wreathed in smiles. It clouded quickly as the merchant's harsh words filled the room.

"What're you doing here, Munger?"

Cord wheeled slowly, settling back again upon the edge of the counter. "Buying and paying cash."

"I don't want your business! Thought I made that clear."

"You have now."

"And you . . . boy!" the merchant continued, pointing a finger at Button, "next time I catch you selling this man something, I'll. . . ."

Munger came up slowly. "You'll what?"

Price Lalicker paused, frowned, his face coloring. "I . . . I want him to know you're not welcome here," he finished.

"All right, you've told him, but let it drop there," Cord said in his quiet, level way. "Don't ever let me hear of you taking out your righteousness on him, understand?"

The merchant's features turned darker as anger swept him. "Now, see here! The boy works for me . . . he's in my charge."

"And you've got full count for every dime you put out on him, don't be forgetting that. You once get out of line with him. . . ."

"What's he been telling you?" Lalicker broke in excitedly.

"Told me nothing, but fact is I know your mind. Think you own him, top to bottom. Been in his shoes myself."

"Boy gets good treatment from me . . . same as if he was my own son."

"Just keep it that way and you and me'll never have any trouble," Munger said, and stopped as a tall, severely dressed woman parted the curtain at the rear of the store and stepped into view.

She glanced around, frowning. "What is it, Price?"

Munger felt her sharp eyes drilling into him and was fully aware of the burning hostility that filled them.

"What's he doing here? I thought you said. . . ."

"I've told him we don't want his trade. He won't come again."

"We want you to stay away from here!" the woman cried as if not hearing. "We won't have you in our store . . . not ever again! And you leave Button alone, too. You hear me?"

Cord Munger nodded. "Be a mite hard not to," he said, and swung his eyes to the boy. "Keep working on that horse," he added, winking.

The youngster came from behind the counter in a rush. "Won't you be back?"

"Sure, I'll be around," Munger said. "Don't worry none about that. If there's a time when you need me, you know where I'll be . . . at the Flying A or . . ."—he finished with a side glance at Price Lalicker—"at the Crossroads saloon. So long."

Silent, he returned to his horse, Zumwalt a step behind him. They mounted and, side by side, cut back into the street. After a bit the old 'puncher squared himself on the saddle, removed his hat, and scratched his thinning hair. "Sure does you good to rag old Price, don't it?"

Cord grinned. "His kind always needs notching a little."

"You think he ain't treating the boy right?"

"Expect he is. Just aim to keep him doing it regular."

They gained the edge of town, broke clear of the last homes, and started the long, gentle pull through the wooded hills for the ranch. The sun was warm, and a faint haze lay over the land, turning it soft-edged and friendly.

"I keep a-thinking about the new marshal," Zumwalt said. "I ain't so sure in my mind he can do the job they've cut out for him."

"It'll take a mighty good man."

Jed considered Munger for a long breath. "And I take it you don't figure he's it."

"Was a good man once, but the years crawl up pretty fast, and they sort of hamstring a fellow. He gets to the point where he has to take a job and maybe do what he's told whether he likes it or not."

"He don't *have* to do it."

"Man like him, one with a lot of pride, has to. Reputation counts pretty high."

"Yeah, kind of thought that had a lot to do with it . . . all them fancy clothes and that big gun he's lugging. Ain't needful for a man to do that if he's downright sure of hisself."

"Don't sell Bledsoe short. Probably still one of the best lawmen in the saddle. Far as clothes go, he always did like that kind."

"Not saying there's something wrong with it, long as it ain't covering up the real man underneath. I expect you know that you and him are going to tangle if things go the way they're shaping up."

"Could be. But Sim's square, and he knows I'm right."

"Right or wrong, it plain don't count this time."

"Because of Lalicker?"

"Exactly. He can't let it make no difference to him if he's going to keep wearing that star for. . . ." Zumwalt's voice broke. He jerked to one side, sagging as the sharp crack of a pistol echoed across the hills. "I'm shot!' he yelled, clawing at his arm.

"Get off that horse!" Munger shouted, and threw himself headlong into the brush bordering the road as the bush-whacker's gun again rapped through the stillness.

VI

Munger hit the ground hard. Breath exploded from his mouth, and, reacting instinctively, he rolled, coming in behind a berm of grassy, rock-studded soil. The marksman—or marksmen, he wasn't sure how many—was to his left, he thought, probably somewhere near the butte he could see beyond the brush and shrub cedars. But searching him out would have to wait. Twisting about, he glanced anxiously at Jed Zumwalt. The old 'puncher lay a dozen steps away. He was moaning softly, and the left sleeve of his blue cotton shirt was stained with blood.

At once Cord began to make his way to the older man, crawling on his belly, keeping well down behind the hump. There was more than one bushwhacker; he knew that now; he could tell by the too-quick succession of shots. There were either three or four men. They were maintaining a steady fire. Evidently unable to see their targets, they were laying a continuing barrage into the general direction in the hope of getting in a lucky shot.

"How bad are you hit?"

At Munger's question, Zumwalt turned to him, his hawk-like face was strained. "Arm . . . somewheres," he muttered. "Burning like all get out."

Cord, lying on his side, probed the man's soaked sleeve, slicing through the fabric with his knife and pushing it aside.

"Bullet went through. Bleeding plenty," he said, tugging

35

at the bandanna around his neck. "Got to plug the hole, then get you back to the doc."

"You see who it is?"

"No . . . can make a damn' close guess," Munger replied, tying the bandanna around the wound and pulling it tight.

"Stringer and some of his bunch."

"You think of anybody else out to get me?"

Anger was pushing hard through Cord Munger. There was no reason for the outlaw to put a bullet in Zumwalt. The quarrel was with him; he had been the one who had gunned down Virg Stringer—not Jed. And it was no accident, no mistake. The old 'puncher had been well over to his right and not in the line of fire.

"That ought to hold you for a bit," he said, lying back. The shooting had not let up.

Zumwalt swore. "Reckon so, but I don't figure we're going nowheres, anyway. They sure got us pinned down neat."

"Not for long," Munger said grimly. "Want you to stay put . . . savvy?"

There was a note of concern in the older man's voice. "You going out there after them?"

"Aim to do some circling around. Can't just stay here."

Zumwalt stirred. "Well, I ain't so bad off I can't cover you."

"No need," Cord said quickly. "One shot from you and they'll know right where you're hiding. Don't do anything except keep flat, out of sight."

Pivoting on his belly, Munger began to inch his way toward an arroyo a short distance ahead. Gaining it, he got to hands and knees and, keeping low, traveled along its shallow depth until he had placed a fair-size hill between himself and the butte where he believed the outlaws had laid their ambush.

Rising, he glanced about and got his bearings. He was west of the formation. By swinging around the hill, he should come out below Stringer and the men siding him. Munger's lips pulled into a bleak smile. He was assuming it would be Ben Stringer he'd find there—probably with Cal Misak and Fritz Thornburg, and possibly another of his gang. It could be someone else. But it didn't matter.

Wedging bits of twigs in his spurs to silence them, he moved on, covering the uneven ground in long, quiet strides. He had no time to spare; Jed Zumwalt's wound, while not serious at the moment, could become so if he lost any large amount of blood—and there was the ever-present danger of infection. He needed the attention of Doc Conrad as soon as possible.

The arroyo behind the hill petered out, and he came up onto a small saddle connecting the rise with another of similar size. Again dropping low, Cord climbed to its highest point, crouched, and threw his glance about searching for the bluff.

From behind he knew it would appear the same as the surrounding land—all rolls and dips thinly covered with brush and grass. It should now be to his left. Quietly he resumed the advance.

"Well, reckon we sort of had the same idea."

At Cal Misak's drawling words Munger froze. A gust of impatient anger blew through him at his own carelessness; he should have realized Stringer would attempt to circle and get to him and Zumwalt—just as he had hoped to do with them.

"Keep your hands raised."

Cord lifted his arms slowly. He heard the sound of the outlaw moving up behind him, and turned.

"Ben's going to be mighty pleased to see you," Misak murmured in a satisfied tone. "Was hoping all along he'd get the chance, personal, to square up with you for Virg."

Munger, slightly hunched, waited for the outlaw to close in and lift his weapon from its holster. He could not see the man, only hear his cautious, slow approach. Misak was being careful, not fully trusting his advantage. Evidently he was not certain his prisoner was alone. Cord seized the opportunity.

"One thing," he said.

The outlaw halted. "What's that?"

"You made yourself a big mistake."

There was a long moment of silence. Then: "Me? What're you talking about?"

"You're forgetting there's two of us. Look behind you. . . ."

In that same fragment of time, gambling on the man's uncertainty and immediate reaction, Munger lunged to the side, pivoting. His arm flashed down and came up again. The pistol in his hand blasted through the summer hush.

Misak, half turned, sought to recover as he realized he had been tricked. He was a fraction late. Munger's bullet caught him in the chest and knocked him back a step. His heels caught against a clump of snakeweed, and he went down hard.

Immediately Cord trotted to where the man lay, kicking the pistol free of his clutching fingers. It was a needless precaution. Misak had been dead even before he fell.

Cord, wheeling at once, hurried on along the edge of the hill toward what he believed was the butte. The others would have heard the gunshot and likely would decide to investigate. He'd be smart to get as near as possible, hoping to take them off guard.

He reached the lower side of the rise and paused. Somewhere ahead he had heard the dry rattle of spilling gravel. He dropped low, waiting. Someone was coming—or pulling out. The rattling ceased. Munger hunched lower, an uncomfortable prickling running along his spine. Stringer or Thornburg—or someone else—could be lining him up in their sights at that very moment.

Impulsively he took a step to one side, cut back, and ducked in behind a thick, storm-twisted cedar. At least he was not in the open now and no longer an easy target. Holding his breath, he listened. He could hear nothing. Whoever it was had either moved away, or he had destroyed his aim when he changed position. The outlaw could now be holding off, looking for a second chance.

Abruptly Munger straightened up, a curse ripping from his lips as the quick beat of running horses reached him. Rushing forward, he gained the opposite side of the hill and halted. He was on the rim of the bluff. The outlaws had been directly below him and would have been easy to take. Realizing that, when they had heard him coming, they had chosen not to fight it out.

Brushing at the sweat on his face, he stared off into the direction of the road. There was no sign of riders, only the gradually diminishing pound of two running horses. It would have been Stringer and Thornburg, he was certain of it.

Holstering his weapon, he dropped off the rim of the low butte and crossed to where Misak's horse stood tethered in the brush. This wasn't the end of it. Ben Stringer had declared himself and his intentions, and he'd not get by that easy, nor would the outlaw chief let it end there. He'd make another try. The only answer was to beat him to it.

Taking the reins of the buckskin, Cord swung onto the saddle and rode back to where the dead outlaw lay. Dismounting, he loaded the body across the hull, secured the hands and feet so that it would not slip off, and returned to where he had left Zumwalt.

The old 'puncher stirred wearily as he drew in beside him.

He studied the figure of Misak draped over the buckskin with filmy eyes. "Heard them others a-running off," he said slowly. "Figured you was all right. Cal trying to sneak up on you?"

"Was what he did. I bluffed him out of it," Munger answered, kneeling beside the suffering man and adjusting the improvised bandage. "Figure you can make the ride to town, or you want me to go get Doc and a buckboard?"

"Can make it," Zumwalt rumbled, struggling to sit up. "Just get me on my horse. I sure ain't laying here a minute more'n I have to . . . not with them danged scavengers hanging around . . . waiting," he added, pointing at a half dozen broad-winged buzzards circling high overhead.

VII

With Jed Zumwalt swaying on his saddle, one hand clutching his bloodied arm, and trailing Misak's horse with its slack burden behind him, Munger turned into the upper end of Hell's Corners' main street and pointed for the quarters of Doc Conrad. Morning church services being over, a small, grim cavalcade moved slowly down the dusty way; persons along the board sidewalks came to a halt and stared, features dark and disapproving. Munger raked them with his sardonic glance, asking for no understanding, and offering none.

Reaching the combination home and office of the medical man, he drew up to the rack. Dismounting, he methodically wrapped the leathers of all three horses about the crossbar, and then stepped to Zumwalt's side, lifting the older man to the ground. Supporting him with an arm around the waist, he half carried him into the physician's house.

Conrad was not in his office. Cord gently settled the old 'puncher in one of the leather and steel examination chairs, stepped to an inner door, and opened it.

"Doc!"

"Coming." Conrad's voice floated back from somewhere deep in the structure.

He appeared shortly, wiping his hands on a towel, spectacles pushed to his forehead. Halting in the doorway, he stared at Munger, expression changing slowly.

"You, eh?"

Cord favored him with a twisted smile. "Tough luck, Doc, it ain't me . . . it's Jed Zumwalt. Took a bullet in his arm."

Conrad tossed the towel onto a chair and crossed to the older man's side. Quickly removing the bandanna that encircled the wound, he examined it critically.

"Missed the bone . . . lucky," he murmured.

Wheeling, he turned to a cabinet placed against the wall, took from it a bottle of brandy and a glass, and poured a stiff drink.

"Drink this," he said, forcing it into Zumwalt's hand. "It'll give you strength." He glanced up at Munger. "Who did it?"

"Was no friend," Cord replied quietly. "He going to be all right?"

Conrad nodded. "Lost some blood. Nothing much more serious than that." He paused, glancing through the window into the street. Hanging lace curtains impeded his view, and he crossed hurriedly and parted them. A half dozen curious onlookers had gathered about the horses and the body.

"Who's that . . . Cal Misak?"

"That's him."

The physician sighed, returning to Zumwalt. The dose of brandy had hit the old 'puncher solidly. He was looking about the room, face screwed into a tight frown. The dull glaze had faded from his eyes.

"You kill him?" Conrad asked, beginning to remove Zumwalt's shirt.

"Was him or me."

"Usually the way it goes . . . and somebody always winds up dead."

"You got a better answer to when a man's holding a gun on you, ready to shoot?"

"Yes . . . don't carry a weapon. Pulling a trigger won't

come so handy when a little argument comes up."

"Don't figure you can call bushwhacking a little argument," Munger said coldly, and faced Zumwalt. "Going to leave you here for Doc to fix up, partner. Be coming back in a bit."

Jed bobbed woodenly. "All the same to you, I'd like to be getting to the ranch, do my laying around there. Smell of this place plumb riles my innards."

Cord glanced at the physician. "He be able to do that?"

"Give him a couple hours' rest, he should. You want to wait, find yourself a chair in the next room."

"Little business to take care of first," Munger said, and wheeled to the door.

Stepping out onto the porch, he paused, eyes coolly inventorying the crowd, which had enlarged, clustered around the horses. He recognized none of Stringer's bunch, and, ignoring the sullen looks cast his way, he crossed to Misak's buckskin, freed the leathers, and headed down the street for the Skull Saloon, a block or so distant.

He was a tense, threatening shape in the streaming sunlight as he walked slowly through the ankle-deep dust, the buckskin's reins in his left hand, right hand hovering, like an eagle poised to strike, above the pistol hanging at his hip. His eyes whipped back and forth continually, probing and searching restlessly. Ben Stringer could try to gun him down as he moved in the open—but he doubted it. The outlaw was more inclined to the ambush, to the shot in the back. Cord would take no chance, however.

He drew abreast the general store and let his brittle gaze rest briefly on Price Lalicker, standing in the doorway, watching him pass in silence. Beyond him Cord could see Button, following his every stride with a strained look covering his youthful features.

He reached the Skull Saloon, led the horse to the rack, and, without taking his eyes from the swinging doors, wrapped the reins about the bar. Hand now riding the butt of his weapon, he mounted the porch, starting to cross. At that same moment the batwings parted. Pete Grinnell, fingers toying with the tooth dangling from his watch chain, halted before him.

Munger settled back. Voice low, firm, he said: "Looking for Stringer . . . and Thornburg. They in there?"

The saloonkeeper was staring at the horse at the rack. "It's true . . . you got Cal."

"You're looking at what was him."

There was motion behind Grinnell, beyond the doors. Munger's eyes narrowed. "Better quick tell your friends inside they'd best be careful. Any of them gets ideas, it'll be you that stops my first bullet."

Grinnell threw a hasty glance over his shoulder, shaking his head. Somewhere in the dark interior of the building a chair scraped noisily against the floor.

"Waiting for my answer . . . Stringer in there?"

Grinnell shrugged. "Was here earlier this morning. Ain't been around since."

"Thornburg?"

"Same goes for him."

Cord studied the man in silence for a long moment. "If you're lying, it'd be no bother starting with you."

"It's the truth! They ain't here."

"Then where'll I find them? Know they're in town. Both rode this way after they tried bushwhacking Jed Zumwalt and me."

Pete Grinnell folded his arms across his paunch. "Well, was I guessing. . . ."

"Don't guess."

44

The saloon man's shoulders stirred. "Reckon you'll find them at the house . . . them and a few others."

Munger nodded and, backing to the side of the porch, away from the doors, stepped down into the street.

"What about Cal?" Grinnell called, pointing at the rack. "You just going to leave him there?"

"He's your boy," Cord answered, and continued on.

Not trusting the man or any of those he knew were inside, Munger drew in close to the front of the adjoining building and chose a course along the inside of the walk on that same side of the street. Should any of the men in the Skull Saloon decide to take him on, they would be forced to come out into the open. He asked for no better odds than that.

He moved on, tension gradually lessening as he drew farther away from the saloon. Grinnell would be right; Stringer and Thornburg likely went straight to the house they had taken over and now occupied at the lower edge of town. Once it had been an inn, a sort of hotel, but Hell's Corners had grown away from it, and now, bleak and run-down, it squatted in the midst of uncared-for trees and a riot of brush and weeds. It would be easy to approach. And approach it he would despite the fact the outlaws would have all the advantages; he'd meet and overcome the odds as the moments presented themselves. The thought of letting the matter slide for a more opportune time did not enter his thoughts. Stringer was out to kill him; he wanted a settlement. He would get it but not on his terms. Better that way than letting it slide, have it hanging over his head and always be watching and waiting and wondering about every corner, every dark pool of shadows along a trail. He. . . .

"Hold it, Munger!"

The cool voice of Sim Bledsoe, coming from a passageway lying between the lawman's office and an adjacent building, brought Cord to a stop. He smiled thinly. Sim had allowed him to pass, then stepped in behind. He'd changed some. In the old days it would have been the other way around; Bledsoe would have moved out ahead and confronted him.

"Keep your hand away from that gun."

Cord Munger nodded. "You're holding the best cards. What's this all about?"

"You . . . and that man you killed . . . and the ones you're going after to kill."

"Was them that started it. Tried bushwhacking Zumwalt and me."

"Don't doubt it."

"Ben Stringer's honing to square up for his brother. Aim to accommodate him."

"Forget it. Stringer's my job," Bledsoe said. "I'll stand for no interference from you."

"Quarrel's between him and me."

"Maybe, but I'm the law here, and there's to be no more of this settling things yourselves. Got to be left up to me."

Cord Munger shook his head. "You know that ain't going to work, Sim. Not with me . . . not with any other man."

"Up to me to see that it does. Get this straight, I'm running things . . . and I'll take care of this Stringer and his whole bunch. Won't need any help from you or anybody else. That clear?"

"What you're trying to do is clear, but horning in like this on a private matter's wrong. No call for you doing it."

"Seems there is . . . in this town. They want the law to be top dog. Expect to give them what they want."

"Be hard to do."

"Maybe, but it's what I'm getting paid for. Now, your word's always been good with me. You tell me you'll climb on your horse and ride out . . . leave Stringer and them others to me . . . and I'll turn you loose."

"Can't do that, Sim. Got to get him before he puts a bullet in my back."

Bledsoe swore. "Sounds like you don't figure I'm man enough to take him."

"Not judging you one way or the other, just know what I've got to do."

"Then there ain't nothing I can do but lock you up," the lawman said, and, stepping forward, lifted Cord's pistol from its holster. "Turn around, head back into the jail."

Anger gripped Munger, turned him stiff. He did not stir "The hell with that," he snarled. "You want me in there, you'll have to put me."

"Reckon I can do that, too," Bledsoe said.

Cord felt the muzzle of the lawman's gun jab into his spine.

"Don't make a mistake," Bledsoe said softly. "I'll pull this trigger if I have to. Killing you'd solve a big chunk of my problems . . . and I reckon I'd draw a vote of thanks from the town for doing it. Move!"

Munger pivoted slowly, retraced his steps along the walk to the marshal's office, and entered.

"Through there," the lawman directed, pointing to an open doorway beyond which stood a row of barred cells. "Be the best place for you until I can get done what I've got in mind."

Cord, utterly silent, stepped into one of the cages, flinching as he heard the door *clang* shut behind him and the lock *click*. ❡

"You're wrong," he said finally, coming around.

"About locking you up, or going after Stringer?"

"Both."

47

The lawman's eyes snapped angrily. "May be getting a mite old, but the day ain't come yet when I can't handle the likes of him!"

"Face it, Sim," Munger countered bluntly. "That day's here."

"The hell it is! I've gone up against better guns than him . . . and I'm still living."

"Just what I'm trying to tell you . . . you did it once, a long time ago. This is now."

"No difference. I'm the same man. . . ."

"Don't try wooling me . . . I know you. Hell, you're half blind. Spotted that when I first saw you this morning."

"Can see good enough," Bledsoe said, lowering his head.

"To handle the Saturday night drunks, maybe, but not good enough to go up against somebody like Stringer and his crowd." Munger paused, moving to the front of his cell. "If you're set on doing it, let me side you."

"Something I can't do. Law wouldn't mean a thing around here if the marshal had to call on a gunny to give him a hand. Obliged to you just the same, however."

"You mean Lalicker and the others wouldn't like it," Munger said. "Listening to them and what they want is going to get you killed. Best you handle this job the way you know it ought to be."

Bledsoe turned toward the door. "We'll see. Just you leave Stringer to me. Handled his kind before, reckon I can do it again."

Munger watched the lawman move through the doorway and pull the connecting panel shut. He stared at it for a time, then shook his head. "You're a damned fool, Sim," he muttered aloud, "but I'm wishing you luck."

VIII

Settling on the cot placed at the rear of the cell, Munger leaned back against the bars. He was sweating freely in the small confines of the room, and the anger that still simmered within him was making matters no better. Bledsoe had no call to lock him up—he'd the same as said so just as he had more or less admitted he was doing it because that was the way Price Lalicker wanted it. That wasn't right. No lawman should cater to the whim of some town boss—he should stick by the rules, enforce the law in the manner prescribed by the law itself—and Sim Bledsoe knew that, knew he was in the wrong. He had been at it too long to believe otherwise. Then why?

It came suddenly to Munger. Bledsoe was a proud man with a tall reputation, but neither could stay the irresistible advance of time, and as was the case in most instances he was refusing to admit to himself that he had reached his maximum and was on the downgrade. Even more importantly he sought to hide it from the world and, desperate in that attempt, was knuckling under to please, laying his life on the line in an effort to prove his worth. Earlier, Cord had suspected such was the case where Sim was concerned, but he hadn't given it any deep thought. It was clear now, however, and the realization moved him to pity. He reckoned few men found it easy to step down gracefully from the heights to become lost in the crowds of mediocrity.

Restless, Munger rose and walked to the single small window set high in the wall. Heat was mounting steadily in the cell-block, and that one barred opening, since the door connecting the office was shut, was the only source of ventilation.

The street was deserted. Grinnell, or some of his followers, had removed Misak's horse with its lifeless rider, and now the silence of a Sunday afternoon lay over the settlement. He glanced toward Doc Conrad's, wondering how Jed Zumwalt was making out, and guessed he was all right. He'd not be making that ride back to the Flying A as early as expected, however. Sim Bledsoe, in his burning hope to please, had voided that.

Bledsoe. . . . His thoughts returned to the lawman. Did he actually have it in mind to go after Ben Stringer and his gang alone? He mentioned something about a plan; did such include bracing the outlaws, single-handed, in their hang-out at the edge of town? It would be a damned fool thing for Sim to attempt—but then he had intended to do that very thing himself.

It was different where he was concerned, Cord assured himself. Bledsoe was twice his age, and he was fully aware of his own capabilities—something Sim was misjudging insofar as he himself was concerned. Would he—if he managed to reach the same age as the lawman—have the same illusions concerning his abilities?

Reaching up, he loosened the top buttons of his shirt, fumbling irritably with the small circles of bone. Bledsoe could have at least left the damned door open. The place was turning into an oven. He paused, frowning as he caught the sound of footsteps in the outer office. A current of relief passed through him. Sim was returning—maybe he could talk a little sense into the lawman. A moment later the panel swung back, and he swore softly. It was Button.

Smiling, the boy crossed hurriedly to Munger's cell. "I heard the marshal had gone and locked you up," he said breathlessly. "Couldn't hardly believe it."

Cord grinned. "Expect he figured I'd be better off in here."

Button reached inside his shirt, produced a can of peaches, and shyly handed it through the bars to Munger. "I . . . I thought you'd be hungry . . . might like this."

"Am, for a fact," Cord said, accepting the can. "Peaches'll taste real good."

The boy pressed against the cell. "It true what they're saying . . . that you shot Cal Misak and was going after Ben Stringer when the marshal stopped you?"

Munger, opening his pocket knife, began to cross cut the top of the can, pressing back the sharp-edged metal triangles with his thumb. "Misak with Stringer and Fritz Thornburg ambushed Jed and me on the way home. Jed got shot up some."

"And you killed Misak?"

Cord forked out a peach half with the blade of his knife. "Was either him or me."

Button's eyes glowed with admiration. "Figured it'd be that way! Ain't nobody good as you with a gun! Sure hope when I grow up I can be like you."

Munger stared intently at the boy for a long moment. Setting the can of fruit on the edge of the cot, he shook his head. "No you don't. I'm no pattern for you or anybody. My kind of living is the wasted kind. You're going to find yourself somebody that amounts to something to be like."

"Who'll that be?" Button asked, his voice falling.

"There's plenty around. . . ."

"But I want to grow up and get myself a good horse and

saddle and learn to be real fast with a gun, same as you!"

Munger reached out and laid his hand on that of the boy, clenched tightly around one of the cell bars. "I'll tell you something for true . . . be smart, forget about guns. Don't ever hang one on and you'll be a hundred times better off than a man who does. Nothing but trouble ever comes out of a six-shooter . . . trouble that don't ever end but keeps growing."

"But a man has to wear a gun. . . ."

"A brave one don't. You can settle a problem without one, and doing it that way won't spade the ground for more trouble like using a gun does. Want you to remember that."

Button stirred, wagged his head. "I reckon I just don't understand. Always thought a gun. . . ."

"It's this way. Man sets out to settle a score with a bullet. He kills somebody. Then that somebody's brother, or maybe a friend, comes to kill him. Maybe he does, if the brother or friend of the first man sets out to even the score for him . . . and it just keeps on going like that, one man dying and then another. Can be no end to it."

The boy looked down. "Guess it's not like I thought it was . . . being grown up to a man, and carrying a gun, I mean."

"Being a man's fine . . . if you're the right kind. But there's no pleasure in always walking soft and looking over your shoulder. Men that enjoy living and having all the fine things are the ones who can ride down the middle of a street any-time, anywhere, and not be wondering if there's a gun pointed at them from some alley."

Button said nothing, but simply kept his eyes down while he scuffed the floor with the toe of his thick-soled shoe.

"I want you to be the kind of man that folks turn to for help, not the kind they back off from because they're scared. Asking you right now to remember that."

The boy nodded slowly. "All right . . . expect I'd better be getting back to the store. Mister Lalicker don't know I'm gone."

"Then I guess you had. Obliged for the peaches. They sure hit the spot." Cord took up the can again, making no offer to pay for the fruit, knowing the boy would take offense.

"How long's the marshal keeping you here?"

"Dark, probably."

"You want me to bring you some supper?"

"No need. He'll feed me if he aims to keep me overnight. Better hightail it back now before Lalicker misses you."

The boy grinned. "He won't. I got a way to get in and out of the place . . . through the cellar window," he said, and, turning, hurried from the room, closing the door. Munger grinned, shaking his head. He'd intended to tell Button to leave the panel open, but the boy was too quick for him.

Picking up the can of peaches, he resumed eating. It was hard to talk to the boy the way he had, to set him down so roughly, but it was best. His was no way of life for any youngster to copy. True, there was a freedom of sorts, but there was a price that had to be paid if a man was to retain it—one never encountered by those who made their way without relying on a gun. He'd never wish on anyone, boy or man, the years he'd spent growing up, the times knocking about the land, drifting from town to town while the reputation that came to him by chance continued to grow as he fought to hold his own and stay alive in a hostile world of violence.

Just as heroes were made and never born, few men start out to be expert with a gun; usually it was thrust upon them by some twist of fate after which, to keep from dying, they were compelled to improve that skill, which resulted in an increasing adeptness that swiftly became known far and wide. Then came the challengers, those intent on purposely staking their claim to fame by downing the master and thereby creating an aura of their own. And there was no turning back, no hanging up of the guns, no disclaiming the distinction they had brought. Always there was someone who remembered, or someone with a long smoldering grudge, and in the end it was that utter aloneness in the center of a crowded saloon, or a dark alley, or the empty street of some nameless town and. . . .

Again the sound of footsteps in the marshal's office caught his attention. Bledsoe this time, he was certain. But it was Rufe Ackerman, owner of the Crossroads.

IX

Ackerman, glancing nervously over his shoulder as if fearful of having been seen entering the jail, closed the door behind him.

"Leave it open," Munger said brusquely. "Hot as hell in here."

The saloon man pulled the panel wide once more and stepped away from it. Removing his hat, he rubbed at his jaw. "Hate seeing you in here, but I reckon the marshal figures it's best."

"You mean Price Lalicker, don't you?" Munger said dryly.

Ackerman looked away, fingering his high, stiff collar. "Well, I don't know. . . ."

"Makes no difference. They can turn me loose any time. If the law wants to get at Stringer first, it's all right with me."

The saloonkeeper's brows lifted in surprise. "Glad to hear you talking that way. It's just what we're trying to do . . . let the law handle things like that instead of a man taking them into his own hands. What made you change your mind?"

It was the things he'd said to Button, Cord realized, and the need to stand behind his words to prove them, but his inner aversion to sentimentality would not permit him to state it. "Just been doing some thinking. You're all asking plenty of Sim Bledsoe. Reckon you know that."

"We told him how things were. He was agreeable. Seemed to think he'd have no big problem."

"That was a man talking out of thirty years ago. He's changed from then."

Rufe frowned. "Don't you figure he's good enough to do the job?"

"No man's good as he was thirty years ago."

Ackerman fell silent. Somewhere along the street a child was crying, and back in the fields west of the settlement a meadowlark whistled cheerfully.

"Well," he said, finally, "he took the job with his eyes wide open . . . like I said. We're all hoping he can cut the mustard, because we're going to get this town squared away, somehow." The saloon man hesitated, then: "One reason I stopped by."

"Yeah?"

"Wanted to explain about what Lalicker said. I appreciate your business and would like to keep it. You never caused no trouble in my place, but if your coming there . . . coming into town . . . is going to keep things all stirred up, then I guess . . . well. . . ."

"You'd as soon I'd stay out, that it?"

Ackerman nodded hurriedly. "Glad you understand. We're taking on a big job cleaning up Hell's Corners. Won't be easy to straighten out a place that's always been a trail town, but we're looking ahead, to the future. Town's set just right, at the main crossroads from all four directions. It don't need trail-hand trade, and, if we clear them out, make it plain they're not wanted, decent folks are sure to move in . . . folks who'll start little farms or maybe go into business . . . things like that. We even aim to change the name of the place, give it one that's more civilized-sounding. Hell's Corners . . . even sounds wild . . . bad."

"It was that kind of town that put a lot of money in your pockets."

"I'm admitting that," Ackerman said, wiping the sweat from his forehead, "but times are changing, and we've got to keep up. Cattle driving's going to come to an end someday, what with the railroads stringing out the way they are, and unless we get set for it, we'll get left high and dry with no business coming from anybody. You've been to a lot of places, you know that for true."

Munger shrugged. "Happens to most towns."

"We don't aim to let it happen here . . . getting left out, I mean. We're figuring ahead so's we'll be ready when it comes."

"Which might be quite a spell," Cord said, and added silently: *When it does, it'll be a fine thing for Buttons. He'll live right.*

"Anyway, that's how it is," Ackerman said, and stopped short to listen as the rapid beat of a running horse and the grating sound of iron-tired wheels slicing into the sandy dust of the street filled the room.

"It's the marshal!" a voice shouted. "He's been shot . . . dead!"

A stricken look crossed Rufe Ackerman's face. "My God!" he muttered in a strangled voice and, wheeling, rushed through the doorway into the open.

Munger, grim set, stepped back to the window. What he had feared had come to pass. Sim Bledsoe had overestimated himself, failing to take into consideration the toll the years had exacted from him.

The buckboard whirled up to the front of Doc Conrad's and stopped. Lalicker, Wilcox, Davidson, a dozen other men and a few women and children were running into the street and gathering around the vehicle. As Ackerman reached the crowd, Conrad came from his office at a fast walk. The driver of the buckboard, a man in bib overalls, was standing up, speaking volubly with many gestures.

After a bit, two of the men lifted the lawman's body from the flat bed and carried it into the physician's quarters. The crowd hung on for a few more minutes and then began to disperse, leaving only Price Lalicker, Ackerman, Davidson, and the barber, Wilcox. They continued to converse for a time and then, in a tight group, moved down the street in the direction of the jail.

Cord drew back, settling himself on the cot. They were coming to open his cell, he guessed, to free him at the suggestion of Rufe Ackerman. He'd be damned glad to get out of the cage, collect Jed Zumwalt, and line out for the Flying A. He reckoned Jed had the right idea, after all. It would be better if they did their gambling and drinking in Oakville. It was too bad about Sim Bledsoe, but, as Rufe had said, he took the job with his eyes wide open—and he knew the Ben Stringer kind. He should have handled it differently, but, being a proud man, his mistake had cost him his life.

Cord glanced up as boots rapped across the floor of the adjoining room. There was a brief silence as the men halted for some cause, and then Lalicker, carrying a ring of keys and followed by the others, came through the connecting doorway.

Face set, wordless, Lalicker stepped up to the cell and, inserting a key, flipped back the lock. Munger, hostility rising within him at sight of the merchant and equally tight-lipped, rose and stalked out of the cage, not stopping until he had entered Bledsoe's office. Pausing at the lawman's desk, he jerked open the top drawer, retrieved his pistol, and dropped it into his holster.

"Munger. . . ."

At Lalicker's voice, Cord wheeled to face the man.

The merchant, sweat beading his forehead, swallowed

hard, glanced around at the others as if for support, and then cleared his throat. "Guess you know Bledsoe's dead. Amos Brian found him laying alongside the road. Was shot three times in the back."

Munger made no comment, simply letting the words hang. Wilcox shifted restlessly, his boots making dry, scraping noises on the dusty floor.

"Was a good man trying to do a good job," Lalicker said. "Guess he wasn't up to it."

"You were wanting too much," Munger commented bluntly in a cold voice.

"Maybe, but he was willing to try. Got to give him credit for that."

"It was trying to please you, live up to what he used to be that got him killed," Cord said, and moved toward the door.

"Thought maybe you'd be willing to finish the job. . . ."

Munger halted, turned slowly to face Lalicker, scorn filling his eyes.

"He told us quite a bit about you . . . and, while I don't approve of what you are," the merchant rushed on, "we think you could do it."

Cord's head came forward. "Let me get this straight . . . you're offering me the job of being your marshal?"

Price Lalicker nodded. "As mayor of the town and with the sanction of the other members. . . ."

"Hold it," Munger cut in, a half smile on his lips. "You're forgetting something. I'm the kind you don't want around. Every one of you made that plenty plain to me."

Lalicker again glanced at the men grouped around him. "Well, now, you've got to understand. . . ."

"I understand, all right."

"That mean you'll take the job? Like to have your answer here and now."

"You've got it," Munger said, looking squarely at the merchant. "Go to hell."

Wheeling, he stepped through the doorway out into the street.

X

Both anger and a sense of satisfaction were running through Cord Munger as he strode along the deserted street for Doc Conrad's office: anger because Price Lalicker had deemed him simple-minded enough to accept the job as marshal after what had been said about him, satisfaction stemming from the pleasure he had experienced in turning down the offer. But he did feel sorry for Sim Bledsoe; he deserved better than what he had got. And maybe Lalicker and the others had learned a bit from his death, and this time would not only hire themselves a lawman on the basis of current ability, instead of past reputation, but be more reasonable and practical in their demands on him.

He reached the physician's house, turned up the weedy walk to the door, and entered. Jed Zumwalt, stretched out on a cot in a room to his right, pulled himself to a sitting position, beckoning with a knotty hand. "In h'yar, Cord. Been waiting."

Munger stepped up to the old 'puncher's side. "You feeling all right now?"

"Finer'n frog's hair. Took most of Doc's bottle of brandy but I'm near as good as new." He paused and cocked his head, studying Munger's cool gray eyes. "Don't see no star pinned on you."

"Not likely to."

"Heard them talking in the street about offering you the

61

job. Figured you'd tell them what they could do."

"In three words. You able to ride?"

"You bet," Zumwalt replied, and, throwing his legs over the edge of the cot, rose unsteadily to his feet. "Hey, Doc! I'm leaving."

Conrad appeared in an adjacent doorway and nodded. "Just take it easy. Don't want that wound breaking open."

"Won't be doing anything but riding. It all right if I make you wait till payday for your money?"

"No need," Cord said, reaching into a pocket. "How much?"

Conrad looked surprised, as if unaccustomed to cash-paying patients. "Why, a couple of dollars will cover it."

Munger handed over two silver coins, picked up Zumwalt's hat, and passed it to him.

"You turn them down?" the physician asked, rubbing the coins together between thumb and forefinger.

"He sure did, just like I said he would," the old 'puncher replied, grinning broadly. "Reckon they learned they can't throw a man out one minute, then pat him on the back the next."

Conrad nodded. "Serves them right. Had no business getting on their high horse with you in the first place."

Munger shrugged but made no comment.

"They meant well," the medical man continued. "Just that their viewpoint . . . Price Lalicker's, anyway . . . is a bit narrow. Afraid the fat's in the fire now, however."

"You mean because there ain't no marshal?" Zumwalt asked, moving toward the doorway.

Conrad nodded. "I look for Stringer and his bunch to really break loose now . . . teach this town a lesson, show who's running it."

"Man takes a stick and stirs up a net of rattlesnakes, he

better be all set to corral them or figure on getting bit," Munger said, and followed Jed Zumwalt into the open.

The street was still deserted as they swung into their saddles and pulled away from the rack. Lalicker and the others were still in the marshal's office, Cord guessed, probably trying to come up with some answer as to what should next be done. Conrad was right; Ben Stringer and Grinnell would likely make them pay dearly for their all-out attempt to drive them from Hell's Corners. That was usually the way it ended.

He glanced sideways at Jed. The older man was leaning forward on his horse, half standing, knees bent as he sought to minimize the jolt of his mount's movements. "Keep to a walk, be easier on you," Cord said, hauling in on his own reins.

Zumwalt slackened the pace. "Feels like this dang' broomtail's got a dozen legs . . . all coming down at the wrong time."

"Take it slow. We've got plenty of time to get to the ranch."

"Expect I'll need it," the old 'puncher muttered.

It required a full hour to reach the Flying A. Munger, pulling up in front of the bunkhouse, helped Zumwalt from his saddle and saw him to his bed. Then, retracing his steps, he led the horses to the corral, leaving the older man to answer a barrage of questions voiced by a half a dozen or so members of the crew who happened to be present.

When he returned a time later, Jed had completed the story of what had taken place in the settlement, even to the point of Munger's refusing the offer to pin on the marshal's star.

"Wish't we hadn't rode out early," said one of the 'punchers who had made the trip in with them. "Damned if I ain't always missing the fun."

"Can't see no reason why we can't still take a hand in it," said a squat, dark-faced man called Ollie. "That Stringer bunch bushwhacking a couple of Flying A boys is something we oughtn't to let pass. I'm all for saddling up and riding into town and learning them a thing or two. Besides, them counter-jumpers are going to be needing some help."

"They don't want it that way . . . not from us," Zumwalt said. "They're wanting it all done by the law. Ain't that right, Cord?"

Munger sank onto his bunk and stretched out. "Made that plenty plain to us."

"But they ain't got no lawman," Ollie protested.

"Probably already sent for one. Meantime, they'll crawl into a hole and just wait for him to come."

"If Stringer and Pete Grinnell let them," Munger said. "Bringing in Bledsoe sort of surprised them, I figure . . . and riled them plenty. Like as not they'll be out to do the teaching and maybe make the town forget about cleaning itself up."

Zumwalt twisted, easing his wounded arm in the sling Conrad had fixed for it. "Got a lot of crazy notions, that Lalicker and them others. Seem to think a man ought to take on the whole Stringer bunch and do it without no fuss . . . just take them by the hand, polite-like, and invite them to leave town. They ain't realizing that what they're wanting done's going to call for a lot of bleeding . . . and some dying."

"They know better . . . leastwise Lalicker's smart enough to," Munger said. "Only turning their backs to it . . . got the wagon in front of the team. They won't get that kind of law until after the town's cleaned up, and it's going to take some gun play to bring that about."

Ollie was not convinced. "Still think we ought to ride in, work that Stringer gang over. There's enough of us."

Cord, idly listening to the buzzing of a bluebottle fly in the window above him, stirred. "Best you drop it," he said. "Town don't want us . . . and Stringer's beef is with me. We'll settle it someday. There's no sense in you going to war over it."

The 'puncher turned away. "Well, putting it like that, I reckon there ain't nothing we can do. What about Saturday nights?"

"Spending mine in Oakville, starting now."

Ollie halted abruptly, wheeled. "That dump?" He glanced about at the other riders. "You letting Ben Stringer run you off?"

Cord raked the man with a cool glance. "Not the way of it. Rufe Ackerman asked me decent-like. Told me what they want to do, cleaning the town up and such. I won't hinder them none."

There was that deeper, more important reason, too—the one pertaining to Button, but, as before, he made no mention of it.

Ollie drew out his bandanna, mopped at his face and neck. "Well, if that's the way you all want it, it's jake with me. Never liked that Oakville much, but I reckon poker and women are the same everywhere."

"There ain't no difference," Jed Zumwalt assured him solemnly, and swung his glance to the door. "Who's that a-coming? Sure in a powerful hurry."

The riders gathered around the old man's bunk gravitated to the opening, looking out into the sunlight-flooded yard. After a moment Ollie turned.

"It's that there kid that works for the general store . . . Button, I think they call him. Appears like he's bleeding some."

XI

Cord Munger came off his bunk in a lunge and rushed to the doorway. "Over here, boy!" he shouted.

Button, astride an aged mare, riding with only a halter, veered toward the bunkhouse. His youthful features were drawn, his hair awry, and there was a blood stain on the leg of his denim pants.

Munger caught at the horse's headstall, hauling her to a stop. "What . . . ?"

"They've took over the town!" the boy cried, sliding to the hard pack. "Riding up and down the street, shooting and yelling and setting fires. . . ."

Cord seized Button by the shoulders, held him firmly. "Whoa . . . slow down a mite."

The boy swallowed hard, glanced at the 'punchers lined up in front of the bunkhouse, and then looked down. He smiled shamefacedly. "Wanted to tell you in a hurry."

"Plenty of time," Munger said. "Let's have a squint at that leg of yours, first."

"Ain't nothing. . . ."

Munger dropped to a crouch to examine the boy's wound. It was only a scratch—a grazing bullet had broken the skin deep enough only to draw blood, but it had been a bullet. Cord, eyes narrowing, drew himself upright. "Who shot at you?"

"Don't know," Button replied. "Was when I was riding off

I felt a burning down there. Reckon that's when it happened. Everybody was shooting and. . . ."

"Who's everybody?" Zumwalt asked from the doorway.

"Ben Stringer and Billy Siddons and Fritz Thornburg . . . all that bunch that hangs around Grinnell's. They're sure tearing the town up . . . and I rode out to see if you'd come stop them," the boy finished, looking earnestly at Munger. He had calmed considerably, and the breathlessness was all but gone from his voice.

"You mean they're a hoorawing the place?" one of the 'punchers asked.

"Yes, sir. Started doing it right after Mister Lalicker got hurt."

"Hurt? How'd that happen?"

"That Ben Stringer and about half a dozen others come to see him. Told him he'd best forget about hiring a new marshal because they was going to give the job to one of their bunch. Mister Lalicker wouldn't listen. Ben Stringer hit him on the head with his pistol, knocked him down."

"He hurt bad?"

"Well, he got up after a bit, and he's walking around. Then Stringer said he wanted the town to know for sure that him and Pete Grinnell owned it, so they was going to show everybody. They left, and pretty soon they was all galloping up and down the street, shooting out the windows and scaring folks. They set fire to that old house near the hotel, but nobody could go and put it out because they kept shooting at everybody that tried. I snuck out the back of the store and come here while that was going on."

"Doc was sort of figuring this would happen," Zumwalt murmured.

Ollie shrugged. "Expect you could say Lalicker and the rest of them merchants plain asked for it . . . trying to take the town away from that bunch of hardcases." He glanced about. "We doing something about it?"

"Not our fight," Munger said slowly. "They want a clean town, they'll have to go through the hell of changing it."

"Be some folks get hurt. . . ."

"And there'll be some men die if we ride in there, like an army," Munger countered. "Stringer'll fight . . . don't think he won't."

Ollie spat into the dust. "Yeah, reckon you're right. Not our butt-in . . . and we been invited to stay out. Them counter-jumpers had ought've figured what they was going to be up against." He turned away. "Expect I'd best be getting set to work. Riding night herd . . . me and the rest of the boys here."

Button, his small, round face torn by anxiety, watched them move off toward the cook house for a moment, then brought his attention back to Cord. "Ain't they going to help?"

"Not their fight," Munger replied. "What say we go inside, let me put some arnica on the bullet track you've got. Ought to be tended to."

The boy shook his head. "It ain't no bad hurt. Won't you come?"

"Was told flat out me and my kind wasn't wanted around there."

"But they offered you the marshal's job?"

"Only when they found themselves in a tight they came to me . . . and that was after I'd been told to stay away from the town. You think I ought to give them a hand, them feeling like they do about me?"

"I . . . I don't know. I just know they're tearing the town to pieces and most likely Mister Lalicker'll get killed before it's done with. He's going to try and fight them . . . get up a posse or a vigilante committee, or something, and it'll sure get him killed because he don't know how to do things like that. And if he does, I'll get cut loose again without some place to live. Maybe he ain't all that a pa could be, but he's been good to me, and he's seen that I eat and got clothes to wear and a place to sleep. I sure don't want him to die, Cord."

Munger studied the boy closely. "He send you out here to tell me that?"

"Nobody sent me! He don't even know I'm gone. When all the shooting started, he told me to go hide in the cellar so's I wouldn't get hurt. That's what I done, then I got to thinking about what you said . . . about being a man folks turned to for help, so I climbed out the window and took the old mare and rode here."

Cord Munger raised his glance, stared out over the hard pack to the low, smoky hills in the distance. A cicada clacked noisily in the cottonwood that spread its shade over the bunkhouse, and back in the corral a horse nickered.

Jed Zumwalt moved to the forward edge of the porch and squatted on his heels. "Time like this, maybe you oughtn't to hold all them things they said against them."

Munger stirred at the old 'puncher's comment. "I figure when a man says something, he means it."

"Maybe so, but somebody like you . . . us . . . has got to make allowances for regular folks. They's a lot they don't understand about our kind of living. The good Lord sort of divided people into two bunches . . . them that sees things one way, like Lalicker and Wilcox and the other merchants, and them that knows everything ain't all sweetness and light, like us. They never get around to knowing what it's like to have to live by the gun, to shoot a man so to stay alive, and they just plain don't understand. They figure everybody can live by the Good Book, and they can't see it when they come across somebody who can't exactly go by the rules. They ain't that way, so they figure nobody else should be . . . and there being more of their kind than ours, they try to make us over. Just don't work out, and most of what always comes of it is that they get themselves in a mess of trouble."

Munger wheeled to Zumwalt. "All that means you think I ought to step in and help?"

"I ain't feeling no kinder towards them than you are, but I'm saying maybe you should show a mite of understanding."

Cord's shoulders twitched. "The hell with them, all of them. If I do it, it'll be because of the boy."

"One reason's good as another, I reckon," Jed said quietly. "Point is, something's needing to be done. Them folks is in bad trouble, and you're the only one who can bail them out of it."

Button moved nearer to Munger, hope shining in his eyes. "Will you?"

Cord was silent for a time, finally nodding slowly. "If I do, it'll be because you want it . . . and because Jed there thinks I ought."

The boy smiled, happy and relieved. Zumwalt bobbed his head approvingly. "Figured you'd be man enough to see it. You want to call in Ollie and some of the boys? I'll explain to McCoy when he shows up. Reckon he'll say it was all right for them to ride with you when I tell him what's going on."

"Better I handle it alone."

"Against the whole Stringer bunch? There's ten, twelve of them!"

"Makes no difference the way I'll do it," Munger said, opening the box of cartridges he'd purchased and dumping half its contents into a pocket. He handed the remainder to Zumwalt and looked down at the boy.

"Want you to stay here. Jed'll see you get doctored up and fed."

"Yes, sir," Button answered, smiling. "I'll be waiting when you come back."

Zumwalt extended his hand, enclosed Munger's fingers in his own. " 'Luck," he murmured, "and just you be sure you come back."

Munger grinned. "So long," he said, and moved off toward the corral for his horse.

XII

It was still two hours before full dark when Cord Munger reached Hell's Corners. He could hear the gunshots racketing through the late afternoon well before he reached the settlement and the black smoke plumes, rising from several separate points, that had been visible for miles. Swinging wide, he circled in from the west, taking advantage of the brushy, broken country in that area and thus approaching the town from the rear. Unnoticed, he picketed his horse in the trees a short distance from the buildings and made his way to the back of the jail. After making certain there was no one inside, he entered.

Like the early days in Dodge, he thought, walking the length of the building to the front. Taking care not to be seen, he drew up close to the window and looked out. Riders were pounding up and down the length of the street, firing their pistols at random. The clatter of falling glass as bullets smashed into windows was almost continuous, and the smell of burning wood and a dark smoke haze hung in the air. Over near the barber shop a dog lay dead at the edge of the sidewalk, whimsical victim of some galloping gunman testing his accuracy with his weapon. The sign that had swung from the roof of the Territorial Hotel dangled from a single chain, the other having been parted by a marksman. The old shack nearby that Button said had been set ablaze had gone up quickly and was now only a charred, smoldering ruin.

Other fires still burned—ones at Carter's Grocery, the Bon-Ton Bakery, and Weinberg's Clothing Store, but the flames had been brought under control by their owners who, ignoring the riotous riders, were sloshing buckets of water against the wood siding. Wilcox's striped barber pole had been roped and torn from its pedestal. Now riddled with bullet holes, it lay on the porch of the Crossroads saloon where someone had tossed it. Lalicker's General Store appeared to have suffered most of all. One of the gallery roof supports had been jerked clear, allowing the canopy to sag to the floor. There was not an unbroken window in the building, and a blackened flare on the south wall of the structure indicated that an attempt had been made to set it afire, also.

A half a dozen loose horses were trotting about, heads high, ears pricked forward, confused by all of the shooting and racing about. Evidently they had been freed from the corral at Willie's Livery Stable to do their share of damage by trampling vegetable gardens and flowerbeds. At the far end of town Munger could see a half a dozen or so men standing in front of the church and assumed there were more inside. They had probably gathered there to escape the danger from stray bullets. He could find no indication of the vigilante committee Lalicker had intended to organize—and hoped that was a sign the merchant was abandoning the idea. Such would only make matters worse; inexperienced, ordinary, everyday men, despite determination, always came out second best in a head-on encounter with hardcase gunmen for one reason—they lacked the courage to kill when it became necessary.

Munger dropped back to the scarred desk in the center of the room and opened the drawer where he had earlier found his gun. There were two more pistols, and, taking out the better of the pair, he checked the caliber to be certain it matched that of his own weapon, then tested its action. Satisfied, he thrust it under the waistband of his pants. An extra gun might come in handy.

Wheeling, he returned to the window, eyes touching briefly the wall rack in which there were several rifles and shotguns. Both were effective weapons when facing a mob, particularly the latter. But he was more at ease with a pistol, and, dismissing the thought, he looked again into the street.

Munger drew up abruptly. Two riders were swinging into the hitch rack fronting the jail. He watched them come off their horses and move toward the door. At once he dropped back into the adjoining room in which the barred cells stood and took up a place just inside the entrance. A taut grin pulled at his lips. He was about to have company.

"Might as well start getting used to your office, Marshal Gates," the shorter of the two, a husky redhead, said. "How about making me your deputy?"

Both men were unsteady on their feet, probably an indication that all of Stringer's bunch had been drinking heavily.

"Well, now, Mister Jake Fisher, I maybe'll do that," Gates replied in a broad drawl. "Got to find me a star first, howsomever. Ain't never seen no marshal that didn't wear a star."

Gates swaggered to the desk, yanked open the top compartment, and began to rummage about in its contents.

"You ought've grabbed that'n the old man was wearing."

"Didn't know then I was going to take his place," Gates said. "Ben hadn't told me yet. Sure don't see one here."

"Prob'ly weren't but one. Like as not you'll have to send to Denver or one of them big towns to get another'n. Was I you, I'd order one of them real fancy gold ones with blue lettering and. . . ."

"He won't be needing it," Munger said, stepping into the room, a gun in each hand.

Both men whirled in surprise. Fisher made a grab for his weapon. Munger flashed out with his left hand, clubbing the redhead solidly. The outlaw dropped to his knees. Again he struggled to draw his weapon. Cord kicked him brutally in the ribs. The redhead gasped and fell on his side.

Holstering one gun, Munger plucked the outlaw's pistol from its holster without taking his eyes off Gates. Throwing the weapon into the opposite corner, he circled the desk to where Gates stood and relieved him of his six-gun. "Pick up your friend," he directed.

The outlaw hesitated momentarily, then bent over Fisher and, slipping his arms under the redhead, got him to his feet.

"Into that first cell," Cord said, wagging his pistol.

Gates turned slowly, half carrying, half dragging his partner into the cage. Dropping him onto the cot, he swung about as Munger clanged the door shut and turned the lock. "You ain't getting by with this!" he yelled.

"Looks like I am," Cord replied humorlessly.

"Won't for long! Ben'll be coming by here, and when he does. . . ."

Munger slammed the connecting door shut and locked it, also. Fisher and Gates would do some yelling, he knew, but doubted they would attract any attention. He had purposely placed them in the first cell which, unlike the one he had occupied, had no window, and anyone hearing faint shouts above the tumult in the street would have difficulty finding where they were coming from.

Picking up the two weapons he had taken from the outlaws, Munger removed the cartridges, tossed them into the lower drawer of the desk, and dropped the pistols again in the corner. Face expressionless, he crossed once more to the window. He'd lowered the odds a little, but not by much; there were still seven or eight Stringer men, plus Ben himself as well as Pete Grinnell, on the loose.

He must act soon—before dark. Under cover of night the outlaws would probably split up and prowl the town in singles or pairs, looting and doing what they willed with anyone unfortunate enough to encounter them. Separated, bringing them down would be more difficult.

He couldn't see Ben Stringer among the half a dozen riders in sight and guessed he was inside the Skull Saloon with Grinnell. They would be savoring their victory in those moments, congratulating each other on their success in blocking the efforts of Lalicker and the other townsmen to clean up Hell's Corners and their ability to take it over with such ease.

Like as not they would be laying plans as to how they would proceed, how they would force men like Price Lalicker and Davidson and others to bend to their will—or tell them to move on, either abandoning their property and possessions or selling out at a price so ridiculously low that it would be laughable were the offer not made at the point of a gun. It was an old story. Cord Munger had watched it happen a half a dozen times in his life—the strong and the savage simply overwhelming by sheer force and getting their way with men, not necessarily weak, who refused violence as an answer, and then, fearing for the safety of their families and themselves, they took the only road open to them.

That was where they made a mistake, Munger believed—that knuckling under, that bowing down and going to their knees before the Stringers of the world. A man had to fight for what he got—then fight to keep it. Better that he die than just hand it over to somebody like Pete Grinnell or Ben Stringer. He guessed that maybe there was the difference Jed Zumwalt was trying to make him see. He was looking at it from his viewpoint, figuring life the way he thought it should be lived;

too, he had no family to worry about and keep from harm. Lalicker did, just as all the others who were trying to clean up the town—and Button was a part of that, the boy was Price Lalicker's family.

Munger's jaw hardened. Drawing both pistols, he checked the cylinders, making sure both were fully loaded. Then, holding them at his sides, he stepped through the doorway onto the small landing that fronted the jail. Glancing up and down the street, hazy with drifting dust and smoke, Cord placed his shoulders to the wall of the building and, raising both weapons, fired into the air.

XIII

Halted in front of the Bon-Ton Bakery, the four outlaws turned, looking at Munger. For a long breath they stared, surprise blanking their features, and then, as recognition came to them, they yelled, wheeled as a single body, and with guns blazing spurred directly for him. Munger leveled his pistols, aiming at the two men in the center of the oncoming, abreast line. Bullets were thudding into the wall behind him. He felt the heat of a slug as it brushed his neck. Dead calm, he triggered his weapons.

The two outlaws jolted, threw up their arms, and began to fall from the saddle. The men to either side of them stiffened abruptly, hauled back on their horses, and came to a rearing halt. Beyond them, at the far end of the street, Cord could see three more riders. They had paused, watching.

Grim, pistols still leveled, Munger remained silent as the pair he'd shot fell heavily to the ground. "Throw down your guns," he ordered in a cold voice.

The outlaws only stared, shocked into numbness by the sudden turn. Expressionless, Munger fired the gun in his right hand. The man it was trained on yelled, clawing at his arm as the bullet ripped into him.

"I need to tell you again?"

The wounded man, cursing steadily, wagged his head, dropped his weapon. The remaining outlaw, features drawn, eyes sullen, followed suit slowly.

"Climb off those horses . . . walk over here . . . easy."

Both complied, the injured one throwing a leg over the saddle horn awkwardly, sliding off the hull as he clutched his shattered arm.

"Kick those irons over to me . . . then get inside."

The outlaws obeyed, toeing their surrendered weapons to where Munger stood, and then stomping sourly into the marshal's office. They halted while Cord opened the door to the cell-block, watching his every move with narrowed, hating eyes. That done, at a motion from the weapon in his hand they filed into the adjoining room and entered the center cage. Munger slammed the grill closed, locked it, and stepped back as the first two men jailed crowded up to the separating bars. As he wheeled and reentered the office, he heard Fisher's voice, paused.

"What the hell's going on? What was that shooting right outside? We thought it was Ben coming after us."

The wounded outlaw only shook his head. The man with him swore deeply. "He's loco . . . plumb loco! Just stood there flat-footed and blasted Red and Dave right off'n their saddles while all of us was coming at him, shooting. Put a slug in Bud when he didn't move quick enough."

"What about Ben? Where the hell is he?"

"How the devil should I know? Ain't in the street."

"Well, I reckon we'll sure be hearing from him now," Fisher said. "Don't figure he knew we was in here, but after that ruckus he'll catch on mighty quick that something's gone wrong and. . . ."

The voice of Bud, the wounded man, cut in on the redhead's words. "Hey, you out there . . . Munger. I'm needing the doc, bad. This here arm of mine's. . . ."

Cord kicked the door shut and locked it again. The odds were improving. He had cut Ben Stringer's force to about half strength, and the next move would be up to the outlaw chief. There would be no need now to dig them out; they'd come to him. Stringer couldn't afford to let it be any other way.

Crossing to the office entrance, he threw his glance up and down the street. The dead outlaws lay where they had fallen, their horses standing patiently nearby. He'd be condemned by Price Lalicker and the rest of the town elders for killing them, he supposed, but it didn't matter—no explanation he could give would ever make them understand. Men such as those lying there in the dust respected but one thing—violence. It was the code they lived and died by.

The haze-filled, littered strip, hemmed in on either side by its ravaged store buildings, was otherwise deserted. His pistol reloaded and holstered, the spare tucked under his waistband, Munger stepped into the open, collected the weapons of the fallen outlaws and those dropped by the pair he'd made prisoner, and carried them back into the office. Removing the cartridges, he added them to the supply he'd dropped into the desk drawer and tossed the heavy guns into the corner with the others.

The sound of subdued voices came to him, and, stepping to the window, he looked out. His appearance had evidently had a reassuring effect on some of the townspeople. Three men and a woman were standing near the outlaws, staring down at them while talking in low tones. Farther down he could see Doc Conrad coming from the direction of his quarters.

As he watched in dry amusement, Wilcox and Davidson, and then Rufe Ackerman, joined the physician, and all headed his way. Others began to show, emerging from the passageways that separated some of the buildings as well as from the structures themselves.

He frowned. Where was Ben Stringer—Grinnell—the rest

of the outlaw gang? It was folly to believe they had given up and pulled out, as some of the people in the street probably thought.

"Some of you men . . . carry these bodies over to my place. Can't leave them lying here."

It was Conrad's voice. Munger moved to the back wall of the room and leaned against it. Folding his arms, he crossed one booted foot over the other and waited. A moment later Conrad, trailed by the men who had joined him, pushed through the doorway into the room. Ackerman crowded forward, hand extended, a smile on his lips.

"Was the damnedest piece of nerve I've ever seen!" he exclaimed. "Sure put that bunch down hard!"

Cord shrugged. Being complimented for killing a man regardless of whom he might be always stirred a vague anger through him.

"Glad you changed your mind, decided to take the job," Davidson said in his gruff way. "Don't know what we done. . . ."

"You didn't," Munger cut in shortly. "Was the boy."

The men exchanged puzzled glances. Conrad said: "The boy . . . you mean Button Hays, the kid that's staying with the Lalickers?"

Cord nodded. "Rode out to the ranch, told me what Stringer was up to . . . asked me to help."

"He done that?" Wilcox asked.

Cord studied the barber coldly. "Button's a good boy . . . and he's got guts. That some kind of news to you?"

"No, only sort of surprises me."

Davidson bobbed his head, rubbed his hands together. "Sure . . . sure, he did a good thing, and we're grateful to him. You think the trouble's all over?"

"No chance."

The merchant looked startled. "You mean there'll be more shooting?"

"Stringer's not about to give up yet. I'm just waiting for his next move. I've got four of his bunch locked up, and there's those two dead ones you just hauled off. Hamstrings him some but it won't stop him."

Ackerman moved to the connecting door, tried it, and found it locked. He turned away, his interest not sufficient to press his curiosity further.

Wilcox's face was taut. "Then you ain't pulling out on us? You're aiming to see it through?"

"Told the boy I'd straighten things out. Just what I'll do."

The barber relaxed, smiled. "Takes a load off us all. Want you to know we appreciate. . . ."

"Doing it for Button, not you," Munger said bluntly. "Far as I'm concerned, Stringer could have this town, but the boy needs a home and Lalicker's giving it to him."

The men were silent at the rebuff. Finally Conrad said: "Anybody seen Price?"

There was a general shaking of heads. Rufe Ackerman said: "Expect he's working inside his place. That bunch went in there and tore things up something fierce. Hit him hardest of all."

"Could be doing a lot of work for nothing, if it ain't over yet," Davidson said glumly.

Conrad glanced through the window into the street. The men carrying the two outlaws had reached the office and were turning into the yard. He came about, facing Munger. "Well, what do you think we ought to do?"

"What you're doing . . . stay inside out of the way."

"You think they're through raising hell with the town?"

Cord nodded. "For a time . . . at least until they've dealt with me. I'm the one they'll work on now. If they come out on

82

top, you can look for things to get worse."

Ackerman rubbed at his jaw. "You want some help? Ain't none of us no great shakes with a gun, but, if you say so, we'll do what we can. Just tell us what."

A half smile pulled at Cord Munger's lips. That was the heart of the problem—none of them knew how to face another man, a cold-blooded killer such as Ben Stringer and the men who ran with him; it was quick suicide for any of them. "Best you leave it up to me. If I don't make it, then'll come the time to grab your shotguns and rifles and make a stand . . . if you think you ought."

"You figure you've got a chance?" Wilcox asked. "Know you've done plenty good so far, but. . . ."

"That's a fool question!" Conrad snapped before Munger could reply. "He's here, isn't he?"

"I know, but. . . ."

The barber's words trailed off as the rapid pound of boot heels in the street drew all their attention. Davidson walked to the door, glanced out.

"It's Ed Murdo," he said without turning. "Must be something wrong."

Davidson pulled back from the entrance, allowing Murdo, a small, thin man, breathless from his running, to enter.

"It's Lalicker . . . his wife," he said between gasps. "Stringer's grabbed them. Holding them prisoners. Said to tell you if you wanted them to keep on living, you was to turn loose them boys of his you've got locked up!"

XIV

Conrad swore into the stunned hush that had fallen across the room. He reached out and grasped Murdo by the shoulder. "They hurt any . . . you know?"

The small man sleeved the sweat from his sun-dark face, shook his head. "Never said. Was one of Stringer's bunch . . . the one they call Billy Siddons. Stopped me when I was crossing the street below Jamison's. Told me to give that word to you . . . you, I mean," he added, looking at Cord Munger.

"That all he said?"

"No, you're to take them over to Grinnell's saloon and stand them on the porch so's everybody can see them getting turned loose. You got to do it inside one hour."

"Guess that blows everything sky high," Conrad said heavily. "We give in to Stringer's demands, it'll be the same as handing the town over to him as a gift."

"But if we don't, they'll murder Price and Blanche!" Davidson cried, his voice filled with alarm. "We've got to tell Stringer we'll do it!"

"Damn it, I know that!" the physician snapped. "What I'm saying is we've got no way to go now but down."

Rufe Ackerman, his eyes not straying from Munger since Murdo had completed his message, said: "What's your thinking on this, Cord?"

"Changes nothing as far as I'm concerned . . . except maybe what I'll have to do."

"You mean you're going right ahead . . . fight them . . . risk the Lalickers . . . their lives?" Davidson demanded in a strangled tone.

"Seems the choice ought to be ours," Wilcox said. "It's our town, and it's us that's getting hurt." He paused, looking directly at Munger. "It being that it was Price that chewed you out and ordered you to stay clear of here . . . that wouldn't have nothing to do with you going right on, would it? Lead pipe cinch you ain't no friend of his."

Munger's shoulders stirred. "How I feel about him's got nothing to do with it. Fact is, I don't want anything happening to him or his woman. They're giving the boy a home. That's what counts with me."

Ackerman's head came up. "Then you think we ought to do what Stringer says?"

"You do that and you can wave good bye to your town . . . just pick up your hat and move on. That's about all they'll let you get out with."

"Seems to me you're talking in circles," Davidson said with a sigh. "How can . . . ?"

"I aim to play along with them."

"*You* aim to!" Davidson shouted. "By God, we've got some say in this!"

"Ease up, Joe," Ackerman broke in quickly, nodding to Munger. "Seems you've got some idea how you can get the Lalickers turned loose and still not give in to Ben Stringer."

"And Grinnell," Cord said. "Don't think you people realize he's in this deep as Stringer. That because he's a merchant, same as you?"

"He might be in business here, but he's not one of us," Wilcox said. "We all figure he's a rotten apple, but we let things ride where he was concerned because he catered to the toughs, kept them out of the decent places like Rufe's."

Munger's features were inscrutable. "Just be sure of where he stands," he murmured.

"What kind of idea you got?" Ackerman pressed, evidently anxious to get off the subject.

"Whatever it is," Murdo warned, "you'd best get at it. They only give you one hour."

"Just what I figure to do soon as you all get out of here, hole up."

"You're not letting us in on it?" Davidson said, rubbing at his jaw nervously.

Munger shook his head. "You want the Lalickers safe . . . and you want your town back. Happens that jibes with what I want, too . . . on account of the boy. I'll be doing it for his sake, nothing else. All I want from you . . . and everybody else around here . . . is to keep out of my way."

Davidson continued to claw at his face. "I . . . I don't know about this. Way he feels about Price. . . ."

"Already said that doesn't make any difference," Conrad said impatiently. "And it makes sense to me. If he wants to see Button Hays looked after, he sure won't do something to hurt him."

"But what guarantee've we got he'll . . . ?"

"Guarantee!" the physician exploded. "What guarantee you got that you'll live to reach your house the way things are? Far as I'm concerned, his word's good enough for me."

"Same here," Ackerman said, as Wilcox nodded.

Davidson turned away, walked to the window, and glanced into the empty street. "I think we're a pack of fools," he said wearily. "Seems we're putting our faith in the same kind of a man we're fighting to get rid of."

Rufe Ackerman wheeled hurriedly. "Now, wait a damn' minute, Joe. . . ."

Munger waved the saloon man into silence. "Maybe that's

what it adds up to from where you're standing," he said coldly, "but, like it or not, that's what you've got. I'm doing what I figure is needful . . . and I'm starting pretty quick."

Conrad bobbed his head. "And I take it you want us out of here, and off the street."

Cord made no answer, continuing to lean against the wall. Behind it the mumbling of the outlaws in their cells was a low drone.

Ackerman turned, threw out his arms to encompass Wilcox and Joe Davidson, and propelled them toward the door. Conrad, motioning at Murdo to follow, smiled at Munger. "It's your fandango," he said, "and I, for one, am thanking you. Good luck."

The only acknowledgment of the physician's wish was a slight flicker in Munger's brooding gray eyes.

XV

Cord Munger was a man with few illusions—with none insofar as his ability to survive a head-to-head shoot-out with Stringer and his entire gang was concerned. He knew he could account for more than a few of them before it was over, but the sheer power of too many guns would eventually cut him down. His death, unless Stringer and Pete Grinnell and all of the hardcases who sided him also died, would go for nothing. All had now tasted the heady wine of absolute power, of owning a whole town where fear and force combined to grant their every desire, and the thought of forfeiting it was something they would never accept. He could expect a bloody fight to the finish.

In deep thought, the plan he had sketchily formulated when Murdo had first delivered Ben Stringer's ultimatum now being fleshed out in his mind, Munger pulled away from the wall and, crossing to the open doorway, looked into the street. It was softening now, turning gentle as the sun, sinking toward the high hills in the west, spreading a pale amber glow over the land.

The chances were the outlaws held Price Lalicker and his wife in the old inn where they quartered. Storming it, even if he had sufficient men to back him, was, of course, out of the question since Stringer would have taken precautions against such a move. It was no part of his plan, anyway; he could only win by outsmarting the outlaws—and to do that he must play a lone hand.

He had made that choice at the beginning, when Button Hays had first come to the ranch with his plea, and riding in alone had been no act of bravado. He simply preferred it that way; it left him free to act on his own, unhampered by consideration for others, accountable only to himself and able to adapt to any swiftly changing situation instantly without having to warn anyone assisting him.

The street was clear—and time was slipping away. He had a half hour, perhaps a bit less remaining in which to make his move. He'd best set things in motion, otherwise Conrad and the others might think, as Joe Davidson had implied, that he was throwing Lalicker and his wife to the wolves in order to satisfy his dislike for the merchant. Not that it mattered to Cord Munger particularly what any man thought, but it irked him, nevertheless, when he realized that Davidson believed he could stoop so low. He reckoned old Jed Zumwalt had been right when he said men such as Davidson had no understanding of those who were not of the same mind and pattern as they.

Turning, he moved along the narrow hallway that ran the length of the jail to its rear entrance. Stepping out into the warm reflected sunlight, he veered right into the littered alleyway that ran behind the structures lining the west side of the street, and walked quickly to the back of the Skull Saloon.

The town lay hushed beyond the structure, and, pressing up close to the door, he listened. He could hear an occasional voice and the *clink* of glasses. Drawing back, he swept the surrounding area with a glance to reassure himself that he had no witnesses, and then stepped carefully up onto the board landing. Keeping to its edge in order to avoid any squeaking, he quietly closed the iron hasp that secured the door to its frame and engaged the thick padlock that hung from a small chain nearby. He nodded in satisfaction; the door was effectively locked—the only exit from Grinnell's saloon would be by the front.

Moving off the landing, he began to collect a quantity of loose paper, cast-off boards, odds and ends of dry brush and other trash that was scattered close by, and piled it on the stoop and against the door. When it was sufficient for a quick, hot blaze, he turned, heading back to the jail. That part of his plan, barring someone's unexpected arrival and desire to enter the Skull Saloon by the rear, was complete. He had little fear of that, however; the outlaws were all under cover as were the townspeople.

Returning to the marshal's office, he picked up the pistols he had tossed into the corner, checked them once again to be certain there were no cartridges in any of them, and then dumped the lot into a small basket he found behind the desk. Making a final examination of his own weapons to assure himself of their readiness, he opened the door to the adjoining room and entered. Talk among the outlaws ceased immediately, but as he stepped up to the cages, turned the locks, and drew back the grills, Fisher, the redhead, laughed. "See? What'd I tell you? Knew Ben wouldn't leave us in here for long."

"All of you . . . move out," Munger ordered, backing up to the wall, pistol leveled.

The outlaws began to file out, the wounded one nursing his arm tenderly.

Fisher grinned at Munger. "Reckon you know now who's the bull of the woods around this burg."

Cord gave him no answer but simply motioned them on into the office. When they had reached the desk, he said: "Hold it there."

The outlaws halted, wheeling to him angrily. Fisher said: "What's going on? Ain't you turning us loose?"

"Got a deal with Stringer. I'm trading you for Lalicker and his wife."

The redhead stared, then slapped his leg and grinned broadly. "That what he done . . . grabbed them off?"

Cord ignored the question. "Plan is for me to march you over to Skull. You're to wait on the porch until he shows up with the Lalickers. When I see him let them go and get out of the way, I'll holster my gun. Any one of you that don't do exactly what I've said or makes a wrong move . . . dies. That clear?"

Fisher's mouth pulled down into a scornful smile. "Hell, you wouldn't try nothing like that. Be dead yourself."

"Maybe . . . but whichever one of you it was that made the mistake'll go sliding into hell with me."

The outlaws considered him sullenly. Finally the redhead nodded. "All right, we savvy. Them our guns in that basket?"

"You get them when the deal's finished . . . when Lalicker and his woman are turned loose."

The redhead bristled. "What's wrong with right now? We ain't going to be using them . . . not with you standing over us with both your hands filled."

"We're playing it my way," Munger said coolly. "Everybody got it straight? Hate to kill a man just because he didn't understand."

"We got it," Fisher muttered. "What happens when the swapping's done?"

"Be up to Stringer . . . mostly."

"You pulling out? That part of the deal?"

"I'll still be around."

Fisher bobbed his head. "Be smart was you to move on, 'cause it sure ain't going to be healthy for you. Ben don't forget the jaspers that cross him up, and you sure done that . . . shooting down Virg and Cal and getting in his way."

"Ben Stringer's problem," Munger said. "When you step out that door, stay together. Walk shoulder to shoulder . . . and don't be forgetting that this thing ain't over for you until the Lalickers are out of the way."

"Sure . . . we got it."

"Something else. You see any of your bunch lining up on me before the trading's done, you'd better tell them to hold off. From where I'll be standing, right behind you, I can cut all four of you down before I'm dead."

One of the outlaws wheeled impulsively, his features strained. "How we going to know? Some of the boys maybe are hiding and we won't see them . . . won't even know if they're throwing down on you!"

"Might be smart to sing out once we're in the street, warn them to hold off. And don't make a sudden move like that again unless you're tired of living."

The rider swallowed hard and glanced at Fisher. "You do what he says, Jake . . . yell out, make them back off. They'll listen to you."

Fisher gave it a moment's thought, brushing at the sweat on his face. "Yeah, reckon it would be smart. Right now, this bird's holding all the good cards, but I'll tell you this, mister," he added, pointing a finger at Munger, "when it's done with, you'd better make yourself mighty scarce around here because I'm coming looking for you! I ain't ever took this kind of shoving around from no man, and I ain't starting now."

"Up to you," Munger said with a dry smile.

Moving to the desk, he took up the basket of guns and cradled it under his left arm. "Let's go," he said, motioning to the door with his pistol.

XVI

The outlaws filed hesitantly into the empty street.

"String out . . . like I said," Munger snapped, and waited until they had formed a four abreast, shoulder-to-shoulder line. "Now . . . down the middle of the street . . . slow."

The men moved forward, eyes anxiously searching the store fronts, the passageways, the roofs. Tense, his own senses keyed to sharp alert, Cord stepped in behind them quickly, placing them between him and Pete Grinnell's.

"Ben . . . you other boys!" Fisher's words echoed through the hush. "Hold your fire! Don't go trying to pick off this bird . . . you'll get us all killed! Hear?"

There was no reply, only the querulous barking of a dog at the far end of town roused by the shouting. The outlaws began to slow, to hold back.

"Keep moving!" Munger warned.

It was as if he were sitting in on a high-stakes poker game and had played his top card—the fear he had instilled in the four men—and now he waited to see if some unknown opponent would play one higher.

Gates, walking beside Fisher, half turned. "Nobody answered," he mumbled. "Try again."

The redhead sang out his appeal once more, but was greeted with only silence. He brushed nervously at his ruddy face, glaring at Munger.

"God damn you . . . putting me through this! I aim to square up with you when it's over."

"If you live through it," Cord replied softly.

They reached the halfway point between the jail and the Skull Saloon. No one had appeared along the street, and he had noticed no guarded movement behind any of the windows. But there were many eyes watching, he knew, some in fear, some in hope, and others searching for the opportunity to cut him down and leave him dying in the dust. Evidently that part of Stringer's gang that was inside Grinnell's had heard Jake Fisher's words and were heeding them, but Cord was taking nothing for granted. With each measured step his glance continued to probe ceaselessly, overlooking nothing, ready to act at the first sign of a would-be bushwhacker.

The outlaws reached the edge of the porch fronting the Skull Saloon and halted. Munger could see the relief flow through them like a rolling wave of water, and the old cocksure arrogance return.

Fisher turned about, extending his hand. "Be taking my gun. . . ."

"Not yet. Line up there facing the wall."

The redhead swore, but stepped up onto the gallery. The others moved in beside him. Keeping them between him and the saloon's batwing doors, Munger set the basket of guns an arm's length from the end of the porch.

"Keep looking at the wall," he said. "I'll tell you when you can turn around."

Backing hurriedly, he reached the corner of the adjacent building a dozen strides away and drew in close. The structure would afford only a degree of protection from anyone seeking to fire on him from the saloon, as the buildings fronted the street on an almost identical line. He would be much better off farther down near the jail, he knew, but his plan called for being nearby when the exchange was made.

The hour should be up. Munger glanced again to the sky. Night was not too many minutes away and that brought a frown to his face. Darkness would complicate matters, making his task many times more difficult. If he had. . . . Cord Munger's thoughts came to a standstill. Four riders, with two persons walking ahead of them, had turned into the end of the street. It was Stringer. Fritz Thornburg was on his right, two other men he did not know to his left. Lalicker and his wife were trudging wearily ahead of them. That would be the outlaw's idea—his way of humbling the town by forcing its leading citizen to walk through the dust in view of all; he was driving home the message proclaiming his mastery.

Lalicker had a ragged bandage around his head and appeared unsteady on his feet. It was plain that Stringer had given him a bad time. His wife, hair loose in places and trailing down about her face and neck in straggling wisps, looked worn and near exhaustion. Once she stumbled, and Lalicker surged forward, catching her. Thornburg said something to Stringer, and both laughed. They drew abreast the Skull Saloon, swinging toward it.

Ben Stringer's voice, loud, brought them to a stop. "Whoa-up there!"

Thornburg laughed again as they all dismounted. Lalicker placed his arm about his woman and pressed her to him, as if to assure her their ordeal was near an end. There was movement then behind the saloon's doors, and the four men on the porch stirred.

"Stay put!" Munger barked. "You ain't ready to turn yet."

The outlaws froze. Fisher cast a hopeful glance over his shoulder at Stringer, but the outlaw chief had wheeled lazily, staring at the corner where Cord had taken his stand.

"Munger!"

"I hear you. There's your book-lickers. I've lived up to the bargain . . . turn the Lalickers loose."

"In a minute," Stringer replied. "Got a mite of talking to do to the mayor . . . and the town." He took a long step apart from the men beside him and partly faced the street and the buildings that lined it. "Want all you Holy Joes to listen good! This here shows you who's running this town. You get any more ideas about bucking me, you can figure on finding yourself in plenty of trouble . . . more'n the mayor here got hisself into. Now, there ain't no reason why we can't get along. You can keep right on living here, same as always, and staying in business, only everything's going to be run my way. What I say'll be the law . . . and I'll have my own lawman to keep things right. You forget about ever sending for some outsider. I got one of my boys all picked out, and he'll be taking over. Far as this here mayor of yours is concerned, me and him'll get along. 'Course, he'll be taking his orders from me and doing what I tell him, but that don't need to fret you none. You all agreeing to what I'm saying?"

Stringer paused, letting his gaze travel up and down the street, insolence riding the man's shoulders like a broad-winged eagle. There was no sound, no movement, only a stifling, breathless hush.

"All right, I reckon you got it straight. Just want you to know the how of things from now on so's we won't have no more foolishness like went on here today. It does happen again, I might not be feeling so friendly-like and you maybe'll get your mayor and his missus back on a barn door."

A small sound escaped Blanche Lalicker's throat. She turned to Price, burying her face against his shoulder. Stringer came back around and laid his arrogant glance on the merchant.

"Ain't no sense in hashing this all over with you again. We

96

already done some talking, and you heard what I said to the rest of the folks. Just keep remembering this town is mine . . . barrel, bucket, and broom, and we'll get along. Forget it, and I'll cut you down to little chunks and feed you to the dogs. You understand that?"

Lalicker, staring resignedly off into the darkness, said nothing.

Stringer took a step closer, hand dropping to the pistol on his hip.

Munger drew up sharply. Price Lalicker's pride could ruin everything. "Answer him," he muttered, lining up his weapon on the outlaw leader.

Lalicker stiffened, then nodded his head.

"Say it . . . loud! Say, yes, sir, Mister Stringer!"

The merchant bobbed again. "Yes, sir, Mister Stringer," he repeated in a strained, cracked voice.

"That's fine, mighty fine. Now you and your merchants can go. I'll be paying a little visit to you, come morning, fix it up so's my boys can do their trading with you. There'll be a kind of a tax around here from now on, and that's the way we'll be collecting some of it."

Price Lalicker, arm still supporting his wife, turned wordlessly and angled toward the sidewalk. Cord hoped the man had the presence of mind to duck inside the first building they came to and get off the street as quickly as possible. But Lalicker, mercilessly ground into the dust under Ben Stringer's heel, likely was not thinking clearly.

"Now, friend Munger," the outlaw drawled, wheeling slowly to face the corner, "I got a few things to tell you."

XVII

"Don't waste your breath," Cord Munger replied. "What you've got to say don't interest me."

"Ought to. Reckon you know you're a dead man."

"Not yet, Stringer."

"Same as. You shot down my brother, couple, three more of my boys. Nobody gets away with that. Then you went and stuck your nose. . . ."

"Ben," Fisher broke in, "can't we come down off'n this god-damn' porch? Getting plenty tired of standing here looking at that wall."

"Just keep on standing," Stringer said in that same, unhurried way. "You was dumb enough to let him get the drop on you. Maybe this'll learn you to keep your mind on your business next time."

The redhead and his three friends had but to glance his way, Cord knew, to realize that he no longer held a gun on them—a fact that Ben Stringer certainly was aware of. It was evident the outlaw chief was making use of their discomfort and embarrassment to drive home what he considered a well-deserved lesson. "You ain't got a chance of a rabbit in a coyote's den," Stringer continued. "Thing to do is be smart, throw down your iron, and walk over here to me. You don't, there'll be a dozen men turned loose to root you out."

Munger remained silent, letting the man have his say.

"Can make it easy on yourself . . . on all of us. I'll give you five minutes to make up your mind."

"Won't take me that long to decide I don't want to get snake bit. You through?"

"Said all I'm going to."

"Then I reckon it's my turn to do some talking."

Stringer laughed. "Only kind of talking you ought to be doing is praying."

"Made my deal with the Almighty a long time ago," Cord said. "Now, I'll tell you a little something. You gave me five minutes . . . I'm giving you three."

Ben Stringer glanced around at Thornburg and the two men waiting silently nearby, making an exaggerated show of surprise. "To do what?"

"Drop your guns . . . you and all your bunch . . . and walk out into the middle of the street with your hands up high."

The outlaw's jaw sagged. "What?"

"You're all under arrest."

"Arrest!" Stringer echoed in a choked voice, and then laughed. "You gone plumb loco?"

"You heard me right," Munger said coldly.

Stringer wagged his head. "This sure beats all. You got gall, but you just ain't got enough to try that no matter how good you are. Anyways, you ain't the marshal."

"I'll do till one comes along."

"Yeah? Well, you best figure on a mighty short term in office."

"Waiting for your answer, Stringer. You giving up or am I coming after you?"

"You want my answer? All right, I'm giving it . . . you ain't coming, you're going . . . to the graveyard. Get him!" the outlaw yelled, and, whipping out his pistol, triggered a shot at the corner behind which Munger stood.

The bullet splintered wood. Cord dropped low, leaned forward slightly and threw two quick shots at the confused milling of men on the saloon's porch. He leveled on Stringer, lunging for the doorway, ignoring Fisher and those with him as they scrambled to snatch up their guns, knowing he had no need to fear them and their empty weapons. He got off his shot, but Stringer lurched to the side. The bullet caught Fritz Thornburg, knocking him sprawling to the dusty boards. Yells went up, and hands reached out from under the batwings to drag the man inside.

Munger fired again, dropped a second man, and picked off a third with a hurried following shot. His pistol clicked on the empty chamber. Holstering it, he jerked the extra weapon from his waistband and slammed two more slugs into the wall of the now deserted porch. Wheeling, he raced along the side of the building where he had stood to the alley. He had only moments, and, cutting right, he crossed quickly to the rear of the Skull Saloon, fishing matches out of his pocket as he ran. Reaching the landing, he thumb-nailed one of the matches into flame, dropping it into the pile of débris banked against the door. The blaze caught and began to surge upward.

Pivoting, Cord retraced his steps to the street, reloading his weapons as he hurried to resume his position at the corner of the building. Because of the confusion he was sure his absence had not been noted, but to lay to rest any doubts as to his presence he placed two bullets into the batwings, setting them to trembling.

"Munger . . . !"

He grinned as Ben Stringer's exasperated voice came from the darkness beyond the saloon's entrance.

"Right here . . . waiting."

"What the hell are you trying to do? Know damn' well you can't take us all."

"Willing to try," Cord answered, glancing to the roof of the building. He could see no smoke as yet, and the disturbing thought that the fire had gone out, had failed to set the door and nearby wall ablaze, lodged in his mind. If so. . . .

"You're just making it worse for yourself."

"Expect I'm a mite better off than you."

"Doubt that. What I'm getting at is . . . I been doing some thinking. Ain't no use in anybody dying because it'll all come out the same at the end . . . with me on top. How about us doing some talking?"

Still no smoke. The heart of his plan was gone if the fire had failed. "We've already talked. Can't see no sense in it . . . unless you're ready to call it quits."

"Hell . . . you can't keep us pinned up in here! You're a fool if you're figuring that. All we've got to do is come busting out together. . . ."

"And the first ones through those batwings will be dead before they get across the porch. Better think about it, Stringer."

Movement at the end of the street drew Munger's eye. It was Doc Conrad. He had come from his office and was standing at the end of the walk. Abe Florsheim, the hotel man, was hastening to join him. Munger raised a hand, waving them back into the house. The two men hesitated briefly, then retreated into the physician's quarters.

Cord swung his attention to bear again on the saloon's entrance. He could see no vague shadows directly beyond the swinging doors and guessed the outlaws were taking care to stand clear. Raising his gun, he splintered the batwings with two more shots. "Just reminding you!" he called across the separating distance. "That's what's waiting for every man in there unless he comes out with his hands up."

"Go to hell," a muffled voice replied.

Smoke—at last. Munger felt a glow of satisfaction as his eyes picked up a thin spiral of dirty gray twisting skyward from the rear of the saloon. It was thickening steadily. The fire had been burning all the time, he reckoned, but the breeze had kept the smoke low. Raising his weapon, he again drove a pair of bullets into the entrance of the building, and then reloaded. "Going to have to make your choice pretty quick!" he yelled.

There was no response this time. The outlaws would have become aware of the blaze by that moment; likely they had all rushed to the rear of the building and were doing what they could to check it. Their success would be small; the flames, originating on the outside, would have gained headway and be well out of control before finally eating through to the interior.

Glass shattered, the sound breaking the hush, as a side window was broken. Immediately smoke began to pour through the opening. Munger smiled grimly. Whoever had done that had unwittingly performed a favor. The draft created would strengthen the fire.

Once more he targeted the saloon's doors. He could expect results shortly now. The inside of the Skull Saloon was undoubtedly swirling with smoke and heat from the burning building. Raising his glance, he could see tongues of flame darting along the edge of the roof. The tinder-dry structure would soon be a solid mass of seething fire.

"Throw down your guns and come out!" he yelled.

XVIII

Immediately a pistol sailed through the gray haze drifting over the top of the batwings and landed with a thud in the dust of the street. The swinging panels burst open, and a man, fists knuckling his eyes, coughing uncontrollably, staggered onto the porch. "Don't shoot . . . I'm quitting!" he shouted above the popping and crackling of the flames.

He reached the edge of the landing and, blinded, misjudged the step, falling heavily. Behind him others were pouring through the opening as the thickening smoke boiled about them. Through the fog Munger saw one drop to a crouch. Metal shone dully in his hand, and a fraction of a second later a spot of orange blossomed in the murk.

Munger jerked back and swore as the bullet drove into the fleshy part of his leg, spinning him half around. He cursed again, this time at his own carelessness, and triggered a shot at the hunched outlaw. The man threw up his arms and went over backwards.

Others continued to emerge from the burning structure. Gagging, stumbling over the man sprawled in front of the doors, swearing, they staggered into the street. Cord watched them sharply, eyes searching each for a weapon not discarded, alert for another of the gang willing to lay his life on the line in an attempt to escape.

Smoke was now drifting thickly in the cañon that separated the buildings, and heat was beginning to make itself felt while the red glow of the flames turned the windows into sheets of gold. A half a dozen dogs were breaking the late evening stillness with their excited yapping, and someone, fearing the spread of the flames to other structures, was ringing the fire bell.

Munger, methodically counting the outlaws as he crammed his bandanna between his pants and the wound in his leg to stop the bleeding, guessed the saloon was nearly empty. There were eleven men in the street, including the one lying on the porch, and that brought a frown to his sweaty face. He had not expected so large a number.

He frowned again, and straightened up. Where was Ben Stringer—Grinnell? Cautiously he moved away from the protection of the building, crossing hurriedly to where he could stand behind the outlaws, again placing them between himself and the saloon. Off to the right he could see vague figures trotting toward him through the haze and hear boot heels thumping on the street, but he paid no heed. Stringer and the saloon man were not with the others.

Anger pushing at him, he stepped to the outlaws, gathered in a loose group and still coughing and rubbing their eyes. "Where's Stringer?" he demanded, seizing the arm of the nearest man and jerking him around.

The outlaw glanced toward the saloon. "How the hell would I know! Was in there with us."

"Grinnell?"

"Him, too."

Munger searched the crowd again, both pistols held level in front of him as he circled warily around. The two men were not there; they could only still be inside the burning building. He shook his head at that thought. How could they withstand the heat and the smothering pall of smoke that filled it?

He came to a full stop. Was there another way out that he

was unaware of? Could there be a third door, or perhaps a window different from those he'd noticed in the structure— one large enough to permit a man to crawl through? Maybe— but if so, why hadn't the others made use of it?

"Munger . . . !"

Cord turned, faced Doc Conrad. With the physician were Florsheim and Wilcox. Impatience whipped at him; the last thing he needed at the moment, with a dozen outlaws on his hands and Grinnell and Ben Stringer missing, was interference from the townspeople.

"Told you to stay in your homes, out of the way!" he snapped.

Conrad, an old double-barreled shotgun in his hands, jerked his thumb at the pair with him. They, too, were armed, each with a rifle.

"We want to help. . . ."

"Not over yet. Some of them ain't tallied yet . . . could get yourself shot up."

Conrad's jaw snapped shut. "Damn it . . . don't be so bullheaded! You're needing us whether you want to admit it or not."

Munger, his eyes on the doorway of the saloon, let the words register. He could use a few extra hands. If Ben Stringer and Pete Grinnell had somehow managed to escape the burning structure, he should be after them before they could get to their horses and leave. That would have to wait, however, while he took the necessary time to jail the rest of the gang—and during those lost minutes the pair he wanted most to bring down could get away.

"All right," he said, "you're taking over. Herd this bunch into the cells. Be damned sure the doors are locked, then stand watch until I get back."

Conrad nodded, then paused, his glance on Munger's

blood-smeared leg. "I'll have a look at that wound first."

"The hell you will," Cord replied, pulling away. "No time now."

"Wilcox and Abel can start the bunch moving. I. . . ."

"Forget it," Munger said. "Stringer and Grinnell are not with them. Got to be found."

The physician's shoulders lifted, fell in resignation. "You won't get far, that leg bleeding like it is."

"Far enough," Cord said, and moved off, crossing behind the outlaws now shambling in a ragged group toward the jail under the threatening weapons of the townsmen.

Munger drew in as near the saloon as he could before heat brought him to a halt. Dropping low, he looked under the swinging doors. Within, there was a solid mass of roaring flames. No one alive could be in there, he decided instantly.

Coming upright, ignoring the throbbing pain that hammered at him, he moved to the north side of the structure and walked hurriedly down its length. The two windows, small and placed high in the wall that was now beginning to burn, were shattered but intact. No one had attempted to exit through them.

He reached the back and rounded the corner. Where the door had been was a gaping hole rimmed with tongues of flame and giving him a second view of the inferno within. He continued, walking the breadth of the building along the alley, and reached its opposite side. Fire was creeping along the wall, working toward the center from either end. The windows were still visible, one, oddly enough, as yet unbroken by the intense heat. He stared at the doomed building, brushing the sweat on his face. He had been right about it—there were no other openings the two outlaws could have used.

Puzzled, he wiped at his eyes again and shifted his weight to ease the throbbing in his leg. He was positive the pair had

106

not come out of the saloon with the rest of the gang. He had been watching closely. And there was no doubt both had been inside—at least, he was certain insofar as Stringer was concerned. He had watched the outlaw chief rush through the doorway but had missed him with the bullet that instead downed Fritz Thornburg. Then later he had talked to him.

He was fairly sure of Grinnell as well. The man he had questioned in the street had indicated the saloonkeeper was present, and he'd hardly have reason to lie about it. What, then, had happened to them? Turning, he started back up the alley, deciding to have a look again along the north wall. There could have been a cellar—a low-set window he had missed. Halfway his feet came in contact with something soft and entangling. He tripped and went to his knees as pain ripped through him savagely. Swearing, he pulled himself upright, unconsciously looking down to see what it was that had caused him to fall.

A blanket. Munger holstered his gun and gathered up the rectangle of wool, recalling that earlier he had been through there and had noticed the cover lying in the weeds. It was gray with a faint brown cast. He pressed it to his nose as a sudden hunch came to him. The cloth had a dry, scorched smell. The means by which Stringer and Grinnell had escaped was clear now. They had waited until the others started leaving through the doorway, possibly even a bit longer to insure his attention being occupied. Then, taking the blanket from Grinnell's living quarters that were a partitioned-off section in a back corner, they had wrapped themselves in the thick folds and leaped through the charred opening, left by the burning, and out the door. There should be two blankets.

Dropping the bedcover, Munger gave the matter thought. He had found this one south of the building, and whichever of the two had used it had not come to the street; therefore, it was logical to assume he had continued down the alley in the same direction. Munger moved on at once, drawing in as close as possible to the walls of the succeeding structures lining the alley in order to make no target of himself, should the outlaws be waiting for him farther on.

He covered a dozen steps, then halted again as his eyes, switching back and forth seeking some indication of the men, fell upon a second mound of gray . . . the other blanket. Grimly satisfied, he pressed on, his mind striving to come up with yet another answer—where would Stringer and Grinnell most likely hole up, assuming they had not found horses? Searing pain and a solid shock that rocked him off balance as a bullet tore into his left arm came in that next fragment of time. He had found them.

XIX

Munger allowed himself to fall, to sink into the deep shadows banked along the base of the building behind which he was moving. Beyond it he could hear men shouting in the street while overhead the hanging smoke and glare from the fire combined to form an unreal canopy. Flat on the ground he searched the area ahead for the outlaws. In the murky half dark nothing was distinct, only blurred shapes and outlines. To his right he could make out a hedge-like line of brush, but the growth was low, and he doubted the possibility of a man being able to hide there without being seen.

Opposite and farther on he could see the rear wall of an abandoned livery stable. One of the wide back doors was standing partly open. Adjoining it was Jamison's Gun Shop, its rear exit and openings tightly closed and shuttered. Munger grinned bleakly in satisfaction; the shot could only have come from the empty stable.

Drawing his legs up beneath him, biting back the pain such movement created, Cord began to inch his way forward, pressing against the wall of the building and taking advantage of every shadow, each clump of weeds and bit of trash. He reached the stable's doorway, halted, and leaned against the weathered planking to steady himself while he listened. His left side was numb, and the stickiness of blood creeping down his arm matched that of his wounded leg.

He could hear no sound inside the stable, and after a

long minute he drew himself together again and, hunched low, continued his way slowly and silently into the cavern-like interior of the old barn. A partition—the side of a stall was to his left. He rested, completely submerged in the blackness that lay alongside, listening again. Somewhere ahead he could hear the quiet rasp of someone breathing. Squinting, he tried to make out the arrangement of the building. There should be a runway off which the stalls were built, but what was immediately in front of him? A tack room?—feed storage—office quarters, perhaps? It was important that he knew for such separate, closed-in areas would provide an excellent hiding place for anyone lying in wait for him.

The harsh breathing stopped. Either Stringer had moved on, or had become aware of his approach and was now sitting back, waiting. Or was it Ben Stringer? Cord shook his head impatiently; he was forgetting there'd be two men in the ambush—Grinnell as well as the outlaw chief.

He was gaining nothing by holding back—and he couldn't last much longer. He was losing too much blood. Conrad had been right—he should have let him doctor the wound in his leg, but there hadn't been time. Carefully he pulled away from the thick planks of the partition and began to creep along the hard-packed, cool ground, remembering to keep clear of the wood so as to not allow his clothing to drag and set up a scraping noise. He came to the end of the wall, realized he had reached the runway, pausing as his hand encountered a small pile of metal strips and curving boards—a nail keg or small barrel that had been crushed, probably under the wheels of a wagon—and kicked it aside.

Avoiding it, he inched forward a short distance, once more halting as an oblong of pale light off to his left caught his attention—the front doors of the stable at the upper end of the runway. One was standing partly open, admitting the glow from the street.

Catching the edge of the stall, Munger drew himself upright. There was a vagueness in his head, and a feeling of being far removed from himself possessed him. He shook it off, moved into the runway, and started to cross over.

Above and behind him a boot scraped against wood. Someone was in the hayloft. Munger took a long step back into the stall and threw himself tightly against the thick timbers of the partition. In that identical instant a pistol blasted the silence, filling the old building.

Cord snapped a return shot, targeting on the flash of orange light that appeared suspended in the blackness overhead. A voice cried out hoarsely in pain. There followed a long breath of silence, a dry, rustling sound, and then the solid thud of a body falling to the floor.

Stringer or Grinnell? Cord rode out several dragging minutes, and, when it became apparent there was to be no shot from the remaining man, he dropped low, working his way around the end of the stall, careful to avoid the smashed keg, and moving forward until his groping hand came in contact with the body. He probed it hurriedly, wishing he dared strike a match to see which of the outlaws was not out of it; such was of importance to him since Ben Stringer was by far the more dangerous man. His fingers touched the smooth, oval links of a watch chain, and traced it until they found the rounded surface of bone—a tooth. It was Pete Grinnell who wore a heavy gold watch chain with a bear's tooth attached.

Munger settled back. Where was Stringer? Had he, unlike Grinnell who had chosen to hide in the stable and make his stand from the hayloft, kept going and already left the building? Cord glanced to the opposite end of the runway, at the partly open door; the outlaw could have used that as his escape route, but somehow it didn't seem likely. Stringer would be more inclined to hide in the darkness, as had the saloon man, and await a time when he could safely use his weapon rather than chance being seen by someone as he entered the street. But if true, why hadn't the outlaw taken advantage of that moment when he triggered his shot at Pete Grinnell? The flash of his gun had betrayed his exact position. It was an opportunity Stringer would hardly have passed up—if it had been offered to him.

Munger came about slowly. He was suddenly tired. His thoughts seemed disjointed, and he was having trouble putting them together to make sense, but of one thing he was certain—Stringer was still there—waiting. He drew himself back into the runway, aware now of noises in the street, of far-away voices, of a horse trotting briskly toward the center of town. The fire was probably out by this time, he thought absently. Likely no effort was made to check the burning of the saloon, so long a source of problems for the people of Hell's Corners; time would have been spent only to contain it, to prevent its spreading to adjoining structures.

He reached the stall, where he had been when Grinnell had fired, hauling himself into its narrow width, a weariness dragging at him. He must turn up Stringer soon or forget it. In not too many more minutes he'd be in no condition to do anything about the outlaw. With strength ebbing steadily he could not play a waiting game. That was what Ben Stringer was doing.

The realization came to him abruptly. Knowing he was wounded, the outlaw was laying back, allowing time to work for him. Munger swore silently. Stringer could beat him that way, there was no doubt of it. In another half hour he'd hardly be in condition even to lift his gun, much less make good use of it. He must force the outlaw's hand some way.

Slumped against the side of the stall, he tried to think. He could get to his feet, step into the runway, move toward the door at its far end, expose himself, and take his chances on Stringer's missing his shot. The outlaw would in that way reveal his position. But the odds were all against Stringer's bullet not finding its mark; with Grinnell it might have worked; he was much less adept with such a weapon. But there was a thought here. If he could manage to attract the outlaw's attention, cause him to make his move. . . .

At once Cord began to work deeper into the stall, one hand probing, searching along the floor for something that would be of use. He came to the compartment's end. The manger. He drew himself upright by grasping its smooth edge. His exploring fingers touched the cool surface of glass and metal—a lantern someone had tossed into the feed box. He picked it up quickly and shook it. There was a small amount of oil in the reservoir.

Turning, he retreated to the front of the stall, crouching at its corner. Setting the lantern on the ground, he twisted the knurled knob to set the wick and pressed the lever, raising the globe. Reaching into the runway, he obtained one of the barrel staves, laid it close by where it would be quickly available, and then dug a match out of his pocket. Taking a deep breath, he crouched over the light, struck the match, and touched it to the wick. After a long moment it caught. He lowered the glass cylinder with its trip, ignoring the squeak, and, still hunkered over the lantern to block its glow, he forced his left hand to take up the barrel stave and slide it under the bail.

Rising slowly, with difficulty, gun ready in his right hand, he wheeled, holding the stave extended well out in front of him so that the lantern hanging from it was as far removed from him as possible, and stepped into the runway.

The hush was again shattered by a gunshot. A bullet slammed into the wall beyond Munger, traveling a course that would have sent it driving into his chest had he been holding the lantern at a normal distance. He dropped the light as boot heels thudded toward the door leading into the street. Stringer had been hiding in one of the front stalls. He saw the crouched shape racing for the opening.

"Stringer!"

At Cord's yell, the outlaw dodged to one side and spun. Munger fired once. Stringer staggered back, pressed off a shot that buried itself harmlessly in the ground, rocked forward, and fell.

Munger sagged against the upright at the end of the stall. That had done it for him. He'd flushed out Stringer and downed him before he could get away; he guessed that that was about all he could do for the people of Hell's Corners. Next thing was to see to his own needs.

Unsteady, a thick fog swirling in his brain, he made his way to the door and into the street. He halted, aware of several shadowy figures bearing down upon him at a run, all shouting. He shook his head, focusing his eyes on the first to reach him. It was Conrad. He nodded to the physician. "Reckon you'd best be fixing me up a little, Doc," he said thickly.

XX

Sunlight was streaming brightly through a window into the room. Cord Munger stared at the slanting rays and struggled to organize his thoughts. He was on a bed. The air was heavy with the smell of disinfectant, and he could hear voices somewhere. He could only be at Conrad's, he decided, stirring. At once he felt the restriction of bandages on his leg, and arm. He swore, angrily impatient at finding himself in so dependent a condition. Hell, he hadn't been hurt that badly— not nearly as seriously as that night in Matamoros when those two *vaqueros* had taken it upon themselves to carve him into steaks.

Frowning, ignoring the pain, he drew himself to a sitting position, brushing at the sweat on his forehead. It was morning; he'd been there all night, he supposed—or maybe he'd slept around the clock twice. He wasn't too sure of anything—only that he'd had it out with Ben Stringer and Grinnell in the old livery barn, and survived.

"Hey . . . Doc!"

His voice sounded hoarse in his ears, and he cleared his throat, swallowing. A moment later Conrad appeared in the doorway. Others crowded close behind him—Rufe Ackerman, Newt Wilcox, Joe Davidson, Price Lalicker, Jed Zumwalt, others.

"See you're awake," the physician said unnecessarily, and stepped up to the bed.

Munger considered him silently, shifting his glance to the group pushing into the room, then brought it back to the physician. "How long have I been laying here?"

"Since last night . . . most of today."

"Most of today . . . it's morning, ain't it?"

"Afternoon . . . late," Conrad said, feeling his pulse. "You're doing fine."

"No need being here in the first place," Munger grumbled as the physician straightened. "Got hurt worse falling off my horse."

"Wounds weren't severe, I'll admit that. You just lost a lot of blood."

"Reckon I'll be going, then," Cord said, and, pushing the blanket aside, dropped his feet over the edge of the bed to rise. A surge of dizziness swept him. He paused.

"Not yet," Conrad said, and pressed him back. "You'll be here a couple of days, at least."

Munger swore softly, then relaxed. He shifted his eyes to the doorway. A slow grin cracked his lips when he saw Button Hays now standing in the forefront. Jed Zumwalt's big hand rested on his shoulder.

"Hi, partner," he said. "How's the leg?"

The boy smiled broadly. "Doing good. Wasn't nothing bad . . . not like you got. You all right?"

"Thought I was, but I reckon I'm due to stay here a spell."

Conrad leaned forward. "These men came here to talk to you. Feel up to listening?"

A coolness returned to Cord Munger's eyes. His shoulders moved indifferently. At a nod from Conrad, Price Lalicker stepped to the end of the bed, resting his hands on the footboard. There was a neat, clean bandage around his head.

"Want you to know the town thanks you for what you did," he said. "Goes double for me. I've got more to be grateful for than anyone else, I expect, and probably deserve it less."

Munger made no comment but simply lay quiet, his flat glance on the merchant's face.

"We were all wanting too much too quick. I'm ready to admit that, and I'll tell you, too, that you were right about how changing this town would have to be done . . . that first step, I mean. But you made it for us, and we're. . . ."

"Not for you, for the boy," Cord Munger said coldly.

"All right, for Button. Works out to the same end." Lalicker hesitated, looked away briefly, and then continued. "Anyway, now that we've got things headed in the right direction, we're asking a favor of you. We've put out word for a new marshal, but until we can find one we'd like for you to take over. Realize you turned us down before but we figured maybe we could get you to reconsider."

Munger's eyes narrowed. Lalicker and the others were like a bunch of scared rabbits now, and they were turning for help to him—the man they didn't want around. The answer was still the same. He'd done all he'd intended to do.

"We want to go ahead, make this town into a good place to live, just like we planned all along, but we know we can't do it without a strong marshal."

"I'm no lawman."

"We know that . . . and we know how you feel about the job . . . and about us. But you're the only man we figure can keep things from sliding back until we find one we want."

Cord shook his head. "I figure I've done my share . . . and I wouldn't've done that if it wasn't for the boy, there. Doubt if it'd work out, anyway. We don't see eye to eye."

"Be no interference from us, you got our word on that. And whatever you need, or want us to do, we'll agree."

Cord Munger shifted his glance to Button, read the pride,

the hope, in his expression. What the hell, for the sake of the boy, he could stand it for a couple of weeks. He nodded.

"All right, but I'm taking it only till you get yourself a regular marshal."

Relief flooded Price Lalicker's features. He slapped his hands together sharply. "That's understood. There anything else?"

"One thing," Munger said. "Rufe was saying you aimed to change the name of the town."

The merchant stiffened, frowned. "Well, yes, we were planning to. Haven't decided yet on. . . ."

"Making this a part of the deal . . . want you to call it Hays Corners so Button'll have a stake in it. You agreeing?"

Lalicker looked startled, glanced at the other men. They nodded. Doc Conrad smiled.

"Mighty fine idea," he said. "A town called Hell's Corners died last night . . . one named Hay's Corners was born today. Seems appropriate."

Drifter's End

I

Spring was having her wild, young way in the bottom along the Carrizo. Like a woman preening herself for the Saturday night dance in town, she was putting forth her best, wiping away the chilled memories of winter's bitter sojourn, brushing warmness and life into the willows and dog bush, the crisp grass and gaunt cottonwoods, and even the crackling mesquite. The hostile wind with its fierce, slashing drive was gentle now, bringing the smells of greening things from the north where lay the towering Pass country, and from the west, where the ragged edges of the Sierra del Diablo etched their crags against the horizon.

In the thick brush shaping up along the rumbling stream, Frank Brokaw had laid his night camp. Squatting now on his heels in the half dawn, he waited for coffee to come to a boil, mechanically feeding dry twigs into the small fire. He was a sun-blackened young man with a face too old for his years. The coffee lifted to a foaming crest, and he set the lard tin aside. With the blade of his pocket knife he stirred down the froth, waited for it to cool, and then tipped the small bucket to his mouth and drank until there was nothing left but the sack of grounds.

How long had he been on the trail? Almost a year now. Almost a year following a stone-cold trail, hunting a man he did not know nor had ever seen. And a nameless man at that. Matt Slade he had called himself back in Central City where

119

the explosion and all the other things had taken place. But it would not be that now. A man doing what Matt Slade had done would be quick to change his name.

Reaching into an inner pocket for tobacco and papers, he deftly spun up a brown cigarette. With the glowing end of a brand from the dying fire, he lit it, sucked deeply of the smoke, and rose to his feet, throwing his glance out across the brightening landscape. Grass rolled away in all four directions, in hazy, silver-tinged brown waves, reaching even to the savage black edges of the badlands, *malpais* he had heard it called. The Carrizo twisted northerly in a glistening, irregular band. The river was deep, not yet at flood point, but it would become so when the snows in the high country felt the bite of the sun and melted. Then the water would come rushing down to overflow the stream's banks and spread out into shallow lakes on the flats. That was the way of this strange land. Always an overabundance. Always too much of one thing: too much wind, too much snow, too much sun and heat, too much cold. A world of extremes. But it was a strong country, one that appealed deeply to him, and he had a lonely man's brief wish that he might call it his own, that he might settle down on its lush, inviting contours and carve out a home for himself. Instead, he reflected grimly, he was bringing violence to it. He would find no friends in this land of strangers, and he would likely leave none.

Eight years ago it had been different. The war was but a distant, threatening grumble, a far call from the farm of his parents in eastern Kansas, where one day was much like another, and a boy could find his happiness in everything he did, and his dreams in every cloud he saw. Then came Fort Sumter, and the roil of summoning drums spreading their call to the remotest points. Frank Brokaw was seventeen when he joined up.

Four years later it was all over. Sick of blood and vowing never again to lift a gun, unable to get the smell of death from his nostrils, he became a footloose drifter. He saw all of Texas. He rode deep into Mexico. He crossed the bottom of New Mexico Territory and passed through the new one called Arizona. He saw the Pacific's waters from California's shores, turned inland across the glittering deserts, and came finally back to Kansas, four years later.

There, everything had changed. Eight years had made a difference, and the world he had known was gone. People he had not seen before occupied the little farm. His mother was dead, gone of a broken heart, they said. His father, a kindly man, loved and respected by all as town marshal, was a hopeless, mindless dead-man-alive, languishing in the Home for the Insane at Leavenworth. And a man called Matt Slade, responsible for those changes, had disappeared into the vast reaches of the West.

Brokaw dropped the cold cigarette into the ashes of his fire and ground it out. With the toe of a boot he raked moist earth over the embers and trod the dark scar into a mound. He had saddled and loaded his remaining grub on the bay gelding while the coffee had brewed, and now moved toward the big horse, walking in that easy, muscular, swinging way of a man confident of his powers.

He was a tall man, not heavy, but not thin, either. His hips were narrow, pinched in at the waist, giving him a sort of wedge-shaped torso with wide-flung shoulders. He wore the usual range variety of clothing: coarse shirt faded to a light mouse color, sun-bleached Levi's, dust and alkali-stained boots, a wide-brimmed hat that had seen better days. An old, bone-handled Colt revolver, his father's, sagged from a belt around his waist, and his spurs were those of a cavalryman. His face was broad, hard-cornered, placid, tanned to the depths of muddy water. His mouth was wide, his nose prominent, and his eyes were yellow-hazed beneath a shelf of heavy, black brows. Like a dark shadow a measure of cynicism, of arrogance, lay across his features and pulsed through the seemingly careless, but sure, movements of him, as he stalked to the bay.

He stowed the lard bucket in the left hand side of the saddlebags, taking time to thread all three buckles. That done, he checked the double cinches of the old work saddle. He found them to his satisfaction and swung aboard, going up in an easy, fluid motion. For a moment he sat quietly, staring out over the smooth, undulating plains to the west. Far to his right, up a long distance and near the Carrizo, a wisp of pale smoke lifted into the morning sky, marking a ranch or a homesteader, grubbing out a tough living from a quarter section, or, perhaps, the camp of a solitary man like himself. He would not be going that way. He was striking on west, to a ranch called the Arrowhead and a man named Hugh Preston. Maybe this last tip would prove right. Maybe this would be the end of the trail and Hugh Preston would be, in reality, the man who had called himself Matt Slade.

Preston, they had said in Tascosa, had moved into the Scattered Hills country five or six years back. That would be about the right time. He had bought up a run-down spread belonging to a man named Cresswell. He had paid for it with hard cash money, and then had rebuilt it, stocking it well with cattle bought wherever and whenever available. And always paying cash. That fitted, too; Matt Slade would have plenty of cash.

Brokaw clucked the bay into motion and turned him up the gentle incline leading from the stream. That was when he heard the first, fading roll of gunfire.

II

Instantly alert and curious, as any man would be, he jerked the bay to a halt. The shots seemed to have come from his left, from beyond a low ridge lying parallel to the trail he had taken. But sounds fool men in wide-open country, and so he waited. A minute later they came again, three quick reports flatting hollowly in the clear air. Sure of his bearings now, he spurred the gelding to a gallop, striking for the highest point of the ridge a half mile off. The bay horse, fresh from the night's rest on good graze and water, strung out swiftly, gaining the crest in long, easy strides. Brokaw checked there, having to hold the bay, that wanted to continue the run, with a tight rein. He found himself on the rim of a shallow basin that swooped away for a good five miles before him.

Two hundred yards distant stood a canvas-topped wagon apparently halted in its eastward course across the range. Two riders sat their saddles, their opposed ropes suspending between them a man in rough, butternut clothing, pinning him like a calf about to be branded. Their guns were out, and they were lacing the ground about the man's feet with bullets, all the while commanding him to dance.

Brokaw studied the scene with no outward change of expression, its meaning coming quickly to him. A transient homesteader caught on cattle land. It had happened many times before. The riders would rough him up a bit, scare him half to death, and then warn him to move on. But in the end no real harm would be done. He turned back for the trail. It was no affair of his, and there was no call for him to butt in.

His swinging glance caught sight of another rider then, coming in from the south. A distant blur, he was riding hard, attracted also by the gunshots, Brokaw guessed. The homesteader at that moment was down, struggling fiercely. Both 'punchers were laughing as their horses backed away, pulling tight the ropes.

A voice floated up to Brokaw: "Let's build a fire and brand him!"

Another sound reached him. The shrill, faint scream of a woman. He spun the bay around and spurred along the ridge, running hard for a good quarter mile. From a point reached by that action, he could see the front of the wagon. A third horse, hidden from him before by the vehicle's bulk, waited near a front wheel. A thick-bodied man wrestled with a woman, the homesteader's wife likely, on the seat. Brokaw flung a quick glance at the approaching horseman. Still a long way off. And he might be a friend of the three cowboys, anyway. Settling his hat with a hard pulling of the brim, he spoke to the bay, and they went racing down the long slope.

The woman's screams became louder as he drew nearer. He quartered in, keeping the wagon between himself and the two riders with the ropes. But the drum of the bay's hoofs brought the man on the seat half around. He let his hands fall away from the woman's body, mouth sagging a little with surprise. Brokaw swung in close. He reached out with one hand, caught the man by the arm, lost his grip, and clutched at the loose cloth of his brush jacket. The sudden shock almost pulled his arm from its socket, but he hung on, and the man came hurtling off the wagon.

"Look out, Shep!" one of the 'punchers yelled belatedly.

Brokaw spun the bay around, dragging out his gun. He snapped a shot at the closest rider. "Throw down those ropes!"

Both cowboys complied instantly. The homesteader scrambled to his feet, kicked out of the ropes, and lunged for the old Sharps rifle lying near the wagon where he had dropped it. Through all the whirling confusion the woman's voice shrilled on hysterically.

Brokaw heard a growl behind him and remembered the man he had catapulted from the wagon. He tried to wheel away, but hands seized his arm and dragged him from the saddle. He struck hard, losing his gun and hat, and the bay went shying off a dozen feet. He forgot the other two men as the third, Shep by name apparently, began hammering at him with huge fists. The homesteader's rifle blasted suddenly, setting up a chain of echoes, but he could not turn to see if the man had hit one of the cowboys. He rolled, going over and over, getting away from Shep.

The rifle thundered again. One of the riders yelled. Brokaw got his feet under him and bounded up. He saw the two 'punchers standing with their arms over their heads under the wavering barrel of the homesteader's gun. Beyond them, the rider from the south hove into view, his gray horse moving at a long lope. He would be there shortly, and, if he were a friend of the trio's, Brokaw realized he would be in a bad spot. He would have to finish this quickly.

Shep rushed in, and he met the cowboy with a sharp right to the jaw. It rocked the man back, and Brokaw crowded in, driving him to his heels with rapid tattoo of rights and lefts. Shep stumbled away, turning about. Brokaw followed closely. The 'puncher, finally regaining his balance, pivoted fast, for a big man. He lashed out with a swinging, back-handed blow. It caught Brokaw across the neck, grazing his chin, not hurting much, but stalling him temporarily. Before he could duck and weave away, a hard right caught him, and set lights to dancing in front of his eyes.

"Get him, Shep!" one of the riders yelled.

Brokaw slid away from the next broad swing, letting it skip off his shoulder. It threw Shep off balance again when it missed, and he took a stumbling step forward. Brokaw, his head clear once more, allowed him to reel by. Shep was wide open. Brokaw, with a terrific, down-sledging blow to the side of the head, dropped him flat.

He stepped away, sucking deeply for wind. Legs spread wide, knotted fists poised, he waited for Shep to rise again.

"Reckon that'll be about enough," a voice drawled through the hush.

Brokaw lifted his gaze to the speaker. The man on the gray horse. He was an old man, his long hair and trailing handlebar mustache full white, and startlingly offset by jet black, bushy brows. His eyes were a keen blue reaching out authoritatively from a ruddy, hawk-like face. Sunlight glinted sharply off the star pinned to his vest pocket.

Brokaw turned deliberately away, placing his shoulders to the lawman, waiting for Shep to regain his feet. It would be over if Shep said so, if Shep had had enough, and not because a man with a tin badge said it should be. He was poised, ready, willing to carry on the battle if necessary.

"Don't you go turnin' your back on me, mister!" the sheriff barked. "I said this ruckus was over, and I mean just that! You try carryin' it further and I'll put a bullet in your leg!"

Brokaw made no sign he had heard. He watched Shep get to his hands and knees, head hanging like a bushed horse. He watched him shake himself and climb slowly to his feet and pivot tiredly around. Blood streaked from a corner of his mouth, and a heavy, bluish swelling was rising fast along his left cheek.

"All right, Shep," Brokaw murmured. "Right here."

Shep lifted burning eyes to him. After a moment he shook his head and swung away, murmuring: "It ain't because I want it. But the sheriff said we was to quit. I'll see you again!" Retrieving his hat and fallen gun, he moved toward his horse.

The sheriff's satisfied, drawling voice said: "What's been goin' on here? You, Carl, what was this all about?"

The homesteader laid down his rifle and climbed onto the wagon. He took his wife in his arms, awkwardly trying to comfort her. Her crying had dissolved into muffled sobs as she tried, futilely, to cover her shoulders where Shep had ripped her dress away.

The 'puncher, addressed as Carl, said: "Nothin' much, Ben. We caught this sodbuster on Arrowhead range. We was just teachin' him a lesson."

Brokaw whistled to the bay gelding, and he trotted up. He knocked the dust from his hat, picked up his gun, and swung to the saddle, glancing again at Shep who now stood near his two companions.

The sheriff considered that information for a moment. Then he shifted his pale eyes to the homesteader. "What's ailin' your woman, mister?"

The man ducked his head at Shep. "That cowboy tried to force her into the back of the wagon while his friends here held me down with ropes." His voice began to tremble with anger. "Would have done it, too, if that fellow on the bay hadn't come along!"

All the friendliness vanished from the sheriff's voice. His face went flint hard. "That so, Shep?"

The cowboy made no reply, rubbing at the side of his face, his gaze on the ground.

The lawman drifted in closer to him. "I want an answer to that, Shep! How about it . . . you try that?"

Carl spoke up. "Shep wasn't meanin' no harm, Ben. Had hisself a couple of snorts out of a bottle and I reckon he sort of lost his head, seein' that woman."

"And you and Domino was just standin' by lettin' him do it," the sheriff observed with withering scorn. "That don't go in my county! You know that, Shep! All of you do. Any woman's safe around here!"

"Safe!" the homesteader's wife echoed, finding her voice. "Nobody's safe in this god-forsaken country!" Suddenly she began to beat on her husband's chest in a wild, hopeless way. "I want to go home! I want to get out of this terrible country! I want to go back where people are civilized human beings, and not drunken beasts and murderers and thieves!"

Brokaw watched in silence. Shep and his two friends stirred restlessly, shame-faced and ill at ease. A woman's safety on the range was a thing taken for granted, but there were always exceptions, and this was one of those. The homesteader comforted his wife, patting her heaving shoulders, stroking her straw-colored hair. He was a young man, not much older than Brokaw. His wife was a mere child.

The sheriff said: "Like for you folks to drive into town. You prefer charges against these men and I'll see they get taken care of."

The homesteader looked up. "That'd mean days, and I ain't plannin' to spend any more time around here than I have to. All I want is for people to let us alone long enough for us to get out of this country. I had my fill of it . . . it's too hard. Awful hard on a woman."

The sheriff shrugged his thin shoulders. "Just as you say. But a man finds it a hard row to hoe when people won't help him keep the law. Ain't nothin' I can do if you won't make a complaint." He swiveled his sharp gaze to Shep. "I'll be tellin' Preston about this."

Shep stirred. "Go ahead. Tell him. They was on Arrowhead grass, and you know he don't like that."

"We were just crossing," the homesteader cut in. "I never stopped on it."

"Makes no difference," Shep said doggedly. "Arrowhead range is closed."

Frank Brokaw smiled grimly to himself at the turn of his luck. Preston. Shep and the other two men worked for him, and Preston was the man he was looking for—and hoped to get a job with long enough to make certain inquiries. Now there would be the additional problem of Shep and maybe the others as well.

The homesteader pushed his wife gently into the depths of the wagon. He settled himself on the seat and picked up the reins. "How long before we'll be off this Arrowhead land?"

"Couple, three hours at least," the sheriff replied.

"It can't be too soon," the homesteader murmured. "And it'll be the last time anybody'll ever see us around here," he added sourly, clucking his team into action.

"What about Indians?" the sheriff reminded him. "You will be gettin' into Indian country another day or so. Better lay over somewhere until you can join up with a train goin' east."

"I never saw one comin' out, and I don't figure to see some goin' back," the man retorted. "Anyway, don't reckon they'd be any worse than men like these."

"Don't bet on it," the sheriff commented dryly, and turned his back to the departing wagon. "Move on now," he said to Shep and his friends. "I ever hear of you, any of you, botherin' a woman again in my county, I won't wait for this fancy law we now got in this territory. I'll just take matters in my own hands like I used to do! You all hear that?"

They started off at once, pointing their horses due west. Brokaw waited, feeling the push of the old lawman's gaze on him. Now it would come, the usual careful probing.

"You a pilgrim, too?"

Brokaw shrugged. "Possible." He had nothing against lawmen. His own father had been one, and he had been proud of that fact. But experience in the last years had taught him it was wise to talk little in their presence and depend not at all upon their help. Naturally none of them took kindly to a stranger in their midst looking to kill off their townsmen.

"Headin' which way?"

Brokaw waited out a long moment. "There's a law in this country saying I've got to go a certain direction?"

The sheriff clucked softly. "You're mighty proddy, son," he observed with no show of heat. "Happens you're on closed range, and, if you ended up dead, I might try to notify your relations or friends, assumin' you got some. You're a stranger around here."

Brokaw nodded. "That's right."

"Well, it ain't healthy range for a stranger to get caught on. Hugh Preston don't take kindly to trespassin'. You just saw a sample of that."

"Big country," Brokaw replied laconically. "Man's got to cross it somewhere. Anyway, maybe I've come looking to see this Hugh Preston."

The sheriff surveyed him thoughtfully. "Well, you're the kind, all right."

"Meaning what?"

"Meanin' Hugh likes proddy riders. Like Shep Russell and them two with him. Carl Willet and Domino."

Brokaw considered that in silence, not liking the comparison. But Preston was the man he was seeking, and nothing must be permitted to stand in the way, not after all those months of searching. To hell with Shep and the others, and the sheriff, too. He said: "Preston's place to the south? There where the smoke is?"

The old lawman glanced over his shoulder. He ducked his head. "Fifteen miles or so. You goin' there now?"

Brokaw said—"Yes."—and wheeled the bay around.

The sheriff swung the gray in next to him. "Mind if I side along? When a man gets old, he finds lonesomeness a little hard to take. Kind of like he figured there wasn't much time left for talkin' and such, and he don't want to waste any."

Brokaw nodded. He would prefer to ride alone, in the silence that he had come to appreciate as a trustworthy friend in the long hours of the days and nights. He might learn something of value from the old lawman, but he would have to be careful with his own words. He could not afford to create any suspicion other than that any drifter would normally give rise to, and he must use care not to tip his hand.

"I'm Ben Marr, sheriff of this county. Don't think I heard you mention your name."

"No," Brokaw drawled, "you didn't."

Marr waited for him to continue. When, after a time, he did not, he said: "Find this country to your likin'?"

"I've seen better."

"Where?"

Brokaw swung his face to the lawman, grinning at the crudeness of the snare. "Several places."

Marr's bland expression did not change. "You know Hugh Preston?"

"Heard of him."

"Never worked for him before?"

"Like I said, just heard of him. Never saw him, never worked for him."

"He send for you?"

Brokaw shook his head patiently. "No. Why?"

Marr wagged his grizzled head. "You don't know, then they's no use tellin' you. You figurin' to work for him?"

"He hiring hands?" Brokaw asked in a careful way.

"Roundup's getting close. Place like Preston's always needin' 'punchers this time of year. Reckon you could hire on at any of the other spreads, too."

Brokaw made no reply to that suggestion. They rode on silently for the next two miles, the bay a half step behind the lawman's gray. Where the faint trail split, one bearing on toward the distant smudge of Preston's Arrowhead Ranch, the other to the town of Westport Crossing, Ben Marr pulled up. He screwed about in his saddle until he faced Brokaw squarely.

"If you'll take an old man's advice, son, you'll keep on ridin'. They's a lot of new country you can see outside this Scattered Hills range. I don't like to see a young feller get himself mixed up in things like goes on at Preston's."

For a swift moment Frank Brokaw had a fleeting remembrance of his father, of the kindness, the care and solicitation the man had always had for him. Ben Marr, in that fraction of time, was very much like Tom Brokaw. But it was because of Tom Brokaw, and the terrible thing done to him, that he was here now, in the Scattered Hills, looking for Hugh Preston. He gave the lawman a half smile. "Thanks, Sheriff. I can wipe my own nose. Don't lose any sleep over me."

Marr's shoulders lifted and fell in a sigh of weary resignation. "All right. Only thing, someday trouble's goin' to pop like all get-out at Arrowhead. I'm hopin' I won't find you bogged down hock-deep in it."

The hard, tough shell that had momentarily vanished from Frank Brokaw suddenly was about him again, wrapping him with its bitter, cynical shield. "I'll be real careful, Sheriff," he replied in a faintly mocking tone, and swung off down the trail.

III

Hugh Preston's Arrowhead Ranch was no ordinary, run-of-the-mill spread. This was apparent to Brokaw when he topped the last low rise and looked down upon the large, rambling structure with its out-scatter of smaller buildings. The main house was a long stone and log affair with a steeply slanted roof and shining white trim. Rugged, austere, and brutish, it reflected the great power it represented in a solid, foursquare sort of stance, defying man and the elements with its thick walls. It sat well to the fore in a broad clearing with several sheds, two barns, a cook shack, foreman's quarters, and a sprawling bunkhouse ranging out behind it to a grove of medium-age trees on the west side.

Brokaw's studied gaze probed the place for a full five minutes while he memorized the grounds and the complete lay of the buildings, and, too, he was having some dark thoughts about the man who owned it. A lot of money had gone into building it, into stocking it with cattle—how much? He had his own ideas of the amount, and that thought stirred him into action. He clucked the bay forward, going down the long slope.

Unconsciously he pulled the heavy gun at his hip around to a handier position. He had forced himself to learn the use of a handgun. He had never really grown accustomed to having it at his side. He preferred the strength of his arms and hands in a fight, and, if that was not the way it was to be, he liked the rifle now tucked in the boot beneath his leg. But a man couldn't always go walking around with a rifle slung in his arms.

No one was in sight when he approached, which was normal enough. Riders would be on the range working; the night crew would be getting some sleep in the bunkhouse. He reached the wide, hard-packed yard, and pointed for the tie rail at the front of the main house. There was a side door, also, leading into the forward rooms, but he chose the one he thought most apt to open into Preston's office. He had just reached the rail when a figure came into the open from a small building near the bunkhouse. The foreman, Brokaw guessed.

He halted, staying in the saddle, and waited for the man to come up. He was not a young man, somewhere in his early fifties. He wore the usual range work clothes, but he carried himself erect and with a strong show of authority, as though proud of what he was doing. An ancient, worn cedar-handled gun sagged at his hip, and, as he drew closer, Brokaw had a better look at his craggy, pointed features. His eyes were small, a piercing blue, and deep-set. His face was dark from summer's sun and winter's bitter wind and deeply grooved, only partly hidden by a mustache that exactly matched his gray hair. His gaze was cool and level, showing neither friendliness nor enmity.

"You're a far piece from the main trail, cowboy."

Brokaw considered the hard, dry press of the man's voice, wondering if he might be Preston. Too old, he finally concluded; they had said Preston was younger. This man was the foreman, no doubt. He said: "Doing any hiring?"

The old cowboy studied him briefly. "You don't look much like a workin' hand," he said bluntly. "But I reckon we could use some riders . . . the kind that can nurse a cow. That what you had in mind?"

"What else?"

Over in one of the barns a man was whistling tunelessly, and somewhere a horse nickered, getting wind of the bay and recognizing a newcomer. A cricket *clacked* in the dry grass along Preston's house, and, high above the Sierra del Diablo, much closer now, an eagle swooped in a lazy, circling pattern.

"Like I said, you don't look the kind."

"Well, what do I look like, then?" Brokaw asked in a soft voice.

The old 'puncher shrugged. "You didn't get them big arms and that pair of shoulders singin' lullabies to a night herd. But never mind. Always need hands this time of the year, and a man can't afford his choosin's. Forty dollars and chuck. You want it, go over to the bunkhouse and find yourself a bed. What's your handle?"

"Brokaw. Frank Brokaw."

The man thought hard for a moment. "Name's not familiar," he said. Then: "I'm Abel Cameron, foreman for Mister Preston." He paused, as the side door swung in and a tall, spare man came from the main house into the sunlight. "That's him, there," he finished.

Brokaw swiveled his attention to the cattleman, the hair along the back of his neck suddenly stiffening. Here now was Hugh Preston, here was the man he had heard about in Tascosa. Here, by all probabilities, was Matt Slade. He was a good-looking man. He approached in the short, mincing steps of a man unused to walking, and disliking every step of it. He had a squared sort of carriage and good shoulders, but the face failed to fit the body. It was finely cut, almost feminine, and his mouth had a weakness about the corners. His eyes were dark on either side of a thin nose, and his hair, bared to the sun, was a washed-out blond. Brokaw met his glance with a steady gaze.

"Who's this, Abel?"

"Man I just hired on. Name of Frank Brokaw."

Long ago Brokaw had stopped giving a false name. At first it seemed a smart idea when he made his inquiries, but later he decided it was far better to come right out with it—to make himself known. It would serve to bring matters to a quick head once he met the man who was Matt Slade. He closely watched Preston's eyes, his reactions, searching for any signs of alarm or wariness. Preston surveyed him curiously for a moment.

He said: "Good. Could use a half dozen more. Cattle's scattered pretty wide, Abel. We got to get them all in this year." He came back to Brokaw. "You new in this country, Frank?"

"First time around," Brokaw replied.

Preston smiled, showing even, small teeth that were gleaming white. "Glad to have you on the crew. Take your orders from Abel here, and mind your own business, and you'll make out all right."

He wheeled away, striking for the cook shack with its narrow dining quarters attached. Brokaw watched him leave with half-shut eyes, having his suspicions about the man. He was a smooth one and cool as they came. He was the right build and about the described age.

Cameron broke into his thoughts. "One thing about Mister Preston, either he likes a man, or he sure don't. They's no middle ground with him. I reckon he likes you."

Brokaw swung down from the gelding. "I wonder why," he murmured.

Cameron threw a hasty, sharp glance at him. "You think he's got a special reason?"

"He's your friend, you ought to know," Brokaw replied in an easy tone. "My horse has been traveling for quite a spell. I reckon I better draw me another from the corral for the rest of the day. That all right?"

He felt the push of Cameron's blue eyes. The foreman was still trying to fathom his words, read some meaning into them. But he said no more about it. "Sure. Either put him in the corral with the rest of the stock, or take him in the barn. Plenty of horses around here to draw from. You et yet?"

"Not since early this morning."

"Cookie'll have some grub ready before long. Not much sense in you goin' out on the range this late, anyway. Just lay around the rest of the day and figure on ridin' in the mornin'. I'll toll you off to the boys tonight at supper."

Brokaw nodded and led off the bay to the barn. He stabled him, pulled off the gear, and rubbed him down with a gunny sack, afterward pulling down some feed for him. Taking his saddlebags and blanket roll, he strolled through the dim recesses of the barn, throwing his search along the walls until he came at last to the tack room. This would be as good a time as any to look the gear over. There was no one in sight, and he spent a full fifteen minutes going over the rack of hulls. Some were fairly new, some old, and there was one that had been completely shattered by a bullet that had struck the swell, but there was no silver-mounted saddle in the lot. Matt Slade had owned such a saddle when he left Central City. The blaze-faced sorrel they said he rode likely had been sold, or maybe was dead, but the saddle was something else. Something a man usually hung onto after all else was gone, and its being a fancy, hand-tooled, silver-decorated job would make the attachment even stronger. Such a piece of gear Matt Slade probably would keep. Or would he? If he were a smart man, wanting to sever all connections to the past, he might also rid himself of that. Such saddles were not common, but it would not be said they were a rarity, either. Brokaw had seen a few down in Texas and in New Mexico, and some real fancy ones in California. But there was not one there in Arrowhead's

138

tack room, and, if Hugh Preston was actually Matt Slade, he had played it real cozy and had gotten rid of the saddle, or else had it hidden away somewhere else, possibly in the main house.

He left the barn's huge bulk and tramped across the yard to the bunkhouse. It was a large, rectangular affair with double tiers of bunks running along either side and two tables with chairs down the center. Moving softly so as not to awaken the half dozen or more snoring men, he found a bunk that appeared to be unused and, throwing his blanket and bags onto the thin pad, sat down, his thoughts still on Hugh Preston.

The rancher could easily be Matt Slade. He fitted the meager description obtained back in Central City, and he was a smart man, you could see that, one easily capable of controlling his feelings if the name Brokaw had had any special meaning to him. But he had to be sure, he recognized that fact; he had to find more proof, something definite before he broached Preston, bald-faced, with his suspicions.

Thinking of this, he stretched out on his bunk. He fell asleep, passing up the noon meal, and came awake late in the day to the thud of riders pulling into the yard. Rousing himself, he went outside into the falling dusk, nodding to the curious glances of the men he encountered. He cleaned up at the wash house in the rear of the crew's quarters, and, when the supper iron clanged its summons across the graying day, he crossed over to the cook house and entered.

Abel Cameron was there ahead of him and pointed a gnarled finger to a place on his left at the plank table. Other riders began streaming in as the cook, a squat, dark-faced Mexican, started bringing platters of steak, potatoes, hominy, and boiled cabbage. Two large coffee pots were stationed on the table, one at either end. The 'punchers fell to at

139

once, talking little as they ate. Preston was not there, and Brokaw recognized only three men other than the foreman: the man he had tangled with, Shep, and his two companions, Carl and Domino. Twice he glanced up to find Shep's eyes boring him in a hard, angry way.

When the platters were empty and the final cup of coffee poured, Cameron got to his feet. " 'Boys, this here," he said, waving his hand at Brokaw, "is a new man hired on today. Name of Frank Brokaw." He paused, as attention swung around and came to a stop on Brokaw. "He's a Johnny-come-lately to this part of the country so I don't reckon he knows anybody here." He hesitated again, turning now to Brokaw. "Frank, this ain't all the Arrowhead crew, but it'll do as a start. First man here on my right is Jack Corbett."

Corbett, a freckle-faced redhead, acknowledged the introduction with a nod, reserving, as was customary, any further overtures until he became better acquainted.

"Next one," Cameron continued, "is Buckshot Martin. Then Pete Simpson. Then Jules Strove and Carl Willet. Only name next feller's got is Domino. Never heard him mention no others, so I reckon that's all of it." Cameron halted, eyeing the next 'puncher closely. "What happened to you, Shep? Fall off'n your horse and skin up a mite? Or did one them brush-lovin' longhorns take a fancy to you? That feller is Shep Russell, Brokaw."

The old foreman droned on, introducing three more men, the last a powerfully built, handsome cowboy with a neatly trimmed mustache. He was Ollie Godfrey, Cameron said, and he eyed Brokaw with a steady intentness.

The room was quiet after that, as if the final introduction had some deeper, more important meaning. Godfrey ran his fingers through his wavy blond hair. He nodded and in a lazy voice said: "I see grandpa made you right at home."

Brokaw said nothing, suddenly fully aware of a sullen undercurrent in the room. One of the riders chuckled, Shep Russell. He was appreciating Godfrey's small joke and in so doing was letting Brokaw know upon which side he stood.

Cameron's face had gone stiff, and his eyes were glinting, steel-blue points. He said: "There's always a cute one in every outfit, Frank. I reckon Ollie's our boy."

Godfrey made no reply in the ensuing silence. Brokaw recognized then the bad blood that existed between the two and had a brief wonder at its cause. But he gave it little thought, having his own immediate problems concerning Hugh Preston. Two of the riders pushed back from the table, and an immediate exodus of the others began.

Cameron turned to Brokaw. "We start early around here. Breakfast at four-thirty sharp."

Brokaw nodded. His glance was upon Shep Russell. That man had not stirred, but was watching him with a hot, burning gaze. He was not forgetting the affair earlier in the day, where the homesteader was concerned, and it was plain he meant to do something about it.

Brokaw moved by Cameron, his face suddenly dark and still. He well knew Shep Russell's kind—they understood but one thing—toughness and brute strength. He walked to where the cowboy sat, fingers laced across his belly, leaning back in his chair. Lifting his foot, he gave the chair a hard shove. Russell went over backwards in a crashing heap.

Cameron yelled something in his surprise. Godfrey and the cowboy called Jules Strove, and Carl Willet, the only rider still in the room, stepped quickly away from Russell's thrashing shape. Russell got to his feet, his face working with fury, curses streaming from his lips. "Damn you! I'll kill you for that! I'll. . . ."

"You act like a man with something on your mind,"

Brokaw said in a winter-cold voice. "I'm ready to hear it."

Russell's mouth ceased its working. He stared at Brokaw's threatening figure for a long moment. Then: "When I'm ready. I'll pick the place."

"This place is good as any."

A wild temper was racing through Russell, leaving him uncertain and at a loss as to his own abilities. He seemed half inclined to reach for the gun at his hip, but something, some deep and wiser caution, was holding him back. Perhaps it was the absolute calm, the utter deadliness of Brokaw, or possibly the flatness of his eyes. His gaze broke suddenly, and he looked away, glaring angrily at the other men in the room—at the Mexican cook who had entered at the crash of the overturning chair. With a hurried motion, he wheeled away and bolted for the doorway.

Brokaw threw out a broad, hindering hand against his shoulder. He pushed, and Russell fell back a step. In a cold voice Brokaw said: "All right, Shep. I'll let it pass for this time. But keep out of my way. Understand?"

Russell gave him a furious, frustrated look. Nodding, he rushed for the door, slammed through it, and went lunging out into the yard.

Brokaw remained still, letting the tension run from his tall figure. His back was to Cameron and to the others, and there was only the sound of their breathing in the room. Finally Cameron spoke, his voice plaintive. "Didn't know you and Shep had met up before."

"Just once," Brokaw replied.

The old foreman's face hardened. "I ain't knowin' what's between you two, but I want no trouble around here. If you're the trouble-makin' kind, just move along. I got me enough problems without that."

"There'll be no trouble, long as he stays out of my way.

But get this straight, Cameron, I'm of no mind to put up with his foolishness."

Cameron stroked his mustache. "Fair enough. I reckon Shep understands that, too. What's between the two of you, anyway?"

"Matter for us, nobody else."

Cameron's ire lifted again. "Long as you both are workin' for Arrowhead, I say it's my business, me bein' foreman of this crew."

"Then you better ask Shep about it."

"Maybe I will," Cameron said. "Howsomever, I reckon this spread's big enough for both of you. See you in the mornin'."

He moved to the doorway and out into the yard. Jules Strove and Willet followed, but Ollie Godfrey hung back. He walked up beside Brokaw. His face was cold, and his eyes were hard. "You'd be a smart man to move on, drifter. There's no job around here for you, leastwise, a healthy one."

Brokaw favored him with a down-curling grin. "Second time today I've been told that. Fact is, I like it here."

"You may not like it so good later," Godfrey said. "And don't be pinning your bets on old man Cameron. He won't be ramrodding this outfit much longer."

Brokaw said nothing. So that was the trouble between Cameron and Godfrey. The husky cowboy was gunning for the old foreman's job. He found himself not liking the blond, not only because of his cocksure, belligerent manner, but for some other reason he could not quite pin down. "This Hugh Preston's idea?"

Godfrey said: "No business of yours that I can see. But it'll happen. You can figure on it."

"So?"

143

"Take that advice you got and move on. There'll be no job here on Arrowhead for you."

Godfrey turned abruptly to the doorway and walked into the yard. Brokaw stood quietly by the long table for another minute or two, his eyes lost in the dusk outside the room. Then his wide shoulders moved in a gesture of indifference. To hell with Godfrey and Abel Cameron. That was their own fight. He had Matt Slade to find and kill.

IV

Brokaw came out in the wide yard and strolled toward the pole corrals. It was not yet entirely dark, but night's curtain was falling swiftly, and some of the lamps were already lit. Sounds, emanating from a noisy game of stud poker in the bunkhouse, broke the evening's hush at intervals, mingling with an occasional *thud* in the barn where part of the horses fed and rested.

He came to a stop at the wagon shed. Placing his shoulders against its wall, he drew the makings from a pocket and spun up a cigarette. A match flared, orange and bright, under his thumbnail, and, as he held it close, its flame mirrored against the hard, polished planes of his face and gave his eyes a splintery look. Not all of the temper was out of his long frame yet, but he felt better. Shep Russell would stay out of his way for a long time, at least.

He sucked in a deep draft of smoke, tipped back his head, and blew it out in a single, trailing cloud. The spring night was soft about him, only a bit chilly and sweet with the smells of summer coming to life. Once begun, darkness moved in quickly, and the shadows became deep voids of black. Cameron came from his quarters and rapped across the hard pack to the ranch house. He thumped on the door and, to the muffled response, opened it and entered.

Two men came then from the bunkhouse, walking slowly, at ease, their cigarettes small red eyes in the obscurity. They

145

passed under the bunkhouse window's square of light, and Brokaw recognized one as Jules Strove, the other as the redhead, Jack Corbett.

Strove was chuckling. "Man and boy! You shoulda seen old Shep's face when that feller Brokaw knocked over his chair! He looked like a ranny what had just backed into a hot brandin' iron!"

"And Shep didn't take him up on it?" Corbett noted in a wondering tone.

"Uhn-huh! Not Shep, not any of Ollie's bunch. He just stood there quiet as a fly walkin' on fresh butter, and listened while Brokaw told him what's what. Then he skedaddled. Went out the door like a cow critter that had just seen a she-bear with cubs."

"Can't say's I blame him," the redhead mused. "Something about that Brokaw that makes a man think twice before he ups and starts fiddlin' with him."

The men passed on by, enjoying their final smokes before turning in. Brokaw grinned into the darkness. That was the way he wanted it, that was just how he wanted them to feel. Maybe they would all mind their own business and leave him to his. The sooner he got to the bottom of Hugh Preston's past life, the sooner he could wind up his affairs and get out of the country. Ranch life and work no longer appealed to him. It was hard, back-breaking labor in all sorts of weather, and for little pay. He could think off-hand of a dozen better ways to make a living, all of them offering better money. There was a greater depth of danger involved, of course, but a man didn't mind that. It just added zest to the job, and somewhere down the last few years that had become a strong necessity, it seemed.

It had not always been that way. He guessed it was the war that had brought about the change. Before that he had not minded it, possibly because he knew nothing else other than working the small farm-ranch his father owned. With only a couple of men and his mother, he had operated the place while his father carried on with his job as marshal. Then the war fever had seeped into his blood. He remembered the look on his father's face that evening, when he had suddenly announced at the supper table that he was going to enlist. Tom Brokaw, a cup of coffee halfway to his lips, paused, looked keenly at him, and then carefully replaced the cup in its saucer.

"I reckon, if that's what you want, boy, that's what you'll have. I ain't standing in your way. But if you go, I want you to be a soldier, not one of those thieving, raiding cut-throats, killing for the devil of it. A man needs a reason to shoot another man, and, if you are believing in this cause, then, winner or loser, you can come back proud of what you've done, and not be afraid somebody'll remember you for something bad."

It was the longest speech he had ever heard his father make at one time, and he never forgot it. His mother, whom he recalled as a tired, work-worn woman, had cried softly at first when it came time for him to leave. But she squared her slight shoulders, kissed him on the cheek, and pressed a small Bible into his hands.

"You get sick, Son, you come home," she admonished him. She had never fully conceded he was no longer her small boy. "And when the war is over, you come straight home."

But he had not. He was just twenty-one when he had laid down the sword, a boy turned fast into a man by war's harsh and bloody realities. He was sick of fighting, of killing, of hiding, of rain, mud, heat, cold, and the smell of cordite, and the sight of a gun repulsed him. A terrible restlessness had possessed him, and he had given way to its demands. Finally he returned to Kansas, the scars only partly healed, to face a world of cold, half friends and total strangers.

John Tennyson, the banker, had said: "Figured you'd turn up someday. We tried to find you, but nobody knew what happened to you. Some said you were dead. Two, three letters we sent came back."

"What happened? What happened to my folks?"

"Well, this man Matt Slade was a friend of your pa's. Showed up here one day, just passing through, he said. But he hadn't seen your pa for a long spell, so he stuck around, just visiting. Guess he was around here for three weeks or better. Used to see him walking and riding with your pa. Reckon he stayed there at the place with them, too."

"Where did he come from?"

"Don't rightly know. Reckon I never did hear him or your pa say. Anyway, along about that time I had a shipment of gold coin come in. Near ten thousand dollars. Was to be picked up by a land syndicate that was planning to buy up a lot of ground around here. Nobody knew about that money except your pa and me, and maybe the stage driver."

"You trying to tell me Pa had something to do with stealing that money?"

"I'm coming to that. Matt Slade found out about the gold somehow, and only place I figure it could have come from was your pa, because I sure never mentioned it. Then one morning, about four o'clock, we woke up to a big explosion. Everybody went tearing down to find out what it was, and I spotted the smoke coming out of my bank. We saw this man, Slade, leaving on his horse, but he had caught us flat-footed, and there wasn't nobody saddled up to chase him. There was a little shooting, and some say he was hit, but we never did know for sure."

"And Pa . . . what about him?"

"We found him laying there in the bank with his head all caved in. Looked like he had been standing across the room from the vault, and, when the explosion came, a piece of the door flew over and hit him. Poor Tom. Been better off if it had killed him. He didn't know anything. His mind was a blank, and it never changed."

"But there was no proof he had been in on it with Slade."

"Then what was he doing in there with him?"

"He maybe suspected Slade was up to something and followed him there. He might have stepped into the room just as the charge went off. You sure don't think he had anything to do with it, do you?"

Tennyson wagged his head. "I only know what we all saw, and the general opinion around was that Slade and Tom were in it together. Ten thousand dollars is a lot of money. Thinking about it can do things to a man."

"But not to my pa. There's not enough gold in this world to make him do something like that!"

Frank Brokaw was shocked, bewildered, and angered, and for several minutes he vented his feelings in the small confines of the Central City Bank. But after a time a measure of calmness came back to him.

"What did you do to him, after you'd decided what you did?"

Tennyson shrugged. "No point in doing anything to him. His mind was gone, like I said. He stayed out on the farm with your mother. Then that winter she took down and died. There wasn't nothing left to do but send him to Leavenworth where they could take care of him."

The calloused words had ripped through Frank Brokaw, a bitter, steel-hard determination swirled within him and crystallized into an inflexible core. He had said: "Nobody ever heard of Matt Slade again?"

"Nobody. Podie Wilkins did a lot of looking around the country, and the land syndicate sent out an Eastern detective, and they didn't turn up anything. He just dropped out of sight."

"I'll find him," Brokaw murmured, "I'll find him and bring him back here, and make him admit Pa had nothing to do with the robbing of your bank! And then I'll kill him, because that's what he did to them! Killed them both, sure as I'm standing here!"

"Hardly any use. . . ," Tennyson had begun, but Brokaw cut him short.

"What did this Matt Slade look like?"

"Big man, nigh as tall as you. Good-looking, but I just don't recollect anything special about his face. He'd be about forty now, I'd guess. Rode a big, blaze-faced sorrel stallion and sported a silver-mounted saddle. Had silver coins fastened all along the edge of the skirt."

"You sure Slade was his real name?"

"Only thing I ever heard, and that's what your pa called him . . . Matt Slade."

It wasn't much to go on, but Frank Brokaw had filed each detail carefully in his mind, adding to it a few other bits garnered from different townspeople. Podie Wilkins turned over to him his father's gun and belt, and he brushed aside the blood-washed memories of the war and strapped it on. He spent hours practicing a fast draw, and, when he felt he could hold his own in that department, he turned to improving his accuracy. But he spent little time on that; when he found Matt Slade, he would be standing close enough that he could not miss.

So it began, the search for the man who had called himself Matt Slade. At the outset he knew that would not be his name now. He would have changed that just as he would have taken great pains to slash all other connections to the past. But a man with ten thousand gold to spend could not very well hide his glittering light under a bushel. Not in the West anyway, where such things did not escape notice. John Tennyson and Podie Wilkins and many others had told him flatly he was undertaking a hopeless task, that he should forget it, move back on the farm, get it going, and then bring his father to live out the remainder of his days with him. But that was not the way of Frank Brokaw. He would find Matt Slade, drag a confession out of him that Tom Brokaw was innocent of any wrongdoing—then kill him.

In the months that followed he had met a few people who recalled the big red stallion and the fancy saddle, none who remembered the man who rode them. But he did eventually find several who recalled a big man who appeared in the Scattered Hills country around five years back, a man who came from nowhere, who paid cash for the old Cresswell place, and who rebuilt it with an extravagant hand, sparing no cost. That man was Hugh Preston.

Brokaw came back to the present as a curse exploded from the bunkhouse. There was a burst of laughter. A door banged, and one of the riders, Buckshot Martin, it seemed to Brokaw still standing there in the dark, came out and stomped for the wash house. Brokaw heard him stroking the hand pump as he drew for himself a drink of water. Two more came out, Ollie Godfrey and Shep Russell. They drifted into the center of the yard, well away from the crew's quarters.

"How much longer you figure?" Shep was saying as they came within earshot.

Godfrey puffed at his half-burned cigar. "Not much. She's due back in a few days now."

"You're mighty sure of her!"

Godfrey laughed. "I am. She's in the palm of my hand, don't you forget it!"

The side door of the main house swung back, and Cameron came into view. Shep Russell moved off toward the wash house, and Godfrey, hooking his thumbs into his belt, swung full around and watched the foreman approach. Faint star shine flooded the yard, turning all things pale and blurred and deepening the shadowed areas. The Mexican cook's handful of chickens, in their makeshift pen behind the kitchen, chattered sleepily as something disturbed them.

Ollie Godfrey called across the hard pack: "Well, grampa, you get your night's kissin' done?"

Cameron broke his stride and came to a slow halt.

Godfrey's voice, pushing, sarcastic, deliberately pitched to irritate, said: "Not much use in your doing it, old man. You're through. No amount of talking is going to keep you on this job, and the sooner you make up your mind to that, the better off we'll all be."

"I could do a little talkin' on my own, Ollie," Cameron said coolly. "A few things Mister Preston wouldn't much like hearin'."

Godfrey laughed again, in a soft, taunting way. "But you won't, grampa. You'd be a dead man. It would be like committing suicide, and that you full well know."

"Maybe so," Cameron murmured. "Maybe so. Seems to me you're crowdin' things right fast lately. What's eatin' at you?"

"Something you'd not understand, old man. Only thing, don't be making any plans for the future. Leastwise, not as foreman for this outfit."

Abel Cameron thought for a minute. Then: "So that's it. Well, I was foreman when Cresswell had this, and I been the same ever since Hugh Preston took it over. Reckon I'll keep on being same until he tells me different." Cameron finished. Brokaw could see his jutting profile pointing straight at Godfrey, hostility in every angle of his craggy face. "Place like this takes a man, not a slicker, at the head!"

There was a breathless pause, and then Godfrey started forward. "Maybe I better show you what a man is . . . ," he said.

Cameron waited, motionless. Brokaw moved out from the shadows along the wagon shed. He came into the faint shine near the middle of the distance separating the two men. Cameron glanced quickly to him, and Ollie Godfrey pulled to a sudden stop. His face came around, angry and surprised.

"What's this . . . ?" he began.

Brokaw, his eyes reaching out beyond the two men, located Shep Russell over by the bunkhouse and gave his dim shape a momentary survey. He waved his hand, indicating the cigarette between his fingers. "Just having a smoke," he said calmly. "However, you do flap your mouth a little wide."

Abel Cameron chuckled. Godfrey's face went stiff. He flung a hasty glance over his shoulder, saw no one, and came back to Brokaw's languorous shape. "You're horning in where you got no business," he said in a low voice. "Look out you don't go saddling the wrong horse."

"I'll take my chances," Brokaw replied softly.

"That's just what they will be," Godfrey retorted, and pivoted on his heel for the bunkhouse.

Brokaw and Cameron watched him cross the hard pack and stamp into the crew's quarters. When the door had banged behind him, the foreman turned to Brokaw.

"Obliged to you, Frank. But they's no call for you to mix in this."

"I'm not," Brokaw said shortly. "Just happened to be standing around."

Cameron studied him for a moment. "I see. Well, all the same, I'm obliged to you."

He swung away, heading for his bunk. All the lamps were out now. Preston's Arrowhead was quiet. Brokaw rolled another cigarette and cupped his hands over the match. Now there was Ollie Godfrey, he thought. He couldn't seem to stay clear of things. First of all it was Shep and maybe his two friends, Carl Willet and Domino, and, of course, Hugh Preston. If he had recognized Brokaw by name he, too, like the others, would have things on his mind. Briefly he considered his position. A man might find it hard to sleep in a room where others were not exactly friendly.

He flipped his cigarette into the yard, watching its coal flare up brightly and die, then turned about. He moved by the wagon shed, circling it, coming out at the barn where he had stabled the bay. Entering the runway, he followed it out until he reached the ladder, leading up to the loft. He climbed that, gaining the upper level, piled high with fragrant hay. There he bedded down for the night.

V

After breakfast in that chilled, half light preceding dawn, Abel Cameron hailed the Arrowhead crew together. He issued his orders for the day, turning last to Frank Brokaw.

"You take the two-seater and head for town. Missus Preston's comin' in on the stage. Pick her up and bring her back."

At once Ollie Godfrey pushed forward, anger in his eyes. "Why him? None of us been to town in weeks. Why not let me go?"

Cameron said: "Reckon that's the reason. Everybody can't go, so I figure wouldn't be fair to send any of you."

"Rest of the boys won't mind me going," Godfrey persisted.

"Brokaw'll make the trip," Cameron said, and wheeled away.

For a long minute Godfrey stared after the foreman's stiff figure, but after a time he shrugged and moved off toward the corral. Brokaw turned for the barn where the wrangler had the carriage, with its two fine blacks, already waiting for him. Cameron was there ahead of him. Brokaw asked: "How'll I know Missus Preston?"

The old foreman gave him a brief grin. "You'll know her. Never you fret over that."

Brokaw climbed onto the cushioned seat and gathered up the ribbons. "How far to town and which road do I take?"

"You'll be all the mornin' gettin' there. Take the road to

155

the right after you leave the yard. Stay on it all the way."

Brokaw nodded and swung the blacks into motion. They rolled out of the yard, but just as they drew parallel with the front of the ranch house, Brokaw caught movement from the corner of his eye. He flung a quick glance to that point. Hugh Preston was standing at the corner of the log structure, watching him with a studied, careful gaze. How long he had been there, Brokaw had no way of knowing, but possibly for some minutes. It was too far, and the light was much too poor to see the rancher's features distinctly, but Brokaw had the feeling Preston's survey, hard and searching, had been upon him during the entire time he had been in the yard. The thought—*Preston is suspicious.*—sprang immediately into his mind, and that, logically, led to the conclusion Preston and Matt Slade were one and the same, else why suspicion?

He had a moment's urge to halt the blacks, wheel around, and throw his accusations into Preston's face. But a saner force moved in and thrust the impulse into the background of his mind. After all, what proof did he actually have? One or two circumstantial items, and now this close watch Preston had placed on him. You could hardly call that definite proof.

The blacks reached the crossroads and swung south into the deeper, more sandy ruts. It was cool, and they were in high spirits, so he let them have their kittenish way for the first few miles. When they had worked off their steam, he pulled them down to a more comfortable trot and settled himself for the long ride.

He had not known Hugh Preston was married. He wondered if he had been so when he called himself Matt Slade, if Slade he truly was. There had been no mention of a wife in Central City. But that was easy to explain. She would not have been with him, if he had come there with the predetermined intention of robbing a bank. More than likely, he had been a single man at that time, and it was after he had gotten his hands on the money that he took to himself a wife. There is nothing like a wife to suggest respectability.

Brokaw ran his glance idly over the landscape, sliding by at a steady gray-green pace. The bright sparkle of dew still held before the sun's lifting rays. But it would not be that way for long. In another hour or two the heat would move in, drying the tips of the grass, sucking off the juices and changing the prairie to pale tan. The country changed little with the miles. Only slightly more than flat, it stretched out in all directions, broken very occasionally by a lifting hill, a clump of cotton-woods, or a low, frowning butte. The Sierra del Diablo stood aloof and deep blue in the background far to the west. Even at such distance they appeared rough and forbidding, as if trying to repudiate the undulating, regular beauty of the prairies.

It was shortly after eleven o'clock when he reached the edge of Westport Crossing and wheeled into its single main street. It had the same, generally weather-worn appearance of all such towns, Brokaw observed. A twin row of high, false-fronted buildings, all badly in need of paint, stood shoulder to shoulder, facing each other across a dusty, wide avenue. At that hour, few people were abroad, and the narrow wooden sidewalks were nearly deserted.

He headed the blacks toward the far end of town, where a sign jutting out into the street proclaimed **Bell's Livery Stable**. The team was hot and a little tired from the steady run, and he was bone-dry and hungry. He spotted the Longhorn Bar and made a mental note of its location. A little farther on he singled out the Gem Café, looking clean and inviting behind panels of frothy white window curtains, and such information he filed along with the rest.

"Here! You there! Arrowhead!"

The voice of a woman came reaching out from the porch of the Westport Hotel. Brokaw swung his glance to that point, seeing at once the tall, striking shape of the speaker standing next to a pile of luggage. That would be Hugh Preston's wife. He pulled the team in, slanting for the porch, going over the woman carefully with half-shut eyes. She was tall and well-formed in the suit of powder blue. Her honey-blonde hair was caught up and piled high under a perky straw hat, and, as he drew closer, he could see her eyes were blue, slightly almond-shaped, set in a triangular face. He hauled up the team in front of the porch and touched the brim of his hat.

"You're late, cowboy," she stated flatly. "Load these bags and let's get the hell out of here!"

Brokaw's glance flicked her briefly, then a faint humor touched the corners of his wide mouth. He climbed from the carriage and stowed the luggage in the back seat. She did not wait for him to assist her, but was already in the seat when he was finished. He stepped into the vehicle, took up the reins, and continued on for the livery stable.

They traveled perhaps fifty feet before she became aware of it. She whirled on him. "Where do you think you're going?"

"Horses are tired. Need a little rest and feed."

"Forget the horses!" Darla Preston snapped. "Turn this rig around and get started for the ranch. I want to get home!"

"After the team feeds and waters," Brokaw replied calmly. "I'm a bit dry and hungry myself."

She reached suddenly across his arm and grasped the reins, jerking hard with all her strength. But Brokaw's hand was firm, and the team scarcely felt the interference. With his free hand Brokaw pulled loose her fingers and pushed them away.

"Lady," he said then in an even tone, "you might just as

158

well settle down. We're going nowhere until these horses, and I, have something to eat."

She was looking at him in an odd, startled way. Little flecks of anger danced in her eyes, and her full lips were compressed into a stiff line. She said nothing. They reached Bell's, and Brokaw got out and handed her down from the seat, giving instructions for the care of the blacks to the hostler as he did so.

"Be pleased to have you eat dinner with me," he said as they moved back into the street.

"No, thank you," she replied with a quick tilt of her head. She was almost as tall as he, Brokaw noticed. "Who are you anyway? What's your name? I don't remember seeing you around the ranch before."

"You haven't. Just started today. The name is Brokaw."

"Well, Brokaw, you haven't heard the last of this!"

"Horses need attention. No sense in ruining a fine team like those blacks."

"Who cares about the horses? We've got plenty of them. Hereafter, when you're with me, you'll do what I tell you to. Understand that?"

The patience ran out of Frank Brokaw in one final drop. "Look," he said, "I'll be starting for the Arrowhead Ranch in one hour. You want to ride with me, you be standing over there on the porch of the hotel. If you don't want to wait, best thing you can do is start walking."

He wheeled about, leaving her standing there near the center of the street, and headed for the restaurant. He did not bother to look back, and it was only after he had sat down and ordered his meal that he glanced toward the hotel and saw her waiting on the porch. Women like Darla Preston found small favor with him. He had no time to cater to their spoiled whims and notions. But she was a beautiful woman, he had to admit it, exactly the sort you would expect Hugh Preston to marry, and she, in turn, was the kind that would go for a man with plenty of money.

His meal arrived: steak, potatoes, apple pie, and strong coffee. He ate unhurriedly, enjoying the food with the relish of a man sick of his own cooking. When he was finished, he paid the ticket and returned to the street. The sun was full high, bearing down hard, and he paused to brush the sweat from his brow with the back of a hand.

He turned sharply left, striking for the stables at the end of the street, the urgency to settle with Hugh Preston pushing him with relentless force. Thus, he did not see Darla Preston, standing just within the hotel's lobby where she had moved to escape the dust and heat, nor witness the look of puzzled interest on her face. He reached Bell's and entered. The hostler had seen him coming, and was leading the blacks to where the two-seater was parked, when he stepped into the shadowy runway. He helped the man finish the harnessing, and a few minutes later drove to the hotel.

Darla was waiting on the porch. He helped her to the seat, settled down beside her, then they moved off down the street, with the brunt of a full noon heat bearing down upon them. The team had no inclinations to run now, as they had earlier in the day, but was content to trot along at a fair pace.

They drove in silence for the first five miles, Brokaw lost in his own thoughts, Darla a quiet, erect figure, smelling faintly of lilac, at his elbow. He turned to her then, recalling Ben Marr's request, and caught her staring at him. She pulled her glance away quickly.

"The sheriff asked to be remembered."

She murmured—"Oh."—in a way that said it meant little to her.

"He's a friend of the family's?"

Darla laughed, a light sparkling sound tinged at the edges by sarcasm. "Hardly. If he sent his regards, it was for some reason. Why?"

Brokaw shrugged, and leaned forward, placing his elbows on his knees. "The way he talked, I figured him to be your friend."

"He's never approved of Hugh. Or of me. I think he would like very much to get something bad on us. Natural, I suppose. The big ranchers are always targets."

"He been sheriff around here long?"

"Ever since we've been in this country. Little over six years."

Six years! Brokaw smiled his satisfaction. That much of the report was true; he had it now, not from hearsay but straight from Preston's wife. He began a question relative to their previous home, to that time before they had purchased Arrowhead, but she spoke before he voiced it.

"Why didn't Ollie come after me?"

"I was the only one not tied up."

Darla laughed again, having some secret joke about that. Brokaw recalled the young cowboy's obvious disappointment and resentment at not being allowed to make the trip, and he remembered the words spoken by him to Shep Russell the previous evening, wondering what, if any, connection they had.

The blacks trotted steadily onward. The carriage top cut off the strong thrust of the sun and rode easily over the rutted trail. Far ahead, to the right, a ballooning cloud of dust rode the hot air, drifting slowly toward them. Brokaw watched it with interest.

"You a friend of Hugh's?"

To her question Brokaw said: "No. Just came along for a job. Cameron hired me on."

She had apparently forgotten her anger of the morning

and now seemed inclined to talk. "You don't look or act like the usual run of 'punchers."

"No? How does the usual 'puncher look and act?"

She did not reply immediately reply. He knew she was having difficulty in framing an answer. That he did not jump when she commanded, that he did not kowtow to her presence and stand in awe of her majestic imperiousness and beauty—those were her reasons, but she did not express them in so many words. She made a small, upflung gesture with her gloved hands. "Well, you just don't seem like it, that's all. You look more like. . . ."

"Like a gunman," he supplied dryly.

"Yes," she stated flatly, and stopped short.

"Every man around here wears a gun. No call to peg me as a gunslinger because I hang one on my hip. Fact of the matter is, I hate 'em."

Brokaw again felt the pressure of her gaze, searching, wondering, prying deeply. It came to him that she was trying to place him, catalog him, and, woman-like, put him somewhere in the proper niche in her mind possibly for future use.

She said: "Where did you come from, Brokaw?"

He gave her a brief glance. "Around. Texas, Mexico, the Territories. You name it, I probably been there."

"In the war?"

"Four years of it."

"But I meant, where was your home? Where did you grow up?"

He accorded that question the silence it deserved, making no reply. When she saw that she had erred, she said: "Forget I asked that. I know certain men don't like to have their backgrounds gone too deeply into."

He had his own secret amusement at that, but made no comment. They dropped into a shallow valley that was like a broad soup bowl of grass, followed out the road that carved across its floor, and gained the opposite rim. Another basin dropped away ahead of them, and they started the descent, coming suddenly upon a small herd of cattle being driven by a slim girl and a bearded old 'puncher. The herd was about halfway past. Brokaw pulled the blacks to a slow walk.

"Drive on!" Darla Preston commanded, all at once tense and irritable.

The steers began to veer and mill at the appearance of the carriage, which had come so unexpectedly upon them. Brokaw shook his head and hauled them back on the reins, bringing the blacks to a stop.

"Drive through them!" Darla ordered in a terse voice. She leaned forward, grabbing for the whip.

Brokaw, his jaw set, jammed his booted foot against the whip's handle, wedging it in its socket. The slim girl, sitting straight in her saddle and watching them intently, wheeled and loped up.

"Damn you . . . damn you!" Darla gritted through clenched teeth. "Why didn't you do what I told you?"

"Why?" Brokaw said, eyeing her closely. "Those people are having a hard enough time of it without making it worse. Had we butted into that drive, we likely would have got a horse horned, as well as splitting up their herd into a dozen bunches."

"I know that," Darla replied in a tight voice.

The girl on the horse stopped, her eyes sparkling. "I had begun to wonder if I was going to have to put a bullet in one of your horses to make you wait."

"Too bad you didn't try," Darla said coolly.

"Cattle crossing a road take the right-of-way," the girl shot back.

"Not necessarily."

"You mean not necessarily where Arrowhead is concerned. Arrowhead has its way regardless of all others."

The brand on the stock was a Double-R, or R-Connected as it was sometimes called. Brokaw tried to recall if he had heard of it before, but it struck no responsive chord. He turned his attention to the girl. Young, scarcely twenty, he guessed, with dark hair and eyes, and a small nose across which a spray of freckles laid a faint track. She sat her saddle with an easy assurance and a sort of proud arrogance, as though defying the world and all those in it who would dare cross her. She had a will of her own, she would backtrack for no one, particularly Darla Preston, it seemed.

"Why, yes," Darla was saying in honey-sweet tones, "Arrowhead is big enough to do what it wants . . . when it wants to."

"Someday you may find out that it's a mistaken notion you have."

"I'm sure, my dear, it won't be where you and your brother are concerned."

The girl looked away, throwing her glance over the herd now beginning to thin out as it came toward the tail end. Even in her loose, shapeless range clothing of Levi's and too large a shirt, Brokaw saw she was well-built.

"I'll not wait any longer!" Darla announced.

The slim girl swung back to her swiftly, her dark eyes snapping. "You'll sit right where you are until the last steer is across. The last one!"

"Too much dust," Brokaw murmured, striving to keep things at peace. "No use eating dust."

For the first time the girl seemed to notice him. She looked him over carefully, her gaze sharp and thorough. "You're a new one," she stated finally.

Brokaw regarded her with expressionless features. A

vague sort of admiration for her was stirring within him. She had a lot of spirit and all the great power of Arrowhead did not frighten her one whit. He wondered then who she was and what trouble lay between her and the Prestons.

A steer broke out of line and raced off, doubling back in the direction from which it had come. Instantly the girl was after him, handling her pony like a veteran, expertly heading the longhorn, turning him, and starting him back with the others. When she came up again, her eyes were bright with excitement, and the color had risen in her tanned face.

The herd had crossed. To Darla, the girl said: "You and your friend can go now." A look of mischief came into her eyes. "By the way, what happened to Ollie? This your new one?"

"Get this team moving, Brokaw," Darla breathed in a suppressed, furious way.

"Dust's still pretty thick."

"Hell with the dust! Get moving, I tell you!"

"You didn't answer my question, Darla dear," the girl called in a tantalizing voice.

Darla Preston wrenched the whip from its socket and swung it. It slashed through the air with a vicious whine, missing the girl by scant inches. Brokaw snatched it from her hand. He heard the slim girl laugh as she spun away.

"That little snip!" Darla fumed. "That cheap little beggar! She'll get her come-uppance! I'll see to that!"

Brokaw glanced at the small figure, receding into the distance. He didn't know just what it was all about, but, judging from what he had just seen, Darla Preston would have a pretty fair-size chore on her hands doing that.

VI

Brokaw waited out another minute or two, allowing the worst of the dust to spin away and settle, then clucked the blacks forward. Darla was a rigid, outraged figure at his side. He could hear her quick, labored breathing, then realized how deep and far-reaching her hate for the slim girl was. He waited until they were out of sight beyond the ridge before he spoke. "Figuring from what I heard, I take it you two are not the best of friends. Who is she?"

"Ann Ross," Darla said.

"Double-R," Brokaw mused, recalling the brand.

"Place is about twenty miles southwest of us. Small, jackleg outfit. Doing no good. Just wasting grass and water."

"She run it alone?"

"No. Her brother really owns the place. George Ross. She came here about four years ago from some place in the East. *Humph!* She and her high and mighty ways! I'd like to slap her face!"

"You came mighty close . . . with that whip."

"And I would have, too, if you hadn't butted in. I'll thank you, Brokaw, to keep out of my business."

"Had you cut her with that leather, somebody would have been digging a bullet out of you right now, or I'm mighty mistaken about that young woman!"

The thought seemed to sober Darla. After a time she said: "I guess she would at that, and welcome the opportunity."

"What's behind all this trouble?"

Darla brushed at her lap and smoothed out a pleat in her skirt. "You just curious, or do you really want to know?"

Brokaw said: "I work for Arrowhead, I ought to know who its enemies are, and why."

The iron-tired wheels, grating through sand, the steady *clopping* of the trotting blacks were the only sounds for a minute. Then: "I hear you say that, Brokaw, that fine expression of loyalty, and so on. What I want to know now is, do you mean it or are you just talking?"

Brokaw shrugged. "Only a fool tries to play both sides of the table."

At once she turned to him, her face earnest and still. "Brokaw, I meet a man and judge him quick. I think you are what you appear to be, a man that won't back down and that's not afraid to use a gun if need be."

A strange thought came into Frank Brokaw's mind. It had lain deeply and silently within his unconscious for almost a year, since the search for Matt Slade had begun, in fact, but never before had it reached a point of clarification. Now it was out, facing him, posing its disturbance. Could he ever kill a man? Old memories washed back through him, turning him thoughtful and filling him with that vague sickness that brought the sweat out on him. Faint screams and lost yells reechoed in his ears, and somewhere in the distance a face exploded into a mass of pulp and blood, and guns were booming. Involuntarily he shuddered. Could he kill a man— even Matt Slade? Yes, he could!

"What?"

He heard Darla Preston's voice and turned to her. "Sorry, I didn't hear."

"You never answered my question," she reminded him. "About the gun."

167

He said— "I can take care of myself." —and left the matter there.

"We need somebody like that . . . like you at Arrowhead. Oh, I know we've got some tough ones now, Shep Russell and Domino, Buckshot Martin, and maybe one or two more. We have to have them to hold what's ours."

"And take what else you want?"

Darla nodded, absolutely honest about it. "And take what we want and need. You asked about the trouble between George Ross and Arrowhead. It started when Ross bought up a few sections of land lying between the two ranches. When he did that, he got control of some of the best wild hay country in this part of the West. Hugh was trying to buy it, too, but he fooled around and let Ross beat him to it. We need that range, need it badly."

"Doesn't Ross?"

"He says he does. I don't really know, and it's neither here nor there. All I know is that it's a lot more expensive to raise our beef without it. Causes us to drive our stock clear to Rincon Valley for wintering. If we had that hay meadow country, that expense would be out."

The sun was dropping lower as the day waned. They topped a rise, and off in the long distance the darker smudge of Arrowhead, backed against the short hills, became visible.

"George Ross use the meadows?"

"Makes it his winter pasture."

Brokaw shook his head. "Then I guess he needed it when he bought it. Can't blame a man for looking out for himself. And if Pres . . . your husband had a chance to get it but muffed it, you can't very well hold it against Ross."

"Hugh is a fool at times!" Darla exclaimed in an almost savage voice. "But it's land we've got to have, somehow."

"Ever try buying it from Ross?"

"Hugh made him an offer, but he wasn't interested. Said he needed it and would keep it."

"Then how do you figure to get it?"

"With men like you," Darla replied blandly. "He won't sell. We'll force him out and make him give it up. Take it away from him."

Brokaw turned to face her, surprised at the intense quality of her tone. He had a quick recollection of Hugh Preston; he had appeared to be a reasonable sort. He said then: "Does your husband have the same ideas?"

"Not yet. He's inclined to back away from things like that, from violence. But he will come around to my way of thinking. You say you don't know Hugh. Well, there's little harm in telling you this, because you'll find it out yourself after you've been around for a short while. Hugh's a smart man, almost a brilliant one, but he lacks fire. He doesn't have the push that will make him big and carry him to the top of the heap in this country. And that's where I want him to be."

"And if he doesn't want to go there?"

"Then I'll be there in his place. I'll be on top of the pile."

"What happens then to Hugh Preston?"

"Who cares? He can get out. He can go back where he came from, forget all about being a rancher, and about me."

"Where did he come from?" Brokaw asked casually, taking advantage of the statement.

"Where? Oh, I didn't mean it exactly that way. He wouldn't go back there. Probably move on to California. He's talked about selling out and going there several times."

The shape of Arrowhead's buildings became more definite. Far off to the left, behind the scatter of sheds and buildings, a dust roll marked the passage of cattle as the crew worked them northward.

"What if Hugh won't go for that, either?" Brokaw then

said, curious about this frank and forceful woman at his side. "Suppose he won't get out, as you say."

"There'll be no worry about that," she said in a low, confident tone. "It will be my way when the time comes. No matter what Hugh likes, it's what I want that counts. I'll let nothing stand in my way. Nothing!"

Brokaw thought over her words, considered the solid, underlying threat of what she had said. There was no weakness there, he decided. She evidently had been planning for some time and still was carefully laying her groundwork.

"What about Ollie Godfrey?"

Darla skirted a direct reply. "What about him?"

"Seems to have some ideas about being your foreman one of these days soon."

"Ollie has a lot of ideas," she replied with a shrug. "He'd like to be half owner of Arrowhead . . . even owner."

"And Abel Cameron?"

"He'll do what Hugh says. Likely he will quit if matters come to a showdown between Hugh and me."

Brokaw frowned. "How far along are your plans?"

"Far enough that I've got to know who's with me and who isn't. If I can't make Hugh see things my way, then I'll take over Arrowhead. By any means and method I find necessary."

Darla Preston paused. She was looking far ahead, to the buildings of Arrowhead, her eyes dreamy and far-seeing. The afternoon sun reached in under the rig's leather top and glinted off her honey-colored hair, turning her features soft and womanly, a paradox to the strength that lay beneath their smooth surfaces.

"Maybe you think I'm a fool to risk telling you, a total stranger to me, all these things. But I'm not worried. I know men and I know your kind. And I know also that I can make

Hugh believe anything I want him to. You try telling him what I've said and I'll deny it, and make you out a liar and have you run off the place."

Brokaw laughed. "You probably could," he said with a faint bitterness.

"Don't make any mistakes about it! Just as I said before, nothing stands in my way. Anything or anybody that does will get trampled on!"

Brokaw cast a sidelong glance at her. She had not turned her head, but was still lost in a contemplation of Arrowhead. It was difficult to believe such ruthlessness lay behind that calm and beautiful face, that her slim body, with all its gifts, had so great a capacity for hate and violence and greed. Frank Brokaw had known his share of women in his life, but never one like this Darla Preston. She made him think of a gleaming, razor-sharp dagger in a soft, velvet sheath.

"You haven't said where you stand, Brokaw, now that you know the lay of the land."

Brokaw had no intentions of becoming involved in any differences between the Prestons, and certainly he wanted no part of a bloody range war that was sure to follow if the gauntlet was thrown in Ross's face. Anyway, if Preston proved to be Matt Slade, he thought with wry humor he would be doing his part to assist her. The rest would be up to her. But his own needs had to be safeguarded; therefore, it would be wisest to play along. He said: "You don't think I would be fool enough to tell you I was against you, do you?"

"That's no answer," she retorted. "I want somebody like you backing me up, Brokaw. You're a different breed from the others, from Shep and Domino and their kind. And from Ollie Godfrey, too. They're animals, strong and useful like a good horse, but they lack brains, the ability to think. I like a smart man, one that can see ahead and act, not back down

171

when things get rough. I can make it worth your while."

"Money never interested me much," Brokaw drawled.

"I'm not thinking of money alone. I mean all the other things that go with it . . . half ownership of the ranch. And I go with that."

The forwardness of Darla Preston jarred Brokaw solidly. But a thread of irritation also moved through him. She was a woman steering a course for the high-hung star; she was willing to pay any price to reach it. He said: "Thanks for the offer. I'll think on it."

"Fine, fine," she murmured. "We'll talk about it again."

VII

"It'll take well-nigh four days runnin'," Abel Cameron was saying the next morning, "so's ye'd best take along your blanket roll. I've got chuck loaded on a pack horse. We won't be drawin' no wagon."

Brokaw, with Godfrey, Shep Russell, Buckshot Martin, and Jack Corbett turned to make ready for the trip. They were going downcountry a piece to drive back a small herd Preston had purchased from a rancher who was giving up the fight. Godfrey was not liking it, and was saying as much as he walked with the other members of the crew toward the bunkhouse. But Cameron was a firm man. Thirty minutes later they rode from the yard, striking due south, with the rising sun at their left shoulders. They spoke little, each man having his own far-reaching thoughts and keeping them to himself. Cameron, trailing the pack horse with a short length of rope, kept somewhat apart from the others. Brokaw slanted across to him.

Before he could speak, the old foreman said: "Not smart, me bringin' you along with Shep and Ollie and his bunch, but weren't nobody else around. Now, see they's no trouble. You hear?"

Brokaw said: "If there's any trouble, they will be the ones who start it. Much of a herd we're after?"

Cameron shook his head. "Not much. Twelve hundred head or so, Mister Preston told me."

"You figure to stop in town on the way?"

Cameron's faded gaze swung to the tall rider. "You got business there?"

"Not me," Brokaw replied. "Just heard the boys talking. Been a long time since they bellied up to a bar, according to what they said."

Cameron studied the distant hills for a moment, his wind-scoured features sharp against the lifting light. "Well, I reckon it wouldn't do no harm, lettin' them wet their whistles. Ain't none out of the way."

Brokaw nodded his agreement and satisfaction. He had been hoping for just such an opportunity to talk with the foreman. After a shot glass or two of whisky, or a few beers, most men opened up a little. Maybe he could learn a few things about Hugh Preston. The bits of information garnered here and there were beginning to tot up, but he needed more to make it conclusive.

"Want me to pass the word on?"

"No," Cameron said sagely, "you tell 'em now, and they'll bust a gut gettin' into town so's they can have a little more time. We got no spare horses along, and I don't figure to have what we got run ragged. I'll tell 'em when we get there."

But Ollie Godfrey had ideas of his own. When they were still a long five miles from Westport Crossing, he and Shep Russell suddenly disappeared behind a roll of low hills.

Cameron, seeing this, waved the others in. "Reckon we'll stop off in town for an hour or so," he announced. "But don't go gettin' likkered up. I'm tellin' you now, any man that does, is fired."

Buckshot Martin threw his pig eyes toward the point where Godfrey and Russell had dropped from sight in a meaningful way. "Thanks," he murmured dryly, and wheeled away, Corbett following him closely, in the wake of the other two.

It was fully ten o'clock when Brokaw and Cameron turned into the end of the town's single street and rode up to the tie rail in front of the Longhorn. The four other Arrowhead horses were already there. Brokaw swung down, and Cameron followed, more slowly and somewhat stiffly. The old foreman, by all rules, should not have attempted the trip. He could have sent a younger man in his place, but the iron-headedness of him refused to accept any limitations of advancing age, and he stubbornly resisted all intimations that he should follow an easier course of activity for himself.

Brokaw looped the leathers over the tie rail and turned about. He came to a complete halt, seeing Ann Ross pull up in a light buckboard directly across the street. For a moment their eyes locked, and Brokaw saw, or thought he saw, the faintest greeting in her eyes. He touched the edge of his wide-brimmed hat and ducked his head. Ann, trim and fresh-looking in gingham, turned swiftly away.

"Mighty fine little filly," Cameron observed from the far side of Brokaw's horse. "Didn't know you was acquainted."

"We've met," Brokaw said shortly, and stepped up onto the Longhorn's porch.

He shouldered through the scarred, batwing doors of the saloon, holding them back for Cameron to enter. The place was empty except for the Arrowhead riders who were sitting at a far table, a bottle and glasses before them.

Cameron bent his steps toward them. "Now, I'm warnin' all of you, take it easy with that bottle! I'll put up with no drunks on this drive."

"All right, grampa," Godfrey said broadly. "We'll sure be good boys."

Cameron eyed the 'puncher closely. " 'Pears to me you already had aplenty, Ollie."

"Sure, sure," Godfrey replied, and deliberately poured himself another liberal drink.

Cameron's lined face hardened, and the skin, stretched over his cheek bones, whitened. He reached across the table and slapped the glass from Godfrey's fingers, sending it clattering across the floor.

The whisky splattered Buckshot Martin. He yelled and pushed back his chair. Godfrey, eyes blazing, leaped to his feet, hand going for his gun.

Brokaw's level voice snapped through the confusion. "Hold it up, Ollie!"

Godfrey hesitated, his poised, half-crouched shape going rigid. "Stay out of this," he snarled. "The old man's been asking for it for a long time. Don't buy into something you can't handle!"

"I can handle it," Brokaw said quietly. "Now get out of here. You heard Cameron say you'd had plenty. Looks that way to me, too. I reckon he meant it."

Cameron shifted angrily. "Now, wait a minute there, Brokaw. I can run my own affairs without no. . . ."

"Sure," Brokaw agreed easily. But there was no relaxing of his attention upon Godfrey and the others. He waited out the moments, his cold glance covering them all.

Then Godfrey shrugged. "Let's go," he said, and started toward the doorway, the rest trooping obediently after him.

Only then did the coiled readiness of Frank Brokaw fade. He faced the bartender and ordered a glass of beer. Abel Cameron moved up beside him and repeated the request, and together they walked to a table and sat down.

Anger still fanned Cameron's pale eyes. "Appreciate your stayin' out of my business," he said tartly. "I reckon I can look after myself. Been doin' it for a mighty long spell now."

Brokaw said: "I know that. But look at the odds you were

176

up against. Four to one. I don't cotton to that kind of fight."

Cameron's fierce pride was somewhat mollified. "I reckon it was at that. Russell and Buckshot would sure side Ollie, once he started somethin'. And probably Jack would do the same when he saw which way the wind was blowin'." He took a sip of beer, relenting another notch. Wiping the edges of his mustache with a bony hand, he said: "Goes right good after a dusty ride." Then: "That Ollie, lookin' for trouble all the time."

"He'll find it one of these days," Brokaw commented.

Cameron wagged his head. "He sure will at that. Proddy as a spring bull. He givin' you any trouble?"

"None I can't take care of," Brokaw replied. It was a subject made to order for him. He said: "Know him long?"

"Three, four years. He used to work for George Ross but quit him and started workin' for us. He was some sweet on that little Ross gal, I hear tell."

Brokaw considered this information for a moment. Ollie really got around, so far as women were concerned. "You been foreman for Arrowhead ever since Preston bought the place," he said, sticking to the original subject. It was a statement rather than a question.

Cameron nodded. "Was foreman for Cresswell when he sold out to Preston. I went with the sale."

"About five years ago, I guess."

"Closer to six."

"Where did Preston come from?"

Cameron took another swallow of the warm beer. "Don't rightly know. Seems I heard it was Nebrasky, or maybe it was Wyomin'. Why? You heard of him before?"

"Can't say," Brokaw replied slowly. "Name's a little familiar. Did he used to ride a big red sorrel and set a real fancy saddle, one that was all dolled up with silver?"

Cameron gave that some lengthy thought. Then: "You looking to find a man like that, son? That what you're doin' in this country?"

Brokaw smiled ruefully to himself. He should have guessed he could not fool the old foreman for long. He shrugged. "Just trying to place him."

Cameron said: "Well, if it's any help to you, I don't recollect seein' Preston on no red horse, nor forkin' any fancy silver saddle, either. Not since I knew him, anyway. Best I recall, him and his missus showed up in a fancy surrey all loaded down with her duds and things like that. 'Course, he could have shucked his horse and saddle before he came here."

The bartender brought them a refill for their glasses. Brokaw said: "Preston came with a lot of money, they tell me."

"Plenty. He sure fixed up the old Arrowhead. 'Twas about on its last legs when he bought it up." He finished off his drink and got to his feet. "Reckon we better be moseyin'. Wonder where Ollie and them other waddies meandered off to."

"Likely waiting at the horses," Brokaw answered, and flipped a coin to the bartender.

They crossed the saloon's broad width and came up to the doors. Glancing over their tops, Brokaw saw Martin and Corbett leaning against the tie rail. They were watching the batwings with sharp, expectant interest, as if anticipating something not entirely to their liking. Brokaw pressed a hand against Cameron's shoulder, halting him. Motioning for silence, he eased to the far side of the entrance and, bending low, threw his gaze to the outside. He saw the booted feet of a man on the porch standing close to the door frame. He checked the opposite side. There, another pair of legs awaited them.

Pulling back into the saloon, he whispered to Cameron: "We've got a reception committee. Wait here."

"Ollie?"

"Ollie and Shep."

"Let's take the back door," Cameron suggested.

Brokaw's mouth split into a wicked grin. "Might as well let them have their fun."

He stepped softly to the swinging doors and placed a hand, palm first against each. With a sudden, hard push he swung them outward. Immediately he jerked them back in. Shep Russell, caught by the false move, lunged—thinking Brokaw was stepping into the open. He saw his error, tried to catch himself, failed, and went stumbling off. Then Brokaw, coming through the batwings, drove him to his knees with a vicious, chopping blow. Brokaw next moved quickly onto the porch, pivoting to meet Ollie Godfrey who came rushing in.

He took a wild, roundhouse swing high on the shoulder and then returned a sizzling right that cracked against the cowboy's head. Godfrey grunted and grabbed frantically for him. Brokaw knocked his reaching hands aside, then smashed him hard in the face, twice. Shep Russell was struggling to get up, resting uncertainly on his hands and knees, breathing hard. Brokaw placed his foot against the man's ribs, shoved, and sent him rolling off the porch into the dust of the street.

He became aware then of shouts, of men attracted by the fight, pounding up to watch. He saw Ann Ross across the way, on the doorstep of MacGillivray's General Store, her face a tan oval of suppressed excitement as she looked on. Godfrey's knuckles smashed into his jaw, and he staggered back a step. The cowboy came weaving in, his eyes wild, his face set, anxious to finish it up. Brokaw, not napping now, met him coming. He stalled him with a stiff left. Godfrey wavered on his heels and off balance. Brokaw drove a hard right fist deeply into his belly. Wind gushed from Godfrey's mouth. His eyes popped out in pain, and he buckled forward. Staggering backward, he missed the edge of the porch and piled up in the street.

A shout lifted among the spectators. Cameron's worried, insistent voice cut through the dust and swirling confusion. "Get on them horses! Ben Marr'll have the whole bunch of you in the calaboose in another minute."

Brokaw and Cameron moved to Godfrey's side and dragged him to his feet. Half carrying him, they loaded him onto his saddle and jerked the reins free of the rail. The other riders were already aboard and moving off. Cameron swung up, and Brokaw stepped to his own horse. With the sick and heaving Godfrey between them, they started down the street at a fast walk.

Brokaw, remembering Ann Ross, threw a quick glance toward her. She had come farther out onto the porch and was watching him with an odd mixture of admiration and revulsion in her dark eyes. He grinned through his bruised lips, and she swung quickly around, placing her back to him. Even from that angle, he thought, she was a mighty good-looking woman.

VIII

He had learned little, if anything, of value from Abel Cameron. Brokaw admitted that to himself early the morning of the fourth day, when they reached that indefinite boundary of Arrowhead range with the new herd. He did not think the foreman was holding back on him; he just didn't have any information that was of use.

Sitting ramrod-straight on the bay, he let his eyes travel out over the herd, strung in an elongated triangle along the floor of the shallow valley through which they were moving. In the dusty haze he could see Abel Cameron, riding ahead at point position, a hundred yards or so in lead of the first steer. It had been an easy drive. At the very beginning, a red-eyed old longhorn, gaunt and brush-scarred, had forged his arrogant head to the fore and taken charge. From then on it was merely a matter of keeping the knobby-kneed brute pointed in the right direction, and prodding the laggards to keep up.

Brokaw was glad the drive was about over with. Not that he disliked the saddle, but it was preventing him from fulfilling his avowed purpose, from the completion of that relentless, pressing desire to find Matt Slade and bring him to account. Almost a week now, he mused, and only small progress had been made. True, Hugh Preston seemed to fill most of the requirements—and yet he did not, factually. Everything was circumstantial, nothing positive. And Brokaw knew he must be sure before he played his last ace. One wrong move and Hugh Preston would react quickly and be gone like a startled covey of mountain quail. But something must be done soon. Past experience had taught Brokaw it was never wise to remain overly long in one place. Lawmen, by their very nature, had a habit of becoming curious about him and his intentions, just as had Ben Marr. He was glad they had got out of Westport Crossing that day of the fight, before the old sheriff had showed up.

Thinking of Ollie Godfrey, he threw a glance to the tail end of the herd where Godfrey, along with Shep Russell and Buckshot Martin, was holding down the drag point. Corbett, like himself, was at swing, directly across on the opposite side of the herd. There had been no more trouble from either Ollie or Shep. Except for a glowering look from Godfrey on different occasions, there was no further reference made to the affair in front of the Longhorn. But Godfrey was not forgetting it, he knew. He was the kind that could not accept defeat and live with it; he would carry the thought of it in his breast until it became a festering sore, forever looking for the moment when he might vindicate himself in the eyes of others, as well as his own.

Later on, when they were not more than a half dozen miles from Preston's buildings, Brokaw caught sight of an approaching horseman. It was too far to tell who it was. He watched as the rider angled across the range to where Cameron plodded along, halted him, and engaged in a few minutes' conversation. Then the rider swung away, angling around the boil of dust, heading toward him. He saw then that it was Darla Preston.

She approached at an easy canter, riding her horse with a calm expertise. She was wearing a silky, tan riding habit, a jaunty hat perched high on her blonde hair, and a spider-web veil that shadowed her face and gave it a sort of mysterious, brooding quality. She was riding side-saddle. Brokaw remembered a picture he had once seen in a magazine, showing an Eastern lady of quality sitting her mount in just such an elegant fashion. It was a bit incongruous, here on the range, where most women and girls donned split riding skirts, or drew on their menfolks' cast-off Levi's and shirts, and forked a regular stock saddle. But it made a fetching picture. She waved gaily to him as she pulled in alongside the gelding. He touched the brim of his hat, quite frankly admiring her appearance.

"Like what you see?" she asked archly.

Brokaw grinned. "A picture any man would."

She laughed coolly. "Made up your mind about my offer?"

Brokaw made no reply. The herd was moving steadily past. Over his left shoulder he saw Godfrey and the others on a direct line with them now. Godfrey was watching Darla with sharp, mistrusting eyes.

He said: "Yes."

"I'm glad," she answered at once. "I need you, Brokaw. Need your help."

"Don't figure on it."

She turned to him. "I don't understand. You mean you aren't coming in with me?"

"That's right. Don't count on me."

Darla gave a little start. Her face flushed beneath its fragile shield, and a hurrying, brief hardness stiffened it, setting it into unlovely angles. As quickly it changed again. Her full lips parted into a smile. "You are so very positive! But I'm no hand at taking no for an answer. I think you will change your mind," she said, and, with a flirt of her hand, whirled about, and rode toward Arrowhead.

Brokaw threw a quick glance at Godfrey, now less than fifty yards distant. The cowboy was watching Darla leave, his jaw grim and set. She had not bothered to notice him, not even deigning to wave when she departed. Brokaw came back around; Darla was a small shape now far in the distance. His eyes then caught the bit of white lying on the ground near where she had stopped. He clucked the bay closer and, leaning from the saddle, scooped it up. It was one of her gloves, slick, expensively worked doeskin, with the faint odor of her lilac perfume clinging to it.

He stared at it for a long time, having his thoughts about it. She had dropped it deliberately, of course. That was evident. And she believed he would return it to her at a place where she could be found after the ranch was quiet. He smiled, and tucked it into his shirt pocket. He would return it all right, but not the way she had planned. He had needed an excuse to get inside the ranch house and locate Hugh Preston's desk. Now he had it.

Not long after supper that evening he crossed the yard and rapped at the side door of the log building. It was opened at once by Preston, who nodded his greetings, and invited him to enter. "What can I do for you, Frank?"

It was odd the rancher should remember his first name, but some men were like that. His eyes reached beyond Preston into the room, cluttered with heavy, comfortable furniture, brightly colored Indian rugs, elk and deer head trophies on the walls. No desk was to be seen. He withdrew the glove from his pocket.

"Found this on the range this afternoon," he said, handing the doeskin to Preston. "Figured it was your wife's and that she'd like to have it back."

The rancher accepted the glove, turning it over and over in his fingers. "Why, I believe it is hers. Just a moment, I'll tell her."

Preston moved across the room toward a door that led off into a hallway. Brokaw drifted closer to the fireplace, eyes probing his surroundings. There was no saddle, silver or otherwise, in sight, but he did locate the desk. A small porch, on the front of the house, had been converted into an office. The desk, a huge, roll-top affair, stood against its north wall. A door opened off, leading into the yard bordering the front of the structure. There was one window, small and high off the ground.

"Brokaw," Preston said, coming back into the room, "my wife says it is hers and to extend her thanks to you for bringing it in. She lost it sometime today when she rode out to see the stock I bought."

"My pleasure," Brokaw murmured. He glanced up to see Darla, standing well back of Preston in the depths of the narrow hallway. Her face was still, and she was watching him, disconcerted and seemingly at a loss at his behavior.

He turned away then, deliberately choosing the door off the office, and went through it. It led into the yard at the front, as he had suspected. He circled the building, crossing in front of the bunkhouse, and made his way to the barn where he still bunked alone. There he waited until everything had grown quiet, and then returned to the yard.

Drawing off a short distance into the shadows back of the main house, he spent another hour watching and smoking cigarettes. Finally, deeming it safe, he went to the door of Preston's office. It was unlocked, as he had thought it would be. He let himself in quietly and stood there for a time in the utter darkness, listening. Lights had been out for some time, but he had to be certain neither Darla nor Hugh Preston was still up, was there in the front parlor lost to his view in the depths of the heavy furniture. Darla, he knew, had not left the building. She had expected him to meet her in the grove, and, when he had chosen to ignore the invitation, she had remained inside. He wondered then if Ollie was there, waiting.

Convinced that all was safe, he went to Preston's desk. He dared not light a lamp, but used innumerable matches instead, shielding them with a cupped hand to keep their glare from reaching beyond the room. There was little in the desk. Account books, tally records, bills, all orderly and neatly placed. He examined every drawer, many of which were empty. He thought then that there must be a safe or some such depository where valuables were kept, but a search of the room failed to turn it up. When he had finished, he had found nothing of interest, nothing that would indicate Hugh Preston was anyone other than Hugh Preston, and the disappointment turned him still and thoughtful. But it was inconclusive, he told himself as he slipped back into the yard. Any man wishing to bury the past would use extreme care in destroying all things that might link him to another life. He half smiled then, remembering he had given himself that same assurance before. But the inherent honesty and fairness of the man insisted that he be sure, that he be dead certain before he took a life.

He reentered the barn, glancing again to the back room where the equipment was kept. He had examined the gear before, but he checked it again, thinking some additions might have been made. A flaring match revealed no silver saddle.

He pinched out the match, and paused in the felt blackness of the stable. Slade and Preston were one and the same, and somewhere there was proof of it. But time was growing short. He decided then to give it a couple more days, three at the most, and then, if he had uncovered nothing conclusive, he would load Hugh Preston on a horse and take him clear to

Central City. It might prove to be a fair-size job, but it would have to be done. Once in Central City, Tennyson, the banker, could make the identification, could finally say Preston was Slade.

IX

"Pair off," Abel Cameron said that morning at the finish of breakfast, "and work out all them draws and cañons on the east slope of the hills. They're full up with beef hid out there in the brush, and the only way we're goin' to get them down for roundup is to pop 'em out."

Frank Brokaw borrowed a pair of the foreman's leather chaps and joined the half dozen riders assigned the disagreeable task. They rode across the low swells of the range with the sun at their backs: Godfrey, Russell, Jules Strove, the man called Domino, Jack Corbett, and Brokaw. They were slanting for the rough slopes of the Sierra del Diablo, a rugged world of loose rock, buckthorn, piñon, scrub oak, and deep slashes.

When they reached the first outcroppings of badlands, Brokaw found himself lined up with Strove. Godfrey and his ever-present shadow, Shep Russell, had swung away, choosing the lower, more easily worked areas. Domino and Corbett were near them, only slightly higher.

" 'Pears the boys left the easy part for us," Strove murmured laconically, his glance sweeping the ragged territory of the upper climes. "I misdoubt if ary a goat would figure to live up there. But now, a longhorn, he's different. An old mossy'd figure that was pure heaven up there, and I calculate we'll have us a time gettin' what's up there down to the bottom."

Brokaw grinned his agreement, and together they started the steep climb. They rode for thirty minutes, and then paused to allow their winded horses to rest. The little loop-legged rider, hunching against a piñon, drew the makings from his pocket and rolled a lumpy cigarette. Cocking his head to one side, he said: "You see Miz Preston yestiddy, Brokaw? She was sure some fixed up! Reckon she's about the femalest woman I ever set my peepers on!"

"For a fact," Brokaw said.

"You figure she was ever a stage woman? Don't hardly seem like no regular gal would know how to fix herself up like Miz Preston does."

"You have any other reason for thinking she might have been an actress?" Brokaw was immediately alert. Here might be some indication of Hugh Preston's background.

"Nope," Strove said, rising to his feet. "Just don't seem nacheral for a regular woman to fix up and dress the way she does. Takes a lot of know-how, same as everything else."

The going was tough. Stiff brush plucked at them, and the buckskin Brokaw had picked for the day was having a hard time of it. They wormed slowly up the slope, snaking back and forth to make it easier on the horses. They reached a small basin hemmed in with a solid ring of scrub oak. Two steers watched them approach with wild, bloodshot eyes, but Jules Strove sailed right on into the clearing at them—yelling at the top of his lungs and waving his doubled rope overhead. The longhorns bolted, and went crashing through the leafy barrier, headed for lower ground. Strove rode their tails until he spotted Jack Corbett at the next level.

"Cowboy, here's your babies!" he yelled at the redhead, and turned back.

He rejoined Brokaw, and they pushed slowly on, working out every thicket, each hollow. Strove, a little way below

189

Brokaw, commented: "Reckon we ain't goin' to jump any she-stuff up here. Only old mossy horns, too dang' ornery to bed with the herd, will pick this place."

If Godfrey and the other riders had deliberately picked the lower part of the hills for easier going, they were getting the most activity. Watching the small shapes of the riders, Brokaw could see them weaving in and out of the brush, chousing cattle at regular intervals. Godfrey seemed to have assumed the head of the entire operation, however, and had pulled completely off the slope proper and was riding the smoother shoulder of the rangeland.

"Just like old Ollie," Strove observed dourly. "He's too cussed purty to get hisself scratched up."

They rooted out a half dozen more steers, all singles, and drove them down to the men below. It was nearly noon when they came unexpectedly upon a narrow, dead-end cañon. In a narrow clearing of the center, in a space no larger than a wagon bed, they met up with an old renegade longhorn. No victim of the knife and dabbing stick, he was an escapee of a half dozen roundups, and he now prepared to maintain that record. He was an old blue with a multitude of scars patching his hide, and a six-foot spread of needle-pointed horns. He greeted the two riders with lowered head.

"Watch that one," Brokaw warned.

The old blue snorted, and rolled his red eyes. His tail switched back and forth, snapping like a leather whip.

"Bastard's so old he wouldn't even make good taller," Strove said. "Howsomever, Abel said to bring them all in."

Holding his rope folded double to shape a whip, he yelled and drove spurs into his pony. The bull spun away, blowing loudly through widely flaring nostrils. Strove's horse reached the clearing, wild and jumpy from the cowboy's yells and jabbing spurs. Brokaw, coming in from the opposite side, added his own shouts, and the longhorn plunged off into the screen of piñon.

"Head him down slope!" Strove cried.

Brokaw was already behind the bull that was moving fast and quietly as only a wily old longhorn can do when he sets his mind to it.

"Hi-yah! Hi-yah!" Strove's voice sang. "Get along, you danged old rebel!"

He was crowding the bull close, too closely. Brokaw yelled a warning, but it came too late. The bull wheeled, almost rearing upright on his hind legs. Dead branches and leaves exploded in front of him, and he was suddenly charging back at Strove.

The cowboy yelped. His horse came up, unseating him. He struck on his feet and bolted for the brush while his pony scampered frantically out of the path of the bull. Brokaw, a half dozen steps away, drew his gun and snapped a hasty shot into the ground ahead of the steer. The longhorn plowed to a halt, whirled again, and thundered off into the brush.

"Gol-danged stinkin' son of Satan!" Strove raved. "I'll pusonally see that critter gets to the slaughterin' chute, even if I have to ride a cattle car all the way to the packin' house!" Strove recovered his jittery horse and climbed back into the saddle. "I'll nudge him out," he said, his eyes on the brush into which the blue had escaped. "You go on ahead. I'll catch up."

Two rapid gunshots drifted hollowly up from the range. Brokaw, sweating a little from the last moment's excitement, rode forward to a projecting ledge from which he could look down.

"Maybe that old blue devil's already reached the bottom," Strove said, half hopefully, turning his horse to follow Brokaw.

Godfrey and the three other Arrowhead riders had drawn off a short distance from the brushy lip of the slope. Three other riders were facing them over a short space while a small jag of cattle milled around behind them.

"Looks like trouble down there," Strove said.

Brokaw nodded. "Let's take a look."

They rode down the slope, finding a trail that made the descent fairly easy. Brokaw, his glance on the three outsiders, quickly recognized one: Ann Ross. The other two were men he had never seen before, but one was surely Ann's brother, George. The other was likely one of their 'punchers.

"Look what we caught!" Godfrey chortled as they came up. "Real, genuine rustlers!"

The dark eyes of the big man snapped. He was graying at the temples, and his mouth was a hard line. "What are you talking about, Godfrey? We're hunting strays, same as you."

"On Arrowhead range?" Godfrey came back with a knowing lift of his brows.

Brokaw's gaze settled upon Ann Ross. A worried frown puckered her brow and drew her lips into a small, compressed circles; her face had paled beneath its tan. Brokaw shifted his attention to Godfrey and the other Arrowhead men; the incident was far more serious than he had surmised apparently. Faint echoes of Darla Preston's words came back to Brokaw—*Don't miss any chances . . . make something happen.*—or words to that effect had been her orders to Godfrey. This moment had some relation to that command, he realized.

"Ann, ride home."

Brokaw swiveled his glance to the speaker, the big man on the bay. He could see the resemblance to Ann now, the same deeply shadowed eyes, the identical firm jaw and chin. He was struck by another thought: George Ross fitted very well the description he had of Matt Slade. He searched back through his memory—when did they say Ross had come into this country? Six years ago? The figure seemed to stick in his mind, but he was not sure. Yet it was something like that, and that would place his arrival at about the time Slade was supposed to have come.

Ann shook her head. "I'll not leave."

George Ross said: "This looks like trouble, and I'll not have you hurt."

"I'll stay," Ann replied stubbornly.

"Sure, let her stay," Shep Russell said with a wide grin. "She's part of the same thievin' outfit. Give her some of the same medicine."

"Lay a hand on her . . . any of you . . . and I'll kill you," Ross said in a low, savage voice.

"You won't be in no shape to do anything," Ollie Godfrey remarked, "when we get finished with you. Mister Preston don't stand for no rustling on his range, and I figure he expects us to do something about it when we come across it being done."

"What do you mean, rustling?" George Ross demanded hotly. "We're busting out strays, just like you are. A good bit of my stock's drifted onto Preston's range during the winter. Likely there's some Arrowhead stuff on Double-R, too."

"Why don't you wait until roundup? Don't you trust us?" Godfrey asked in a smirking voice.

"Sure, I trust Arrowhead, but we know this bunch was in here, and there was no sense in driving them clear across Preston's range and then having to go after them later."

Ollie Godfrey pointed to one of the steers in the group Ross had been herding. "Looks like an Arrowhead brand on that critter."

Ross nodded. "Probably some more in there, too, along with my own. You didn't give us a chance to cut them out.

You jumped us before we were finished with them."

"Oh, sure," Godfrey said sarcastically, "you were just going to cut out your branded stuff and leave the rest here waiting for us."

"That's exactly right," George Ross said.

"In a pig's eye!" Godfrey snorted. "Come dark that bunch of cows would've been mixed in your herd, and in another week they'd be wearing a new brand . . . Double-R."

Ross said: "You know better than that, Ollie. You know I've never rustled a head of cattle in my life."

"Man's got to start sometime. Looks like you've done just that!"

Brokaw saw the anger flame across Ross's face and his hand drop to the gun at his hip.

"Don't do it, George!" Godfrey barked. "It's six to your two, not counting your sister. You wouldn't have a chance."

"What's all this jawin' for, Ollie?" Shep Russell broke in then. "They ain't nothin' but rustlers. Why ain't we treatin' them like rustlers, instead of doing all this palavering?"

"I'm coming to that," Godfrey replied. He threw his glance along the slope. "No tree fit for a hanging party around here. Guess we'll have to do the next best thing." He swung his gaze to Ann. "You sure you want to stick around here? This won't be pretty."

Brokaw saw Ann's eyes lift to him, bright with their unspoken plea for help. Their gaze held for a moment, and then she looked away, back to Godfrey. "You wouldn't dare hurt us, Ollie!"

"Law's the law," Godfrey said with a shrug. "It says a rustler's got to be strung up. We got no trees big enough, so we'll have to work it another way."

Jules Strove broke in: "You sure you know what you're doin?"

"You bet your life I do," Godfrey shot back. "And if there's any of you that don't agree with me, just ride on off and go about your business!" He allowed his eyes to come to a stop on Brokaw, his meaning plain. Brokaw watched him with a cold detachment.

Godfrey drew his gun and leveled it at Ross. "Shep, you and Domino tie their hands behind them. Then take their ropes and hitch them to the saddle. I reckon a little dragging over these rocks will be about the same as hanging."

There was a long moment of complete hush following that, and then Ann's scream broke the silence. She spurred forward, grabbing for the gun in her brother's holster. Shep Russell threw himself against Ross, blocking her off. He lifted his hand and struck her across the shoulder. Ross tried to spin away, to help her, but Domino caught him against the flank of his own horse and pinned him to the saddle. Russell, laughing, seized Ann by the arm and began to pull her off her pony.

Brokaw had seen enough. "Take your hand off her, Shep!" His voice cut through the confusion.

Godfrey and the other Arrowhead riders swung quickly to face him. He was sitting quietly in the saddle, his gun on Godfrey. "Put that iron away, Ollie. And the rest of you, don't get any ideas. We'll just hold this thing up a minute or two. What Ross says seems reasonable to me."

"Damn you . . . don't you cut in on this!" Godfrey said in a tight, rasping voice.

"I'm not standing by and see two men murdered just to please you," Brokaw snapped. "Jules," he called to the cowboy waiting off to his right, "take a look at that stock Ross gathered up. See how much of it is Double-R stuff."

Strove rode forward and made his inspection. In a few minutes he reported: " 'Most all Ross stock. I see only two, three Arrowhead."

"So what?" Godfrey demanded. "One steer's all it takes to make a man a rustler."

"Depends," Brokaw murmured. "Depends a lot on who the man might be. Right now I think you're all wrong, Ollie. If Ross wanted some of Preston's beef, he could find it a lot handier place than here in this brush pile."

Ross, silent through it all, said: "If I wanted to, that's true. But there's never been an Arrowhead steer on my ranch unless he drifted over of his own notion. And Preston always got him back. Which is more than I can say about some of the stuff of mine that has wandered onto Arrowhead range."

"That I don't know anything about," Brokaw said. "Preston's the man to take that up with." He threw a glance to Strove. "Cut those Arrowhead steers out, Jules, and head them back up this way."

Strove immediately fell to work, hazing the stock that bore Preston's brand out of the bunch.

In a strained, angered voice Godfrey said: "You'll be sorry for this, Brokaw! You've stuck your nose into it once too often. I'll not let this pass!"

"Maybe," Brokaw said without interest. "Right now just sit tight, with your hands in plain sight there on the saddle horn."

"We don't have time to take this off him, Ollie," Shep Russell said then. "One of us can get him."

"Sure," Brokaw drawled. "And you'd like to be the hero that makes the first move, I take it. You'd die, Shep. You and Ollie, because I'd get you both before you could pull your guns. And there's Ross and his man . . . what do you think they'd be doing all that time?"

Shep glanced about the silent group and turned slowly for his horse. He kept his hands high, well in view as he climbed aboard.

"On the horn, Shep, like the others," Brokaw said with a careless wave of his gun.

Russell, placing one hand on top of the other, dropped them as he was ordered. Strove, finished with his chore of cutting out the Arrowhead stock, four in all, rode up. There were still a good twenty-five of Ross's beef in the jag.

"You can move out now, Ollie," Brokaw said. "Take your boys and get back on the job."

Godfrey, the seething fury turning him white, jerked his horse savagely around and started up the slope, the others trailing after him.

Ross got back onto his horse and rode in close, a smile on his lips. "Much obliged to you, Brokaw," he said. "Looked a little close there for a minute or two."

Brokaw nodded, still thinking there was a possibility, a remote possibility, that Ross could be Matt Blade. It hardly seemed likely, being Ann's brother, but you never knew for certain about anything. He decided then he would do some checking into the man's life.

"This will probably mean trouble for you with the Prestons," Ross said then.

"Don't worry about it," Brokaw murmured. "It's no stranger to me."

Ann came up to side her brother. She, too, was smiling, relief strong in her dark eyes. "I want to thank you, too. We owe you a great deal, Mister Brokaw."

She turned to her brother who was watching Brokaw with an odd, half smile. "We've met before, George. This is the man I was telling you about."

Ross nodded. "I see," he said slowly. "Seems I'm indebted to you twice over. My thanks again." He wheeled away, heading back to the stock where his rider was getting them under way.

"Sometime ride over," Ann said, "and we'll try to thank you properly." She, too, swung away and followed her brother.

Brokaw turned about and headed for the slope. Jules Strove was waiting for him.

"When you was doin' that namin' off there a while ago, how is it you didn't count me in?"

Brokaw said: "I'm not ringing in any man on trouble unless he wants it that way."

"Anytime," Strove said in careful, distinctly spaced words, "they's some sidin' to be took again' Ollie Godfrey and his bunch, just count me in! I'd take it as a right smart favor. Now, how about a bit of that chuck there in your saddlebags? I'm hungry as a ground squirrel with a sore tooth."

"Then I guess we'd better eat," Brokaw said with a broad grin.

X

Hugh Preston was angry. It showed in the grim, tight set of his jaw, in the glitter of his eyes, and the small spots of white on the drawn skin of his face. Ollie Godfrey had lost no time telling of the Ross incident, and now, shortly after supper, Brokaw stood in the parlor of the ranch house, facing the rancher. Godfrey was there, a knowing smirk on his features. Cameron, as foreman, was present, also, and Darla. She stood quietly to one side, taking no part in the conversation, but the power of her presence was undeniable.

"Is what Ollie tells me a fact?" Preston asked in his quick, clipped way.

Brokaw shrugged. "Hard to say, not knowing what he's told you."

"That he had some rustlers red-handed on our range this morning. That you threw a gun down on him and made him turn them loose."

"Not rustlers. George Ross. I just stopped a murder."

"Killing a rustler is not murder," Preston came back. "I've been trying to pin something on that man and his bunch for months. And when we finally do, you spoil it. Whose side are you on, Brokaw? Theirs or mine?"

"Long as I'm drawing pay from you, I'm on your side . . . up to a point, and that point is cold-blooded murder. Which is what that amounted to this morning. Far as Ross is concerned, I don't believe he's a rustler any more than you are."

"You don't believe!" Preston cried in exasperation. "You been around here one week and already you know all things! What makes you so sure Ross couldn't be helping himself to my beef?"

"We had him red-handed," Godfrey broke in. "I reckon anybody would call that proof."

"He was going to cut out the Arrowhead stuff in that herd, if you'd given him a chance."

"You believe that?" Godfrey demanded.

Brokaw's hard gaze settled on the cowboy. "Ross was telling the truth. Any fool could see that."

Anger pushed at Godfrey's eyes, and his face flushed slightly under its tan. After a moment he said: "He's just got you buffaloed. Him and that sister of his."

"Where were you when all this happened?" Preston asked, whirling upon Cameron. "Why weren't you there?"

"Little hard bein' two places at one time," the old foreman said dryly. "You had me workin' up on the north range."

"You got opinions on this?"

Cameron wagged his head. "George Ross ain't no rustler. I'm plumb sure of that."

"He'd say that," Godfrey observed sourly. "He'd take Brokaw's part, no matter what. Him and Brokaw's real pally. Brokaw's stood for him two or three times."

"Nobody's got to stand for me," Cameron said defensively. "I reckon I can take care of myself."

The room was quiet, only the slow breathing of Cameron, harsh and rasping, being audible. Brokaw slanted a glance at Darla. She seemed completely beyond the argument, wholly disinterested, but Frank Brokaw knew that was a surface impression only. She was vitally concerned, and he had the feeling she had had much to do with whipping Hugh Preston into the state he was in. But Preston had cooled considerably.

He stood in the center of the room, idly pounding one fist into the open palm of the other.

"Little use in crying over it now," he said finally. "It may be some time before we again have a good case against Ross such as this one. But when we do . . . ," he added, lifting his gaze to Brokaw, "I want you to stay out of it. Let Godfrey, or whoever is handling it, alone. They understand the problem. Don't interfere."

Brokaw said: "Just as you say, but I'll not be a party to a murder."

Godfrey spoke up. "Maybe you'd better take my advice, friend, and move on. Maybe you ought to find yourself another job."

"No need for that," Preston snapped. "I want good men. Need them, in fact. You stay on the job, Frank, but do the things you're supposed to and don't get in the way when there's something you don't understand."

"All right, Mister Slade," Brokaw said, and watched the rancher's face.

Preston's glance swung slowly to him, a frown knitting his brow. "What? Slade? Who is Slade?"

Brokaw shrugged. "Slipped out. Used to know a man named Matt Slade. You remind me of him, I guess."

Preston seemed to be studying. He shook his head. "Can't recall hearing the name before. He from around here?"

"Farther east," Brokaw said, and turned for the doorway. Preston's expression looked sincere enough. But you could never tell about a clever man.

Behind him Cameron said: "If they's nothin' more, Mister Preston. . . ."

"That's all," the cattleman said curtly.

Brokaw moved into the yard and came about, waiting for Cameron and for Ollie Godfrey. The foreman was close on his heels, but the cowboy made no appearance.

The foreman pulled to a stop beside him. "That damned Ollie!" he grumbled in his deep voice. "Hightailin' it to Preston like that. Why didn't he come to me first like he should have?"

"Too big a thing for a foreman," Brokaw said with a dry smile. "Things like murder go to the head man."

"That's sure what it would've been had you let Ollie have his way. George ain't no rustler."

"I know that. But why does Preston want him out of the way so bad?"

"Not hard to figure. Preston wants that land and water, 'specially the meadows. And I figure there is a mite of personal problem there, too."

"Missus Preston?"

"Sure. Who else? I've caught them talkin' once or twice. She'd sure like to see the Rosses out of the picture, one way or another. She can do about what she wants with the boss."

"I'm believing that," Brokaw murmured. "You better keep your eye on Ollie. He wants that job of yours in the worst way, and he won't stop until he gets it."

"I've been figurin' that," Cameron said in a tired voice. "Reckon I am gettin' a bit old for the job."

Godfrey came out of the house and stalked by, saying nothing, taking little notice of them. He struck for the barn, walking fast.

"Now, where you figure he's headed?" Cameron wondered, a light worry in his tone.

"To cool off, likely," Brokaw said.

Cameron thought that over for a moment. He shrugged. "Prob'ly right. If I know Hugh Preston, he gave Ollie a dressin' down for lettin' you get the drop on him and messin' up that deal this mornin'. You hittin' the hay now?"

"Not yet. Think I'll have a smoke or two first."

"Good night," said Cameron, and clomped heavily off to his quarters.

Brokaw watched him depart. The yard was silent, and the only lights were in the cook shack and in the main house. Presently these, too, went out, and the ranch lay in the soft, silver glow of the main and bright stars. A horse blew wearily in the barn, and a man's low-voiced curse rumbled from the bunkhouse for some cause or another.

Godfrey came from the stable then, astride the black stallion he generally rode. He came across the yard to Brokaw and halted, facing him at a distance of a half dozen feet. His features were stone cold, and hatred burned in his eyes at slow flame. His right hand rested on the butt of his gun at his hip.

"I'm through talking to you, Brokaw. I told you it wouldn't be healthy for you around here. Now, I'm saying it no more. Get out. Get off Arrowhead and stay off. If you don't, you're a dead man."

Imperceptibly Brokaw had squared away in the half light of the yard. In a soft voice he said: "You back your own talk, Ollie? Or is there somebody else that does it for you?"

Godfrey stared, hard and pressing, at Brokaw. Then he moved his shoulders slightly. "Don't be around here, come nightfall tomorrow, that's all," he said, and swung the black out of the yard.

Brokaw watched the man leave. There had been no idle talk in the cowboy's warning; it had been a genuine and solid threat, and, while he might never push Godfrey into drawing on him, Ollie had other means for getting the job done—Shep and Domino and several others, and a bullet in the back while he was riding across the range. From this time he would have to watch his back trail.

He was far from sleep after that. He started across the hard pack, thinking back to Hugh Preston's reactions when he had deliberately called him Matt Slade. There had been no visible jar, no alarm leaping into his eyes or over his face. But a smart man would play it that way. He would be difficult to catch off guard, particularly if he were expecting something. There had to be a better way of testing Preston, something that would prove or disprove definitely whether he was Matt Slade or not. But if there wasn't, he still could force Preston back to Central City. That would be a final resort. He moved on by the bunkhouse, by the other sheds, and came to the grove at the edge of the clearing. Settling back against the thick trunk of a cottonwood tree, he drew out his muslin sack of tobacco, papers, and rolled himself a thin, brown cigarette.

She appeared before him so suddenly, so unexpectedly, that he was momentarily startled. He stared at her, outlined sharply in the pale moonlight.

" 'Evenin', Missus Preston," he murmured.

"I've been waiting for a chance to talk to you," she replied, stepping closer to him. She was wearing a robe drawn tightly about her slim body.

"You think this is a good place?"

"Makes no difference now," she answered. "I've run out of patience with Hugh. He's a silly, weak fool. I'll do better without him."

Brokaw glanced at her speculatively. "When he was known as Matt Slade, there was nothing weak about him."

"Matt Slade?" she echoed. "I heard you call him that before. Why? Who is Matt Slade?"

"Maybe it's another name for Hugh Preston. I'd like to know for sure."

Darla shook her head. "He's never been anybody but Hugh Preston. I'm sure of that."

"You never heard the name of Slade before?"

"Not until you said it tonight."

Brokaw considered that in silence. Dead end. Maybe it was a blind trail, after all, for who should know a man better than his wife, than the woman who had lived with him for years?

"But I didn't come here to talk to you about some Matt Slade. I came to see if you had reconsidered, if you had changed your mind about throwing in with me." She paused, eyeing him closely. "Brokaw, I need your help in getting what I want. Hugh's weak, and it will take very little to get him out of the way. You saw how he acted about that affair with George Ross. If I had been Hugh, I would have killed you for spoiling a chance like we had. And so would have you. But that can be fixed. There'll be another time, and we won't slip up. You know better now, and we'll have all of Double-R to add to Arrowhead. It will be the biggest ranch west of the Mississippi! And the strongest and most powerful! We will control everything . . . even the politics of the territory. Brokaw, I'll be plain about it. I need you with me. Help me and I'll see you get everything you want!"

Brokaw's glance was reaching beyond her, to the deeper shadows of brush a dozen yards away. Without moving his head he whispered: "There's somebody in the piñons across the way. Could be trouble. Turn and walk away from me, slow and easy and, when you reach the other side of the feed barn, run for the house."

Darla did not move. There was no fear in her tone when she spoke. "Why? Why should I run from anybody?"

"You want Hugh to find you here? With me?"

"Why not? I'm finished with him. The sooner he knows about it, the quicker matters will come to a head."

Brokaw shook his head. "No, not yet. Better that you go.

We don't want the rest of the crew to know about anything. Can't tell which way they might lean."

His words had no real meaning to him. He simply was striving to send her away. She hesitated for a long moment, as if that question might also be settled then and there. But she turned away finally, and moved off, keeping to the deep shadows. Brokaw let a deep sigh run through his lips.

"All right. Come out of there!'

There was no reply, no answering movement in the brush. Brokaw kept his eyes riveted to the spot where he first had seen the dim outline of an eavesdropper. Hand near his gun, he called out again. There was no response. When he made a careful search some minutes later, he found no one, and so he returned to his pallet in the barn.

XI

Cameron was awaiting him the next morning. He stood just outside the cook shack, a puzzled, wondering look on his craggy features. Other riders moved by him, going in to breakfast. He stopped Brokaw with a lifted hand.

"Preston wants to see you," he said. "You get in some kind of trouble last night?"

Brokaw shook his head. "Not that I know of. Do I eat first?"

Cameron said: "No, he wants you first thing."

Brokaw pivoted on his heel and crossed the yard, a fine thread of warning running through him. The front door banged, and he saw Ollie Godfrey leave, swinging to the left so as to not meet him. The cowboy flung a quick, triumphant glance over his shoulder and disappeared around the far corner of the building. Anger stirred swiftly through Brokaw. So that was it—Ollie Godfrey again. He was getting fed up with Godfrey, his patience wearing thinner, as one incident with the cowboy piled up on another.

He reached the side entrance and rapped. Preston's voice, high and strained, said—"Come in."—and Brokaw twisted the knob and entered. The room was flooded with lamplight, and warm from the flames in the fireplace. Preston stood in the center, his face mottled fury. A pistol was thrust into the waistband of his creased, woolen trousers. Darla, tall and cool with faint color showing high in her cheeks, was near the

207

heavy library table, her fingertips drumming lightly upon its polished surface.

A strong caution laid itself upon Frank Brokaw. Here was trouble; here was something he had not anticipated, something that smelled mightily of a trap of sorts. He pulled to a halt in the big room and settled himself squarely on his two feet while the angle of his jaw stiffened.

"You sneaking saddle bum!" Hugh Preston burst out at once. "I might have known what to expect from you!"

Brokaw's gaze shifted to Darla. There was no explanation in her eyes, only a smooth detachment, a satisfaction in a victory that was beyond understanding. He came back to the rancher.

"Seems to be something wrong here. Before you go any further, let's hear it. I'd like to know what it's all about."

"So you will know!" Preston echoed, his voice lifting. "As if you didn't! You think you could get away with this?"

"With what?"

A spasm of fury wracked its shuddering way through Preston. "Don't play with me, Brokaw! I know what you've been up to." The man's words reached an hysterical pitch, and Brokaw, watching him narrowly, expected him to snatch at the gun in his waistband any instant.

Patience fled from Brokaw. "Get on with it, Preston! What's on your mind! I'm not standing here and listen to you rave much longer!"

"Tell him! Tell him!" Darla suddenly cried, and began to weep.

"You'll stand there until I'm through with you!" Preston shouted. "Or I'll kill you!"

"Maybe," Brokaw replied evenly. "And maybe you won't. Point is, if you don't say what's bothering you, you may get your chance."

The rancher turned to Darla and laid his hand on her arm. "Never mind, dear," he said. "You won't have to be afraid any more." He wheeled back to Brokaw. "You're a cool one. But you don't frighten me any. You may look tough, but I know your kind."

"So you know my kind. If that's all you wanted to tell me, then you've done it."

"I called you here to tell you to get off my ranch. And if I ever see you around here again, I'll kill you. I'll give my men orders to shoot you on sight. Understand that? You show up anywhere in this country, and I'll put a bullet in your black heart. I should anyway . . . right now! It's a hell of a thing when a man's own wife can't be safe on his own ranch!"

Brokaw's glance flicked again to Darla. She had been watching him closely, and now she turned quickly away.

"Yes," Preston said, noting the exchange, "she told me. And if that isn't enough, you were seen by another member of the crew. You deny it? You deny you met up with my wife yesterday morning on the range? You deny you forced yourself upon her last night when she stepped out for a breath of air?"

Understanding came swiftly then to Frank Brokaw. Godfrey, somehow, had forced Darla's hand with Preston, and she had, in her desperation, swung all blame to him. It must have been Godfrey in the thicket last night. Now he was caught in the squeeze.

He said: "She tell you that?"

"She did. And so did Godfrey . . . one of the men."

"Let your wife tell me the same thing," Brokaw said then, looking at Darla.

The rancher swung to his wife. "Go ahead, dear. Tell him. Everything you told me."

Darla whirled around, placing her back to him. Sobbing, she said: "I didn't tell you all, Hugh! About the trip from

209

town. The day you sent him to meet me. . . ."

Anger blazed again across Preston's face. "Get out of here!" he cried. "Get out of my sight before I shoot you where you stand!"

Darla's wracking sobs filled the room. "Oh, Hugh! I'll never live it down. There'll always be the shame, and then, if he's alive, he'll talk . . . he'll tell other men. . . ."

Brokaw, never taking his eyes from the rancher, said: "Don't touch that gun, Preston! You haven't got a chance!"

Outside in the yard Brokaw could hear the 'punchers coming out of the cook shack, their morning meal over. He heard the dull *thud* of hoofs as the wrangler brought up the horses, ready for the day's work, and turned them into the corral. But those things were below the surface of his senses. He was thinking of Darla Preston; she had trapped him neatly, she and Ollie. He had played right into their hands. From the very start, it would seem.

"I'll take that chance," Preston murmured, coming around to face Brokaw. His eyes locked with the tall rider's and for a few moments held, and then fell away. A look of hopelessness crossed his face. "I can't do it," he said in a lost voice. "I couldn't kill any man."

A shrill cry wrenched from Darla's lips. The deafening blast of a gun in her hand rocked Brokaw. He saw an expression of surprise, and then disbelief, pass over Preston's agonized face. The man pulled himself to his toes, reaching up, twisting half around until he was looking at Darla, and the smoking pistol again, firing at point-blank range at Brokaw. It missed by inches and *thudded* into the wall. Brokaw leaped for her, and the gun roared once more. Yells lifted outside in the yard.

"You've killed my husband!" Darla's voice went echoing through the house and out the open windows.

Brokaw struck her full on, and they went down in a crashing heap. He wrenched the gun from her fingers, then threw it into a far corner. Darla, screaming steadily, was like a writhing snake, pressed beneath his body. He slapped her soundly and struggled to his feet, dragging her with him. The yawning door to the hallway was before him. He half threw her into its cavern, slammed the door, and pushed a heavy chair against it.

"You murdered him!" Her voice, muffled and insistent, came through to him.

Brokaw whirled into Preston's office. Fists were hammering at the side door. It swung open, and the vague shape of a man was outlined there. He drove him back with a snap shot that crashed into the nearby door frame. He leaped through the office entrance and out into the yard. It was just breaking daylight, and shadows were beginning to lift. Around the structure, on the hard pack, he could hear shouts and the pounding of boots. He circled the house swiftly, placing it between himself and the sounds.

Running lightly, he traveled its full length. At the end corner he paused. Faintly he could hear Darla, still imprisoned, screaming. She was making it look good. He smiled grimly; the whole plan was clear to him now. Darla would goad Preston into shooting it out with him. If both died, all would be well and good. If one survived, she would see that he did not leave the room alive, and her story would be, in either event, that both had been killed in a gun duel.

Only Preston had failed to come through, even after so fantastic a tale as had been told him. So she had shot him, and then turned her gun on Brokaw. Even her failure to accomplish that had not stalled her clever, scheming mind. She had immediately cried murderer for all to hear, and now he was a target for all their guns. They would be after him, hunting him down. She would see to that, and with Ollie Godfrey at their head there would be no let-up until he was dead. Their only hope of safety lay in his death.

He laid a close survey on the bunkhouse, lying a short distance ahead. It was deserted, he was sure. All those who had not already ridden onto the range, to begin the day's work, would be there in the yard or in the main house. Even at that moment, no doubt, they would be starting their search for him. He hurried across the narrow open space that intervened, reaching the north wall of the bunkhouse. He passed around that building, coming to its extreme southwest corner. If he could cross to the barn without being seen, he might gain entrance, and once inside that building there would be horses. If he could get astride his gelding, he would have half a chance of escaping. But there was little time. It was steadily growing lighter, and Ollie and the crew would be working closer.

He decided it was wiser to double back and go completely around the barn instead of risking the shorter, more open route. He was too likely to be seen running across the yard. He wheeled about and raced along the back of the bunkhouse. Cutting left, he went around the tool sheds and feed house and came to the grove where he had met Darla the night before. He heard a yell go up from the front of the house. Somebody had seen him.

He ran a long fifty yards through the brush, thinking it might draw them off, believing him to have taken refuge in the grove, and then cut left to the barn. The wide, double doors at the rear were closed, but there was a window, empty of glass, shoulder-high above the ground. Without hesitation he launched himself at it. He would have to take a chance on there being someone inside.

He gained the sill and pulled himself through into the

gloomy, dim cavern of a building. A broad square of light marked the open doorway at its far end. He dropped lightly to the floor, still wary of somebody hiding in the deep shadows, and started forward, looking for the bay horse. Shouts were a running chorus in the yard, coming from all sides, it seemed. No one yet, apparently, thought he was far from the main house, that he was in the grove.

He located the gelding, and his hopes dropped. The horse was not saddled and bridled, and there was not time to throw on his gear. Two stalls farther along he found a buckskin ready to ride. One of the mounts of the night crew's riders, not yet relieved of its tack and turned into the corral. Without hesitating, he stepped to the stirrup and swung up.

Wheeling into the runway, he walked the horse quietly toward the front doorway, gun in hand. He would have to break out at a fast run, counting on catching the men in the yard by surprise. While they rushed to get their own horses, he would gain precious distance toward the hills to the west. He wished heartily for the bay, having a brief wonder if he should gamble the extra time it would take to get him ready. A voice, coming from the side of the barn, gave him his answer. He had run out of time—there was none left. The buckskin would have to do, and that was not good, for he knew the horse was already dog-tired.

He reached the doorway and halted, settling himself in the strange saddle. The stirrups were too short, and his knees stuck up awkwardly. He was lucky to have even found the buckskin, he told himself. Bending low, gun ready, he drove spurs into the buckskin's flanks. The little buckskin bolted through the door in a long, startled leap.

Ollie Godfrey was waiting for him. Godfrey's gun blossomed red-orange. Brokaw felt the burning shock of a bullet slap into his leg. He snapped a shot at the big cowboy.

Godfrey staggered, his arm jerking back behind his crouched body. Brokaw drove another bullet at him, hastily, but he was having a hard time of it with the plunging buckskin, and the shot went wild.

Yells broke out. One or two guns flatted in the early morning air, but he was already out of the yard, going into the grove, running hard for the distant bluish haze of the Sierra del Diablo. The buckskin, thoroughly frightened by the crash of gunfire, was going at his top speed, and Brokaw let him have his head.

Hooking the reins over the saddle horn, he punched the empty cartridges from his gun and reloaded from his belt. When this was done, he shoved the .45 into its holster and turned to the wound in his leg. The initial anesthetic of shock was beginning to wear off, and sharp pain was making itself felt. The hole was about halfway between hip and knee, bleeding freely from both openings. The bullet had made a complete passage, going through the fleshy part of his leg at a slightly upward angle. Luckily it had missed the bone. He glanced down at the saddle skirt. A fresh scar showed where the lead had emerged, struck a solid surface, and glanced off into space.

He ripped his handkerchief into strips, making two pads that he bound against the puckered holes. The hard running of the buckskin made the job impossible insofar as a tight bandage was concerned, so after a time he gave it up. The pads would stay, perhaps, until he could reach some sort of shelter. Then he would pause and do the job properly.

He crossed completely through the grove and broke into the open prairie with the bulk of the mountains still miles in the distance. Twisting about in the saddle, he threw a glance at his back trail. No pursuers were yet in sight. He came back around, growing a little giddy from the swinging motion.

Shaking his head to clear away the mists, he cursed softly. A little nick in the leg like that should not give him much trouble. He must be getting soft.

The buckskin began to tire, to slow down. His long, reaching gallop dropped to a run, then to a fast trot. He was blowing hard, and flecks of foam came back on the wind and plastered against Brokaw. He was trembling badly, and Brokaw realized he was good for little more at his present pace. He pulled the little buckskin in. He could take no chances on the buckskin's going down now. The horse would have to last, to carry him at least until they gained the shrouding safety of the brushy hills, for Brokaw knew he was in no condition to walk.

He looked again over his shoulder. He was still alone on the vast roll of flat land. But it would not be so for much longer. Arrowhead riders would be pounding through the grove on fresh horses, even at that moment. They would soon gain the edge and break into sight, and, when they caught sight of him, they would ride in earnest. He let the buckskin idle along, trying to conserve his strength. The horse was not blowing so badly now, but he still shook from his earlier exertions. Brokaw would need every ounce of strength and speed the horse had when Arrowhead's men began to close in.

It came to him then with jolting suddenness. Hugh Preston was dead—and he would never know for certain now if the rancher was actually Matt Slade. The blast from Darla's gun had stilled Preston's lips, and he would take his secret, if he had one, into the grave with him. If he were Slade, the chance to clear Tom Brokaw's name was gone forever. But should he assume that was true, that the rancher had been Slade? Should he give up the search now, satisfied in the knowledge the man had received his just reward and mortal punishment at the hands of his wife? Or should he go on looking for a shadow, as he had been, being suspicious of every man he met who fit a vague description, who had money to spend freely?

The description, he had discovered, fit a multitude of men. He could think of a half dozen who fitted the same general outline besides Preston. There was George Ross, the man called Domino, Ollie Godfrey—even Abel Cameron, except he likely was too old. The money narrowed it down considerably, but even that could have vanished in the past few years, and Matt Slade could be a poor man again. But that would all have to wait for a time now. He was a hunted man himself, one with a murder charge hanging over his head. A posse was at his heels, thirsting for his blood, and Darla Preston, now a powerful and ruthless force in the Scattered Hills country, was driving them after him. She would never let them rest until she had him lying at her feet; he alone was the sole remaining threat to her safety.

Where should he go? In the blazing heat of his escape he had not given it any consideration other than the immediate need for reaching the mountains and hiding there. But he could not remain there for long. There was the matter of food and water and care for his leg, and Ollie Godfrey and Arrowhead would search every foot of it. He might escape them for a time, but not for long. He thought then of making his way to Westport Crossing, to Ben Marr, and telling the sheriff what had happened. He shook off that suggestion with a curling of his lips. He had no proof to back his own statements and who would the law believe—the bereaved widow, or the word of a stranger? The law was not the answer.

The sun was warming to his back. He reached for the canteen hanging at the saddle. Shaking it, he found it to be about half full. He took a swallow, rinsing his dry mouth thoroughly before he permitted it to drain down his throat. There should be water available in the mountains, but he must take no chances. He would have to hoard his small supply until he located some.

He pivoted again in the saddle, more slowly and with greater effort. He supported himself with one hand on the saddle horn, the other on the cantle while giddiness slogged through him. The posse was in sight now, well out of the grove and streaming across the prairie. They were no more than dark blobs, but coming fast, and taking on definite shape and outline with each fleeting second. He twisted back around. The mountains were closer now, not over two miles at the most. He patted the buckskin's sweaty neck in a dazed, addled way, unaware that he yet clung to the horn to stay in the saddle.

"I'm real sorry, old horse," he muttered.

He peered ahead through the mistiness flooding his eyes, selecting a cañon opening onto the prairie that would afford sanctuary. He was heading almost directly into the largest, and the approach was gradual and not steep. Brokaw settled himself lower on the buckskin, trying to brush away the weariness that was overtaking him. He kicked his spurs into the horse, and the game little animal broke into a gallop. Pain wrenched through Brokaw, but he clamped his jaws tightly and hung on. After the initial spasm, the pain flattened out into a solid, running string of fire coursing all through his body. His eyes began to glaze under it all, but he hung on.

The posse was a distant scatter of riders when he leaned forward and urged the buckskin to greater effort. A half mile from the cañon's mouth the horse began to flag, leaning heavily to one side as he favored his left foreleg. Brokaw pushed him cruelly onward, up the lifting slope, every step of the animal's adding to and multiplying his own misery and pain. But mere pain was beyond him now; there was only the necessity to reach the sheltering depths of the cañon.

He was vaguely conscious of finally getting to the top of the grade, finding himself on a sort of ridge that ran for miles in either direction along the foot of the mountains. A shallow valley lay between, and he drove the fading buckskin down into it. Behind him a gunshot echoed, a signal of some sort.

More from instinct than any conscious thought, he swung left and traveled along the floor of the swale until another cañon broke off to his right. He guided the limping horse up this, looking desperately for a place that he might turn and remain safely hidden. At every hand, small gullies fed into the main wash, but these he avoided, knowing they were dead ends and would form a trap from which he might not escape. He heard another shot, off to his right. The posse had crested the ridge. They would pause there, uncertain, trying to find the direction he had taken. A few more minutes' time would be recovered.

A large arroyo cut off at an angle to his left. Without hesitation he turned into it, barely conscious that it curved back toward the prairie. It was thick with cedar and oak brush, and the buckskin labored with every step of the climb, plunging along like a horse in deep snowdrifts. Brokaw knew the sounds of their passage were loud, but there was no help for it. There was no turning back now, no seeking an easier, less overgrown trail. He pushed on, clinging to the saddle horn with both hands.

The buckskin scrambled up a steep bank and came upon a ledge, too beat to go farther. Brokaw hung for a long minute, and then slipped from the horse's back, catching himself with his hands. For another long minute he clung there, upright against the heaving buckskin. This was the limit of travel, the stopping point for both himself and the valiant horse.

He released his grasp and stood for a moment, swaying

slightly. His head had cleared somewhat as the pain lessened when the buckskin stopped plunging beneath him. He would have to make some sort of stand here. He did not know how well hidden he was; he might be out in the open for all he knew, but it would have to be all right. There was no reserve left in either him or the horse. Suddenly the starch went out of his knees, and he sat down, his legs simply folding beneath him. The buckskin shied away, too tired to move far, and coming to a halt a half dozen steps distant. He was still breathing heavily, sucking for wind with his head low between his legs.

Brokaw dragged out his gun and tried to focus his eyes toward the end of the cañon. That would be the point any searching posse member would first appear, he figured. It was an indistinct, fuzzy blur, and all things seemed to be moving in a slow, swirling motion. He shook his head savagely, trying to halt the confusion.

He heard a shout then. It seemed far away, far to the north. But he could not be sure if it actually was in the distance or only seemed so to his reeling senses.

XII

The sun was his friend. It reached down from a clean, steel sky, wringing from him the little moisture left in his fevered body. It stirred him restlessly on his rocky pallet, twisting him first one way, then another. It popped beads of sweat from his brow that rolled off his dark face, and down onto his chest. But finally it awakened him.

It was nearly noon, he judged. He had lain there for three, maybe four hours. Somehow the posse had not yet discovered him, and that in itself was some sort of miracle.

His head throbbed sullenly, and a rivulet of fire traced up and down his injured leg like a continuous flash of jagged lightening. He was kitten-weak from the loss of blood and lack of food. When had he last eaten? Last night? Or was it the night before that? It was all mixed up and confused in his mind.

He turned his head slowly, and caught the buckskin a dozen paces away, cropping at the scanty grass on the ledge. His teeth made hollow, clacking noises as they closed, and the saddle leather creaked with his movements. Brokaw wished he had loosened the cinch. It would have eased the tired horse. The fact of the matter was, he recalled, he had not been able to do much of anything.

He pushed himself to a sitting position. His mouth was parched, and he glanced to the canteen hanging at the saddle. He got to his feet then, moving unsteadily and favoring the leg. It had stopped bleeding sometime during the hours he had lain on the bench, but at his first attempt to rise he felt it start anew, a warm, sticky feeling.

He hobbled awkwardly toward the horse that watched him with tired, suspicious eyes. *All I need,* he thought, *is for that damned horse to spook.* But the buckskin remained where he stood, too tired to shy off, and Brokaw eventually reached him. He hung again to the saddle, appalled by his own inadequate strength while all things swam in front of his eyes.

The water in the canteen was hot. But it was wet, and it eased the stiff dryness in his mouth and throat. The buckskin, smelling water, turned to watch. He took his bandanna from around his neck, pouring a quantity of the liquid on it. Working his way to the buckskin's head, he rubbed the animal's quivering lips and nostrils, managing to squeeze the cloth dry in his mouth. The horse made loud, sucking noises and tried nervously to get more, but it was all Brokaw could spare for the time. He rubbed the buckskin's neck and eventually quieted him down.

His head had cleared again, and this aroused a vague worry in him. He was too keen, too alert, and he was fearful he was not far from fever deliriums. He groaned. He could not allow that to happen now. It would be dangerous to remain there on the ledge overlong. Luck had been with him so far, but it would not last. The posse, failing to find him in an area they knew he had entered, would backtrack and search more diligently. He hobbled to a slab of granite and sat down. He must think calmly and act rationally.

Deliberately he built himself a cigarette, rolling it with hands that were far from steady. He spilled considerable tobacco, but finally it was made, and after the first few drags he felt some better. He decided the thing to be done next was to tend to the hole from Godfrey's bullet. The pads he had made and crudely fastened in place were now stuck to the skin, and it took several painful minutes before he got them loose. This done, he refolded them, placed them over the angry vents, and bound them tightly in place. It was not the best treatment, hardly any treatment at all, but it was the best he could do. He could not continue to lose blood indefinitely. What he needed was hot water, and something with which to cleanse the wound. He would have to find a ranch house.

A faint halloo drifted to him through the hot, still air. It came from below, from the prairie. He was instantly alert. Gun in hand, he moved off the slab and made his way to the edge of the shelf, going the last few feet on his hands and knees, to avoid being seen by anyone scanning the slope—or looking upwards. Reaching the lip, he found he was on a sort of eyebrow that overlooked the entire side of the mountain, and afforded a balcony-like view of the flat land below. On his belly he let his gaze run out over the prairie.

A half dozen horsemen were gathered below, holding some sort of council, it appeared. He immediately picked out Ollie Godfrey, the bandage of his left hand standing out startlingly white at that distance. He could also make out Shep Russell and Buckshot Martin and Domino. The other two riders were not distinguishable. Off to the right a single horseman was loping leisurely toward the group. They were in no hurry. They knew he had little time left, while they had plenty. He was wounded and could not go far on a tired horse.

The lone rider joined up, unrecognizable to Brokaw, and for a long ten minutes the meeting held. It broke up with the men fanning out in different directions, but all pointing into the flanks of the Diablos. One, however, soon pulled away from his companions. He dropped into the swale, lying between the ridge and the foot of the mountains, and rode northward. Brokaw watched him thoughtfully, coming to the conclusion that his task was to find a trail that led to the topmost point of the mountains from which he could look down, and from there Brokaw knew he would be spotted.

He could remain here no longer, that became immediately clear. They would find his hiding place now, without question. They would work deeper into the cañons from below and watch from above, then in the end they would flush him out and shoot him down. He crawled back to the slab, ignoring his throbbing leg and the faintness that now seemed to be continuous.

He threw a glance along the rim of the hills towering above him. He was about a third of the way up. It appeared rough and steep—he doubted if the buckskin could make it. The north and the east were closed off to him, with posse members swarming all through it. The only route open was to the south. That would take him farther from the riders so eagerly probing the draws and arroyos. It would also take him off Arrowhead land and onto the range owned by George Ross. He gave that brief thought, thinking he might head for that point. But it would not be wise. Failing to find him in the mountains, Double-R would be the first place Godfrey would look. But beyond the Double-R, there would lie other ranches. If he could reach one of those, he could obtain aid for his leg, food and water for the buckskin and himself.

He got to his feet too quickly; the motion sent a wave of nausea flooding through him, and he sank back onto the slab of granite. He waited out what seemed a long time, then tried again, moving with more deliberateness now. This attempt succeeded, and he half walked, half crawled, to the waiting horse. He was breathing hard when he reached the animal, and he clung to the horn and cantle for support, gathering his strength to climb aboard.

It was then his flagging mind remembered the buckskin had gone lame back on the prairie. It was like a blow from the edge of all hope, and it left him sagging against the horse, limp with despair. But after a minute the will to fight came back, and he sank to his knees. He patted the buckskin's foreleg until the horse lifted it for his inspection. He examined the hoof, hopeful it was nothing more serious than a wedged-in pebble.

There was no stone visible, and he let the hoof fall. A tendon, maybe. He felt the buckskin's leg, but it seemed firm and straight, with no swelling, nor did the horse try to pull away. He struggled to think clearly, to remember. It had been the left, he was positive. What then was wrong?

He raised the buckskin's leg again. There was the faintest chink of metal. Loose shoe! Feverishly he looked it over. He found the fault, a bit of gravel lying between the hoof and shoe. He searched his pockets for his knife, opened it, and dug about until he flipped out the offending bit of stone. The shoe was really loose, but he feared to do anything about that. Hammering at it with a rock would cause a noise bound to be heard by someone.

Then he led the buckskin to the slab of rock, thus giving himself a three-foot lift above the ground. Standing upon it, he crawled into the saddle, the effort sending his senses rocking back and forth in his head, like loose shot in a bucket. He managed to find the stirrups, resting his weight heavily upon his right leg until he was settled. The buckskin started up the faint game trail leading off the ledge.

For the first hour or so he managed to hang grimly to consciousness as hunger and pain, thirst and weakness slogged through him relentlessly. The buckskin plodded slowly on, guided only by the narrow path itself. Finally it became too great an effort for Brokaw to hold his eyes open, and he sagged forward in the saddle. Only the rigidity of his wounded leg and the death-like grip on the horn kept him from falling.

Off to the south, a far distance from the hills, Ann Ross pulled her spotted horse to a halt and watched thoughtfully the slow, graceful glidings of the vultures. There were four of the huge birds circling high above the mountain's slope, dipping, rising, weaving in the noonday sky like leaves caught in the vagrant whims of a summer wind. They were still high which meant their intended prey was not yet ready, not entirely dead. But they knew, they always seemed to know, possessing some uncanny sense of doom. She wondered about their victim. It could be a calf lost from its mother, but that seemed hardly likely. It was too far up the slope. It could easily be a steer down with a broken leg, or possibly a horse or deer or some other unfortunate animal, pulled to the ground by a lion. Or it could be a man.

Her mind came to a full halt on that thought. She was marking strays, locating the singles and jags of stock drifted from the range and lost in the brush and thickets. Later she would report the locations to her brother, and he, or another of the men, would go after them. It worked out well; it saved the crew from spending so much time poking around the edges of the range. There never was a big enough crew on the Double-R, it seemed.

Ann frowned. It was late to start for so distant a point as the mountain slope where the vultures circled in their tireless way, but the thought that it might be one of their own beeves down, and the almost certain possibility that more would be nearby, was pressing her sense of duty. It would be well after dark when she reached the ranch, and George would be angry and worried. He had been that way ever since that affair with

Godfrey and the other Arrowhead riders. But she doubted if any Arrowhead men would be that far south. This was, she thought, Double-R land, and the slope of the mountain still lay on it, or very nearly so.

She put her pony to a slow gallop, crossing the prairie at an easy, ground-gaining pace. Thinking of Hugh Preston's crew, she wondered again about Frank Brokaw. She had made no headway with George in her efforts to get him hired on as foreman. At first he had seemed mildly interested, telling her he would think about it. Then, yesterday morning after the incident with Ollie, he had come to a decision. They had talked about it on their way back to the ranch.

"That's the man I was telling you about," she had said. "The one that stepped in and stopped Ollie."

George had nodded his head. "Brave man. Maybe a little on the fool side, but plenty of nerve."

"He's probably looking for a job right now. Preston will never keep him after Ollie gets through talking."

"We couldn't afford him."

"Why? He'll likely work for regular wages. I'll bet Preston's not paying him any more than that."

"If he would work for nothing," George had said with emphasis, "we still couldn't afford him."

"But why not?" she had persisted, somehow disappointed and not at all understanding his reasoning.

"Hiring him would be like waving a red flag in Hugh Preston's face. We'd have Ollie and that bunch of hardcases down on us before dark. It would be inviting trouble, and we've got all we can handle along that line now."

"I doubt if they'd try much with him around."

"Maybe not," George had said. "But there's little we would gain. We might even win out, but there'd be mighty little left of the Double-R to crow over. You can figure on that."

It had ended there. Ann had recognized the futility of saying more, at least for the time. But she had not given up. She remembered the way Brokaw had sat there, his strong face so still, so calm, speaking low in such a way that men did not hesitate to comply quickly with his orders.

She reached the first outcropping of rock and halted, lifting a glance to the sky, to the black-winged silhouettes biding their time in fluent flight. They were nearer than she had thought; whatever it was they watched was somewhere on the side of the slope, about where the trail laced across its rough terrain.

She touched her pony with her knees, and they moved ahead, beginning the ascent. It was country she had been over many times in the past, and she turned now for a steep break-off at the end of the long parallel ridge. Here she could double back and reach the path. The pony made it easily, scarcely breathing hard from the effort, then she headed him around for the north.

In another half mile she reached the larger timber, pines and a few spruce. A screen of brush to her right shut off the prairie from view, but she was paying little mind to that, to the thought she might now be on Arrowhead range, and therefore in danger. Her glance was on the buzzards, almost directly overhead at this point.

She reached the cañon where the spring lay shallow and cool in a small clearing and halted there. She allowed her horse to drink while she probed the slope ahead with careful, painstaking eyes. She could see nothing but the glistening, heat-slapped rocks and the gray-greens of the underbrush. There were no sounds, her approach having stilled even the forest's wildlife. Urging her pony away from the water, she continued on, knowing she could not be far off now. If whatever it was the vultures watched was on the trail, she would find it soon. If it lay off and hidden in the welter of draws, thickets, and tangles of brush and rock, it might take some time to locate it.

She climbed a steep stretch, the horse stumbling a bit on the weather-polished stone of the trail, and rounded a bulging shoulder of rock. Her breath caught momentarily. There, dead ahead, was a man on a horse. He was folded forward in the saddle, head sunk deeply onto his chest. The worn buckskin horse he forked was near collapse, standing with legs braced wide apart, half on, half off the trail.

Ann studied the exhausted pair for a full minute, something about the man stirring her memory. The buckskin, sensing the other horse, lifted a tired head and took a faltering step. The rider's hat fell off and rolled away in awkward, loping fashion. Ann gasped. Brokaw! The man Frank Brokaw!

A wild sort of fear raced through her, something she had no immediate understanding of, or explanation for. She saw then the dark crusted blood along his leg. This had been his reward for helping them yesterday morning! With a little cry she leaped from the saddle and ran to him, snatching up his hat as she passed by it. She placed her hand under his whisker-stubbled chin, and raised his head. His eyes were closed, sunken. Stricken with a nameless fear, she unbuttoned the top of his shirt and laid her hand upon his heart. She felt the strike, slow and light. He was still alive.

It was a long quarter mile back to the spring. She unhooked the reins from the horn, seeing he was safely in the saddle, anchored by his own locked hands and stiff muscles, then led the buckskin down the trail. Her own pony fell obediently in behind, and minutes later they were in the cool glade where the spring bubbled noisily from beneath its overhung, moss-covered ledge.

She could not hold back the buckskin when he got his first smell of water. It was all she could do to keep Brokaw in the saddle when he lunged past her, but somehow she accomplished it. While the horse sucked his fill, she pulled Brokaw's feet free of the stirrups, pried loose his hands, and dragged him from the saddle.

His weight was solid, more than she bargained for, and he struck the ground hard. A groan escaped his cracked lips, but his eyes did not open. She laid him out in the shade on the cool grass, then turned to the buckskin. It took her leather belt applied as a whip to drive him away from the stream, but it had to be done. She could not allow him to founder himself. There would be need for him later.

She filled the canteen with water and let a small amount of it trickle into Brokaw's parched mouth. Making a compress of her folded handkerchief, she soaked it and draped it across his forehead. He seemed feverish, but not in too bad a condition. He stirred when the coolness of the cloth penetrated the fog in his mind, and he opened his eyes. But he was not conscious, she knew that. A dozen questions were crowding her, but there was no time to think of them now. That leg would have to be attended to, and then food, from her own lunch that, luckily, she had not paused to eat. And more water, as soon as he could drink.

XIII

He became conscious first of the coolness on his brow. He had been going through a sort of dream, in reality a fever nightmare in which he visualized himself again at Arrowhead, standing completely alone in the empty yard near the main house. Darla Preston faced him from the doorway, calm and beautiful as she leveled the pistol at him. Involuntarily he cried: "Darla!"

He was aware then of someone bending over him, the indistinct, blurred face of a woman. He knew it was a woman because of the halo of hair, and he thought then it was Darla, that it had not been a dream at all, that she had shot him down and was preparing now to finish the job. He tried to squirm away, struggling with little strength. Light fingers began to stroke his face, his cheeks, feeling odd and remote, as they traced across the wire-stiff whiskers along his jaw. He managed to bring his eyes into focus, trying to separate the nightmare from actuality, the true events of the last hours from the confused ramblings of his mind. The posse! Where was the posse? What had happened to them? And where was he—where was this place? It was dark and cool; he could be back at Arrowhead, a prisoner? The last thing he could recall was climbing onto the buckskin and starting along the mountain trail. What had taken place since that moment?

Vision came into his eyes. Ann Ross was beside him, a soft smile on her full lips. Her face was turned half away as she looked out over the prairie. Somewhere in the stillness a

230

squirrel was scolding, and he could hear the steady, contented cropping of a horse as it grazed. The late afternoon sunlight filtering down through the screen of trees glinted upon Ann's dark hair and deepened the tan of her skin, giving it a sort of golden softness. He noted with a start that her shoulders were bare; she wore no shirt, and the curve of her breasts was visible above the undergarment she wore.

He lay there quietly, wondering at the strangeness of that. He felt much better. The pain in his leg had subsided to a dull ache, and the few hours of sleep he had garnered had worked wonders for him. Ann, he decided, must have accidentally stumbled upon him as he came down the trail. But he could not recall their meeting, or how he had arrived at the shady place where now he lay.

Wry humor moved through him. "If this is heaven and you're my special angel, I reckon I'll like it here fine."

She turned to him at once, quick light springing into her eyes. "How do you feel?"

"Better. A lot better."

She felt the press of his gaze on her shoulders and read the question in his eyes. "I had to have bandages for your leg. The shirt was all I could think of."

There was no embarrassment in her tone, no false modesty, only a matter-of-factness that bespoke her practical side. It was something that had to be done, and so she did it. "I thought you might lend me your jumper," she added after a moment.

Brokaw glanced to his leg. His Levi's had been slit from knee to thigh, and the wound was bound tightly with clean, white cloth. A strip of lacy, eyelet trim stuck out from beneath one fold. "I'll bet that's the fanciest bandage ever a man wore," he commented with a grin.

With some effort he raised himself to one elbow. She

helped him get an arm out of the jumper, reverse the process, and pull free the other. The jacket was twice too large for her, and she became momentarily lost in it, but this she finally whipped by tucking the tail, woman-like, into her skirt's waistband. It didn't look quite so large then. During that he lay back, watching her pull and tug until she was satisfied with it. When she turned back to him, he said: "How did you find me?"

"Buzzards," she said. "I saw them circling and figured something was down. Maybe one of our own steers. I never thought it would be you."

That brought an immediate alarm to him. If she had spotted him by such means, others would have noticed the birds and arrived at the same conclusion. "Where are we now? How far from where you found me?"

"About a quarter of a mile. If your buckskin had gone on just a little farther, he would have got wind of the water and brought you here himself."

"He was about done for."

"And so were you," she murmured. She was waiting for him to make some explanation of his condition, of why he had been there in the Diablos, of what had happened at Arrow-head. But she was patient. He would tell it of his own accord, if needed, if he wanted her to know about it. She would ask no questions. "You didn't wake up during all the time I was working on you . . . not even when I poured the whisky in the bullet hole to clean it."

"Whisky?"

"I found a little in a bottle in your saddlebags."

"Not mine," he said. "I borrowed the buckskin in a hurry."

"I see," Ann replied, but she pressed it no further. "Are you hungry? There was a lard bucket and a sack of coffee grounds there, too. The coffee has been used so many times it's about worn out, but I made you some anyway. It's ready if you want it."

He had not thought about food, the surprise of the first moments being so great, but now he realized how hungry he was. "Go mighty good," he said.

Ann moved away at once to where she had built a small fire of smokeless, dry twigs. Brokaw managed to pull himself to a sitting position. His head spun a little, and he was short of breath when it was done, but it was not too bad.

She brought him the tin of coffee. He tipped it up and drank it empty without pausing. She was right; it was weak as rainwater, but it had some strength, and it tasted good. Almost at once the hot liquid made him feel better. She handed him two cold biscuits and a few strips of dried beef. "Part of my lunch. I wish there was more."

He ate it without question, and, while he was doing so, Ann took the lard tin and refilled it from the stream. She set it back over the fire and replenished the fuel. He watched her busy herself at the task, but as he slowly became his old self and reason once again took hold, worry began to haunt him. It was growing late; he had been there on the mountainside almost the entire day, and the posse could not be far off. They had not given up. Godfrey would never face Darla with the word that he had escaped, and he did not want them to find Ann with him. He said: "We should be getting out of here."

"As soon as it's dark," she replied over her shoulder.

"Have you seen any riders around?"

She shook her head. "Nobody has been by here, and I haven't seen any on the slope. I did hear a yell, but it was to the north."

"How long ago was that?"

"Over an hour, at least."

Brokaw glanced to the sky, arching blue and clear above the Diablos. The sun was beginning to swing low, not far above the highest ridges and peaks. It would be a full two hours until dark, he judged. "We've got to get out of here," he said. "That posse can't be far off."

He started to rise, turned restless by the urgency and danger, and, finding he had miscalculated his strength, he settled back on the ground. In an angry sort of helplessness, he shook his head.

Ann, watching him, said: "What posse?"

He thought he detected a lifting change in her tone, sort of disappointment, or perhaps it was dismay. He said: "Ollie Godfrey . . . Arrowhead."

He told her then of the events at the ranch, leaving out a large portion of the story, giving her only the pertinent details. She listened in silence, the tan oval of her face serious. When he was finished, she said: "So Hugh Preston's dead, and Darla owns Arrowhead. That's what she wanted. I knew it would happen someday, but I thought it would be Ollie she used."

"I think that was the way it was planned. Ollie forced her hand for some reason."

Ann was silent, still busying herself with the fire. Without turning to him, she said: "What does Darla mean to you?"

"Mean to me?" he echoed. "Nothing, except that I need her to clear my name of a murder."

"Is that all? Do you know you called out to her, cried her name while you were still unconscious?"

Brokaw's dark face was still, puzzled. He shook his head. "I can't explain that. I don't know what would make me do something like that."

"Perhaps it was just a dream."

"A bad one," he said with grim humor.

"And she means nothing to you, no more than being a witness who can prove your innocence of Hugh's murder?"

"That's all. Once I get clear of Ollie and his bunch, I'm going back after her and make her tell the truth about it."

"You think for a moment she'll do that? She has too much to lose. She'd never do it."

"Not willingly, of course. But I'll force her to somehow. She made her use of me, now I'll have my time."

"She will keep Ollie on your trail until he runs you down. And they'll kill you."

Her voice broke slightly, and Brokaw threw a sharp glance at her. But she was not looking at him, her eyes lost in the dancing flames of the fire.

"First they'll have to catch me," he said in a reassuring voice. "And as to the killing, I'll have a little to say about that."

After a time she said: "Did she send for you to come and work on Arrowhead?"

"No," he said, "I came looking for a man named Matt Slade. I thought Preston might be him, and still think it might be so." He remembered then his suspicions regarding her brother, George Ross.

"This Matt Slade, you must want to find him very badly."

"I do," Brokaw said. He told her then of Central City, of his father and mother and of the endless trails he had followed. When he had finished, he came up to a sitting position, again restless and anxious to be moving. He managed to get to his feet and tried a few, experimental steps. The jagged pain returned at once, but he kept at it, feeling his way, favoring the injured member.

Ann watched him, saying nothing. Her eyes were dark and deep and filled with thought, her face serene and still. There was a tenderness about her as she viewed his first painful efforts, but she was wise enough to offer him no help, knowing he would not want it that way. He hobbled out of the small clearing, finding a length of branch that he converted into a cane. He paused at the trail where he could see beyond the slope, out onto the prairie now fading into pale gold under the lowering sun.

She said: "This search for Matt Slade has almost cost you your life. It may yet before it is done with. Why don't you forget it?"

"Forget it?" he echoed in a surprised voice. "How can a man forget such a thing as that?"

"Vengeance is a bitter thing," she murmured. "It will affect and color you as much as it has Matt Slade. And if you catch up with him, what good will it do? It won't bring back your mother, or change what has already happened to your father. It can only result in a death, yours or his, and at best it can end with your becoming an old, broken man, hating everything and everybody and each day of your life."

"You think a man like Slade deserves to live? To enjoy what he has taken at the cost of two lives?"

"I think he likely has already paid for what he did in many ways. He could be dead himself, and you might be wasting your life chasing a shadow, but if he is not, his days cannot be pleasant ones, not with that memory in his mind."

He came slowly back into the clearing, back to where she still knelt by the fire. The coffee was just beginning to boil, and she added another handful of twigs to the flames, extracting all the remaining strength from the overworked grounds.

"It sounds simple, the way you put it," he said, settling down beside her. "But it's a thing I could never do. I live for one thing . . . to settle with Matt Slade. I'll find out, somehow, if Preston was Slade. If he wasn't, then I'll start to look again."

A small sigh passed through Ann's lips, and her shoulders fell slightly. She lifted the tin of coffee and placed it on the ground near him. "There is little of anything you'll do until that leg is healed."

"I'll manage," he replied. He took up the coffee, offering it first to her. When she shook her head, he tipped it to his wide mouth and drank it down. He said then: "How far are we from open ground?"

"Two miles, more or less."

"It will be dark by the time we reach it, if we start now. We'll have to chance their seeing us on the trail. I've a sudden feeling we had better get out of here."

She rose and stamped out the fire. That done, she walked to where the buckskin and her own pony were picketed at the edge of the clearing. Brokaw, back on his feet once more, checked the loads of his gun and shoved it back into the holster. He could not remember replacing the spent cartridges, but somewhere along the way he had done so. A sort of reflex action, he guessed. He was feeling much better, the combination of hot drink, rest, water, food, and his own immense vitality coming to his rescue.

Ann moved up with the horses, and he prepared to mount. He forgot the leg momentarily, shifting his weight so that it fell fully upon it. It gave away as a solid sheet of pain swept through him. He staggered back, coming against Ann. He threw out his arms to catch himself, and her arms went around him, steadying him, and for a moment they stood that way, locked in embrace.

A sudden gust, wild as spring wind, went through Frank Brokaw. He dipped his head downward and crushed his mouth against Ann's lips for a breathless, sweet space of time. She did not resist, did not pull away. And then some of her calmness touched him, and he released her. He took a short, half step backward, his eyes serious as he studied her face.

She met his gaze straight on, the whisper of a smile on her lips. "Don't regret that," she murmured softly.

He shook his head. "A thing I'll never do."

For a moment they stood there, two people fully aware of each other for the first time, and their own deep emotions—and being unafraid. But the urgency of time was pressing hard at him. He turned again to the buckskin.

Pulling himself into the saddle, he waited for her to mount and take the trail ahead of him. His own horse, rested, fed, and no longer harried by thirst, dropped in behind Ann's spotted pony willingly enough. The first flush of recovery had passed with Brokaw's extra efforts, and he was again feeling the drag of his wound and loss of blood. But he made no mention of it. Riding was painful, and at each step of the buckskin, bracing itself with stiff knees on the downgrade, fire rocketed through his body. When Ann glanced over her shoulder to see if he wanted a minute's rest, he shook his head.

The going was slow along the slope. Brokaw tried to maintain a sharp watch to the rear and along the sides of the mountain, but the brush was thick, and he had little success. He heard nothing that caused any alarm. That assured him somewhat; a single rider, much less a whole posse coming along the rock trail, would be certain to set up a loud clatter. It was just closing dark when they came to the end of the path and broke onto the prairie. He saw then the first indication of the posse.

A lone rider. He was high on the mountain, sitting his horse on a ridge that circled the highest peak and furnished him with a broad, far-reaching view of the entire country. Brokaw spoke his warning to Ann, and they halted, watching the silhouetted horseman with close scrutiny. After a long five minutes the rider swung about and struck northward.

They followed him for a short time, then he was gone from sight, dropping behind a bald knob that thrust up from the piling rocks.

"Did he see us?"

Brokaw shook his head, easing himself to one side of the saddle. "Hard to say. My guess is that he did. We were pretty much out in the open that last half mile. But if he did, we've got the advantage of time. He's got to come down off that mountain and get word to the others. That will take an hour, even more."

"We can get to the ranch before then," Ann said.

Brokaw said: "No, Ann, I'm heading on to the west. I'll make the next ranch and hole up there until my leg gets better. Then I'll be back."

At once she said: "That's foolish! It's more than fifty miles to the McCausland's, the nearest ranch. At least a hundred beyond that to the next town. You're in no shape to travel even the fifty."

"I can't hang around here. That's what they are figuring I'll do."

"You can come to our place, to the Double-R. If just for the night. Then I could tend that leg properly, and you could get some rest. Besides, you'll need supplies."

It made sense, Brokaw had to admit. But if Godfrey found him at the Double-R, the wrath of Arrowhead would descend with full force upon Ann and her brother. He said: "I can't do it, Ann. There would be no end to the trouble it would cause if Ollie found me there. And if that rider spotted us, it will be the first place they will look tomorrow."

"That's just it," she said. "Spending the night won't be dangerous for us. And you'll be gone early in the morning. Anyway, we're only guessing that Ollie's man saw us, and we won't be seen now. It's too dark."

Brokaw again considered the man on the horse etched against the night sky. Perhaps he had not seen them, and he would be a long time getting down the mountain, if he had. He nodded. "All right. We'll ride to your place and talk it over with your brother. If he's agreeable, I'll stay the night and be glad for your kindness."

He saw her face lift suddenly to him, as if his words had hurt her, as if they carried a far lesser meaning than she had hoped. But she said nothing. She wheeled her spotted pony around, and together they started for the ranch.

XIV

They rode into the yard at Double-R shortly after nine o'clock. George Ross met them, a tall figure holding a lantern above his head. He was worried, and he showed it on his face. He stopped short before them, recognizing Brokaw. "Ann... where the hell have you...?"

"Help me, George," she broke in, sliding from her saddle. "He's been shot."

Ross set the lantern on the ground and moved up to assist her, placing his hands under Brokaw's shoulders and pulling him off the buckskin as gently as possible. Brokaw, breathing hard from the pain, grinned his thanks to the rancher, and in that same moment the inconsistency of his own feeling struck him. Here he was accepting the aid and hospitality of a man he had come to suspect as one he might be forced to kill!

"What happened? Who shot him?" Ross asked of Ann.

"Ollie Godfrey," Ann replied. "We must get him inside where I can doctor that leg."

With Ann on one side, Ross on the other, they started for the house. Ann sketched briefly the things that had taken place at Arrowhead and, later, on the slope of the Diablos. At the doorway George Ross halted. In the pale moonlight his face was sharp, his gray hair pure silver. He said: "You shouldn't have brought him here, Ann. You know that. This man means trouble."

241

Ann lifted shocked eyes to her brother. "But he's hurt! Don't you understand that . . . he's been shot, probably as a result of what he did for us. We can't refuse to help him!"

Ross changed his attention to Brokaw. "Nothing personal in this," he said. "But we haven't much show against Arrowhead, once they take it in mind to crawl us. I have to try and avoid all the trouble I can with them."

Brokaw nodded, but he was having his own thoughts about the matter. Was George Ross truly afraid of Godfrey and Arrowhead—or did he have another reason for not wanting him around? But Ann was involved, and she could get hurt if Arrowhead struck. He would not have that, regardless of the cost to himself. Before he could speak, Ann said: "It will be just for tonight. Long enough to get him ready to travel. He plans to leave in the morning."

"Makes little difference," Ross answered. "When Ollie and his bunch can't find him, where will they look next? Right here, of course. They know there's no other place he could go."

"He's right," Brokaw said then. "This is no good, Ann. Help me back to my horse and I'll move on."

"No!" Ann said in a flat, determined voice. "You will do no such thing. You'll stay here until I can get that leg dressed. We can do that much . . . even if we are afraid of Arrowhead!"

For a moment George Ross said nothing. Then: "You're right of course, Ann. Maybe it's time to stop running from Arrowhead." He turned to Brokaw. "Forget what I said. You're welcome to stay here until you're ready to travel."

Brokaw saw pride move into Ann's eyes, as if she was glad her brother had finally stopped and was at last going to face up to his trouble. They helped him on into the house and to a back bedroom. Her own, he guessed, judging from the bottles and other feminine gimcracks on the dresser. He sat down heavily on the bed and lay back, dead beat from the ride.

"I'll stay here a short while," he said, brushing at his eyes. "That's understood."

"We'll see," Ann murmured, and left the room.

He came awake minutes later to her touch. She was removing the improvised bandages from his leg. A low table had been dragged up to the bedside and a pan of steaming water, several medicines, and a supply of fresh white bandages lay upon it. George Ross, his face expressionless, stood quietly in the doorway.

Ann smiled at him, soft and sweetly, when she saw his eyes were open. She continued to work, washing the wound with the hot water, swabbing it with some sort of fiery disinfectant that caused him to stiffen and squirm a bit, and then salving it over with cool ointment. Finished, she got to her feet and set the table back out of the way. Brokaw struggled to sit up. At once she turned to him, pressing him down into the comfort of the bed. "Not yet. Not until you've had another hour's rest. And something to eat."

From the door Ross said nothing, but the tight lines of his face reflected his thoughts and the worry in his eyes was undeniable. Again Brokaw had his wonderment at the man's true reason for nervousness, was he actually afraid of Godfrey and Arrowhead—or did he fear to have Brokaw around? He then said: "It's no good, Ann. My being here. I won't stay and cause you trouble."

"We've had it before," she said lightly. "More of it will be nothing new."

"Not the kind Ollie will bring this time," Brokaw said. "And I won't have you hurt because of me." He swung his attention to Ross. "If you'll stake me to a sack of grub and a canteen of water, I'll pull out of here."

Ann was looking at him, her eyes stricken. Her shoulders

went down with their despair, and she shrugged in a hopeless, tired way.

"It's the only sensible thing to be done, Ann," Ross said.

"There's no sense to anything," she replied. "No reason, at all."

Ross wheeled away, going to fill Brokaw's needs. Brokaw came to a sitting position and worked himself off the edge of the bed. He crossed to where Ann stood and took her gently into his arms. "You must understand this . . . I can't be found here. I can't let myself cause you trouble."

"It wouldn't matter, as long as we were together," she whispered in a faraway voice.

"I know, but can't you see, I could never live with myself if something happened to you, because of me. It's the best that I leave now, but I'll be back. You can depend on that. Nothing is as important as seeing you again."

"Not even your looking for this Matt Slade?"

He waited out a long minute, studying his answer to the question. He said finally: "I can't answer that, Ann. I don't know yet. It's a problem that will take some thinking. But I will come back."

"How can you be so sure?" she cried, holding tightly to his arms. "How can you be sure you'll reach the next ranch or town? That Ollie won't follow you and hunt you down? Against him, in the condition you're in, you wouldn't have a chance!"

"I don't kill easy," Brokaw said with a short laugh. "You know that now. And believing that you will be here, safe and sound, waiting for me, will give me that much more strength."

"I'll be worried, wondering. . . ," she began.

Brokaw bent down, checking the words with his kiss. For a long minute he held her close, soaking in the feel of her body pressed against his own, the softness of her, the freshness of her hair. He was having his own great difficulties in comprehending the moment: why, when he had found the solitary thing in his life that really mattered to him, was he being forced to leave it? But it would not end here; he would find a place to hide, to rest and recover from his wound, and then would be back. Nothing could keep him from Ann. "You'll be here?" he asked softly.

"Until you come back," she replied. "No matter how long it takes."

From the doorway George Ross said: "Everything's ready, Brokaw. Grub in your saddlebags. Canteen is full. You got plenty of ammunition?"

Brokaw stepped away from Ann. "I've plenty."

Ann turned from him, and he followed her to where her brother waited. Ross said: "We'll help you to the barn."

They crossed the yard to the large, sprawling building. The ranch was still, almost deserted it seemed. Ross, seeing the wonder on Brokaw's face, said: "Crew's all out on night herd. Three men's all we hire."

They reached the barn and entered. A lantern hung inside the wide, double doors, throwing a fan of yellow light down the runway and into the first stalls. The buckskin, saddled and ready to travel, munched at the manger, getting in a final meal. Farther along, Ann's spotted pony waited to have his gear removed.

Ross said: "I hung a little sack of grain for the horse on the horn. You may need it before you get where you're going."

Brokaw turned away from him, from Ann, a breathless sort of feeling closely akin to fear racing through him. He moved deeper into the first stall that had been made over into a tack room for the gear and other equipment. His eyes were upon a saddle racked upon the bar, a saddle with heavy silver trimmings, with silver dollars mounted along its skirt just as he had been told they were. He reached out a hand. It trembled slightly from the emotion that ripped through him as he ran his fingertips over the deep, handsome tooling. There was no doubt. He came back to face them.

"Who," he asked in a tight voice, "does this belong to?"

XV

In that suspended fragment of time, following his question, Frank Brokaw remembered many things: the way George Ross had reacted to his presence at the ranch, his anxiety to have him out of there and on his way, the swiftness with which the rancher complied with his request for food and water. But most of all he recalled Ann's words back in the shaded glen on the slopes of the Sierra del Diablo: "Vengeance is a bitter thing. It will affect you as much as it will Matt Slade." It would be better forgotten, she had meant. Was she thinking of her own brother when she spoke those words?

He could not believe it; he would not. But he faced them both with a stiff mask that covered the torment raging through him. Ann—the one woman who had, in a lifetime, come to mean more than a passing fancy to him—the sister of a man for whom he had searched and sworn to kill. "Yours?" He pushed the question at Ross.

Ann said: "No, it's mine."

Brokaw stared at her unbelievingly. "How can it be yours?"

"It was given to me. Why?"

Relief began to flow through Brokaw. "Who gave it to you?"

She gave him a wondering look. "Is it so important? It was given to me by a man who once worked here. As a birthday gift. And then he left, went away."

247

"Who," Brokaw said again, "who gave it to you?"

Ann said: "Ollie Godfrey."

Godfrey!

A sigh passed through Brokaw's lips, and the tension slipped from his taut frame. The alleviation that came with the knowledge that it was not George Ross, not Ann's brother, was like the lifting of a dark and heavy cloud from his mind, almost overshadowing the fact that he knew who Matt Slade was, that the trail had come to an end.

Ann was regarding him with disturbed eyes. "What is it, Frank? What's wrong?"

"Ollie is Matt Slade," he said.

Realization came swiftly to Ann. Her eyes spread into wide circles of surprise as the meaning and its implications grew upon her. "But you can't . . . not in your condition."

Brokaw shook his head. "This changes it all. But I'll not wait here for him. I'll find him and have it over with."

George Ross spoke for the first time in many minutes. "What's this all about? Who is Matt Slade?"

"No time to explain it," Brokaw said, moving toward the stall where the buckskin waited. "Ann can tell you later. You say Ollie worked here for a time. Know much about him?"

"Only that he came with a lot of money. Wanted to buy in with Hugh Preston, but Hugh wouldn't hear of it. I think they were acquainted before they came into this country."

Ann had turned and now blocked his way. She looked earnestly into his face. "I won't let you do it. You won't have a chance. At least wait until tomorrow, until we can go in to town and get Sheriff Marr. He will listen to you."

Brokaw shook his head. "It's too late for the law, Ann. They'll have nothing to do with it."

"But if we all go. . . ."

"No," said Brokaw in a final tone, "it's my affair. I'll handle it my way."

He pushed her gently aside, moving toward the buckskin. There was a sudden rush of horses in the yard.

A voice yelled: "Ross!"

Brokaw came around in a swift, circling motion. Ann clutched at his arm, staying him. Ross gave them a quick glance and moved to the doorway. He pushed half the double width again a yard or so, and stepped outside. "Yes?"

There was a sound of horses coming nearer. Ollie Godfrey said: "You've overstepped yourself this time, Ross. You've got a killer hid out here somewhere. I want him. Either you turn him over to me, or I'll burn this place down to find him. Make your choice."

Brokaw said: "Get out of the way, Ross. This is my fight."

The rancher did not turn or make any sign he had heard. To Godfrey he said: "Who says he's here?"

"I do," another voice spoke up. "Watched him and that sister of yours ride off the mountain and head this way."

Brokaw thrust Ann roughly back into the stall. "Stand back, Ross!"

"No!" Ann cried. "You can't go out there! You can't stand against them all!"

"What'll it be, Ross? You trottin' him out or do we come after him?"

Ross said—"You'll have to come after him!"—and drew his gun. He snapped two quick shots at the riders and leaped back, dragging the door closed with him. There was a blast of gunfire. Bullets splintered through the planking of the barn and slammed into the thicker boards of the stalls. Ross, caught in the runway, staggered against the wall and dropped to one knee. Ann cried out, and Brokaw, heedless of his leg, leaped to the man's side. With Ann's help, he dragged him into the shelter of the stall.

"You damned fool!" Brokaw said in a furious, savage voice. "This is no quarrel of yours!"

Ross smiled up at him. "Always has been but I didn't want to face up to it. Should have called Ollie's hand a long time ago."

"Stay with him," Brokaw said to Ann.

He moved back into the runway. More bullets splatted against the doors and front walls of the structure. He kept low, pointing for the small window that offered a vantage point from which to shoot. Reaching it, he looked out. A half dozen riders were wheeling about in the yard. They had started a fire, and flames were licking at the sides of the main house and the wagon shed. A man, a torch blazing in his hand, came toward the barn, his intent plain. Brokaw leveled a shot at him. The cowboy dropped the torch and folded out of the saddle, his horse shying off into the darkness beyond the flare of light.

An answering hail of bullets came after that, setting up their cracking sounds and thudding into the thicker timbers.

"There any other way out of here?" Brokaw called over his shoulder. He was firing regularly, keeping the riders clear of the barn on its front side. It would not be long, he knew, until they began to concentrate on the other walls. There would be no holding them then.

Ann said: "No. Only the windows and they're too small and high. Like the one you're at."

"We've got to get you out of here. And your brother. He needs a doctor bad." He turned back to the shattered window. "Ollie!"

Godfrey's answer came back to him. "Yeah? That you, Brokaw?"

Brokaw said: "Ann's in here. And her brother is with her.

He's been hit. Hold your fire and let them out. You've got no cause to hurt them. It's me you're after."

"Ross shot one of my boys there a minute ago. And there's a few other things I've got to settle with him."

"Let Ann pass, then."

"I'll not go," Ann said firmly from the depths of the stall. "I won't do it!"

Godfrey's voice said: "You'll all come out together, or none of you'll come out. Makes no difference to me."

A shot followed his words. A bullet smashed into the remaining glass of the window, showering Brokaw with stinging slivers. The main house was a roaring inferno. Flames were leaping high into the night, casting weird, dancing shadows in the yard. Somewhere a dog barked hysterically, and riders whipped in and out, shooting at will, paying little heed to Brokaw's single gun. He was at a disadvantage, his scope for shooting hampered and limited. Maybe, if he could get into the loft, he would be in a better position to keep them at a distance away from the structure.

He emptied his gun at the Arrowhead riders and ducked back into the stall where Ross and Ann were. The rancher was sitting up, holding one hand to a stain on his left breast. His face was gray, the muscles sagging, but his eyes burned with a feverish brightness. "I'll give you a hand in a minute," he said as Brokaw dropped beside him.

"How bad is it?"

Ross said: "Hard to tell. Lots of blood but we've about got it stopped."

Brokaw was not hearing him. He was getting his answer from the rancher's drawn features and the slow drag of his breath.

Ross said: "I think I can manage it now. Just help me up."

Together they got him to his feet. He leaned back against

251

the stall, grinning. Sweat lay across his face in an oily shine, and the effort to stand was costing him dearly. He drew his gun and pointed it at the door.

"I'll hold the fort," he said with a pretense of jocularity. "You two take a look in the back of the barn for another door. Seems to me like there's one there somewhere. Near the northwest corner. Look behind all that stuff that's piled there." He paused, coughing a little. "Stay close to the wall," he cautioned.

Brokaw was watching him with narrow suspicion.

Ross caught his gaze and gave him a brief, hard grin as Ann slipped out of the stall. "It's all right," he murmured. "You look after her."

Ann tugged at Brokaw's arm, and he followed her into the runway. The yelling and shouting had increased outside, and there was a *thump,* as something struck the front of the barn and fell to the ground. Probably a torch. They kept close to the stalls, past the second one in which the buckskin stood, the third that sheltered Ann's little pony. The runway turned to right angle.

"I can't remember seeing any door," Ann said. "That will be the corner George spoke about."

Together they crossed to the point indicated by Ross, piled high with old wagon wheels, harness, broken tools, and other such items.

"Take an hour to move all that stuff," Brokaw observed. "And we don't have that kind of time. We've got to figure another way out."

A yell lifted near the front of the barn, near the doorway. Brokaw wheeled and hurried as best he could toward the runway. The door was swinging back, opening onto the confusion and glare of the yard. George Ross, astride Brokaw's buckskin and leading Ann's pony was momentarily outlined blackly against the lurid background. The gun in his hand roared, and the buckskin leaped into the open, dragging the pony after him.

"George!" Ann screamed, and started for the doorway.

Brokaw seized her arm and pulled her to one side as guns cracked and bullets sang by them. Ross, bending low in the saddle, weaving uncertainly as he fought to stay on the buckskin, cut sharply right through the smoky gloom. A chorus of yells sang out as Godfrey and the others caught sight of the plunging horses. Another welter of gunshots ripped through the night, and then all went thundering across the yard in pursuit.

Understanding came then to Frank Brokaw. He took Ann's hand in his own. "Come on!" he cried, and started down the runway.

They reached the doorway, and paused there. Brokaw threw a searching glance over the yard. It was empty, all the riders having given chase to Ross. To Ann he said: "Any more horses around?"

"In the lower corral," she replied in a dazed, wooden voice. "To the left."

They slipped through the doors into the open. The front of the barn was starting to burn in three or four places, and they were compelled to swing out a distance from it to escape the rapidly climbing flames. Moving as fast as he could, they reached the corner of the doomed building and turned. The corral was still a long distance away, a hundred yards at least, but it was beyond the fire's glare.

A spatter of shots came from the south, from the direction taken by Ross. They seemed to be some distance away, indicating the rancher had drawn Arrowhead's riders off considerably.

Ann, at his shoulder, said: "George did that . . . made a

break for it to pull them off so we could escape."

Brokaw said: "Yes. Knew he didn't have much chance of making it with that hole in his chest, so he chases us off into the back of the barn and then runs for it."

"Why did he take my horse, too? That slowed him down. He would have had a better chance if he hadn't done that."

"I guess he figured Ollie would think it was the two of us. He knew George was shot. When he saw the two horses come out of the barn, he probably thought we were all that was left. That's what your brother wanted him to think, otherwise he would have left some men in the yard."

They reached the corral. A half dozen horses milled nervously about, sticking into a bunch in the far corner. In the dim starlight, aided only slightly by the fire's glare, they caught two of the animals. Both were haltered, but there were no saddles available.

"Can you manage bareback?" he asked.

Ann nodded. "But what about you? How can you ride with that leg in the shape it's in?"

He said: "Don't worry. It seems a lot better. I guess a little exercise is what I needed. . . ."

She was looking away from him then, back toward the burning Double-R. He knew she was thinking of her brother. "Don't worry about him," he said, laying his arm around her shoulders. "It was the way he wanted it. The last thing he said was for me to look out for you."

"He was the kindest man I ever knew," she said, and began to cry softly. But at once she checked herself. Brushing away the tears with the back of her hand, she said: "What do we do now? We can't stay here. Ollie and the rest will be back when they see they've been tricked."

"Can you ride to town?"

"If that's what you want me to do."

"Good. Get Ben Marr and bring him to Arrowhead. I'll be waiting there for you."

She studied his face for a moment. "Will that be wise? Won't Ollie go there, too? And the rest of the Arrowhead riders?"

"Maybe," Brokaw replied softly. "But you get Marr and bring him out. I want him to hear Darla Preston's confession."

He helped her mount, and, when she was seated, she leaned down and gave him her kiss. "Be careful," she murmured, and rode off into the darkness.

XVI

It was well after midnight when Brokaw reached Arrowhead. The ranch was a silent cluster of darkened buildings except for the main house, where the windows of the front room showed their squares of yellow light. He pulled up in the deep shadows on the north side and slid wearily from his horse. It had been a long and painful journey, one that had done his injured leg no good.

He stood for a time in the pool of blackness, formed by a spreading cedar thrusting its branches against the starlight, and let the stiffness fade from his muscles and a measure of life work back into the wounded leg. Walking was a difficult task, and this worried him. He had no plan, having given it little thought until this moment; there was only purpose— force Darla Preston to clear his name, then settle with Ollie Godfrey. Darla would be in the house now, alone. Godfrey would come later.

Moving quietly and with involuntary slowness, he crossed the narrow intervening ground and reached the corner of the house. He followed along the wall until he came to the door leading into Preston's office, and there he paused, praying that luck was with him, that the door would not be locked. He placed his fingers on the doorknob and, with infinite care, twisted.

The slab panel opened without sound. Gathering his faculties, he stepped inside, pushing the door to, but not closing

it, fearing the snap of the catch. He threw his glance into the parlor. The back of Darla Preston's head was partly visible above the thick roll of one of the leather chairs. She was alone, as he had suspected she would be, alone and awaiting Godfrey to return and tell her Brokaw was dead, that the Double-R was gray ashes blowing in the wind, and George and Ann Ross were finished.

He moved a step closer to the portièred archway separating the office from the front room, still unsure as to his best course of action. He came to sudden halt, hearing the rapid drum of a horse coming into the yard. It came to a sliding halt near the rail, and a moment later a man's boot heels beat a tattoo of approach. Darla had risen from her chair and stood now facing the door, her face stilled by expectancy, lamplight spilling over her blonde hair, turning it yellow gold.

The door swung back, and Ollie Godfrey came in. A wide smile was on his mouth, and, as he came to a stop just inside the room, he brushed his hat to the back of his head, giving him a young and reckless appearance. "It's done with!" he said. "Finished."

"Brokaw's dead? And the Rosses?"

"We got Ross in the barn. Brokaw and the girl made a break for it. We went after them, the whole bunch of us. Chased them for miles. When I saw the girl's horse with an empty saddle, I turned around and came back. Be just a matter of time, a few minutes maybe, and they'll have Brokaw."

"But you didn't see him dead?" Darla pressed.

"Not exactly, but he didn't have a chance. Don't worry about it."

"You should have stayed there until you knew for sure," she said, anger sharpening her tone. "I don't like things only half done."

Godfrey crossed to her and threw his arms around her

shoulders. "I've told you, there's no need to worry about it. Brokaw's out of the picture. Now we can go ahead."

Darla pushed him away, falling back a step or two. She was not satisfied, and it showed in her face. Trusting no one but herself, she had utterly no confidence in the promise of things done, only in the actuality.

Godfrey said: "The boys will be here soon. They'll tell you it has all been handled, just the way we wanted it. It's all ours now, sugar . . . Arrowhead and any part of the Double-R we want. We can go right along and do what we planned. I'll ride to Santa Fé tomorrow and get my money from the bank, and then we'll be partners. Partners in the biggest ranch in the country!"

Brokaw stepped from behind the heavy folds of the curtains, coming to a solid, square-shaped stance in the open archway. "No, Ollie. Not tomorrow, not ever."

Godfrey spun about, surprise blanketing his face and dragging down the corners of his mouth.

Darla whirled with him, throwing a hand to her lips to choke back a cry. "You said he was dead!" she shrilled. "I knew you would slip up somewhere."

Godfrey had recovered from his shock. A sly grin crossed his face. "Song's not sung yet," he murmured. "There's still another verse."

Brokaw said: "Don't fool yourself, Slade. This is the end of the road for you. I've hunted you from one end of the country to the other. You'll not get away from me now."

"I can try," Slade said.

"Anytime you're ready."

Darla said: "I'm glad you're not dead, Brokaw. I'm glad you didn't let them kill you. It proves what I've thought all along. You're the one man I can depend on. Our deal still stands."

Brokaw was hearing only words, only sounds. His eyes were on Matt Slade, watching that man with a close and narrow surveillance.

"You hear? You and I will be the partners. We'll own Arrowhead and everything else we want, just like I have said before! We will control this part of the country!"

Darla's voice was a nearly hysterical drone. Matt Slade had slipped into a half crouch, his hand spread-eagled and poised above the gun at his hip. There was no smile on his face now, only a frozen grimace.

"Kill him, Brokaw! Kill him and get him out of our way! And then I'll swear you didn't shoot Hugh, that it was him . . . that he did it, and then ran outside!"

Brokaw saw the break in Slade's eyes, that slight tip-off that telegraphed his intentions. His hand swept up his gun, and Brokaw fired. Slade's own weapon crashed. Brokaw felt the solid wallop of the bullet, like a blow from a massive fist, somewhere high up on his right breast. He shot again at the buckling shape of Slade, dim and wavering in the boiling smoke, and through it all Darla's voice was a high, shrilling scream, overriding all else. And then he felt himself falling backwards. He clutched at the portières, hung there momentarily, until the cloth ripped and gave way, and he dropped heavily to the floor. He remembered nothing else.

They found him that way, lying half in the parlor, half in Hugh Preston's office, the heavy drapes all but covering him. There was Ann, Sheriff Ben Marr, Abel Cameron, and Jules Strove. They carried him into the bedroom and made him comfortable, while Strove went to Westport Crossing for the doctor. Ann, not waiting, dressed the ugly wound and gave it the care it needed.

Slade was dead, shot twice. Darla Preston, her mind

giving way under the fierce pressures that lashed it, broke down and told Marr all he wanted to know, and Frank Brokaw was a free man. There had been letters in Matt Slade's pocket that cleared up the matter in Central City.

"Your daddy's a free man, son," Ben Marr told him. "Things in these here letters from Missus Preston to Godfrey . . . I mean, Slade . . . prove he had nothin' to do with the bank robbery. Reckon it proves somethin' else, too. Slade had a mite of conscience, after all. Looks like he wrote her to send your ma some money to tide her over. Darla's letter says she sent it, but I reckon we won't ever know if she did or not."

A deep peace had settled in Frank Brokaw. He was seeing Ann, sitting close by and thinking it was all over, that the long trails had ended, and there were no dark shadows in the background or waiting in the future. There were new things to talk of, things like a trip to Leavenworth and getting a fine old man released to their custody, the farm in Kansas that was waiting to be worked, or perhaps it would be the rebuilding of the Double-R. It was good to dream of the days ahead. Good to make plans. It was especially good to know he would be making them with Ann.

About the Author

Ray Hogan was an author who inspired a loyal following over the years since he published his first Western novel, *Ex-Marshal*, in 1956. Hogan was born in Willow Springs, Missouri, where his father was town marshal. When he was five, the Hogan family moved to Albuquerque where they lived in the foothills of the Sandia and Manzano mountains. His father was on the Albuquerque police force and, in later years, owned the Overland Hotel. It was while listening to his father and other old-timers tell tales from the past that Ray was inspired to recast these tales in fiction. From the beginning he did exhaustive research into the history and the people of the Old West, and the walls of his study were lined with various firearms, spurs, pictures, books, and memorabilia, about all of which he could talk in dramatic detail. "I've attempted to capture the courage and bravery of those men and women that lived out West and the dangers and problems they had to overcome," Hogan once remarked. If his lawmen protagonists seem sometimes larger than life, it is because they are men of integrity, heroes who through grit of character and common sense are able to overcome the obstacles they encounter despite often overwhelming odds. This same grit of character can also be found in Hogan's heroines, and in *The Vengeance of Fortuna West* (1983) Hogan wrote a gripping and totally believable account of a woman who takes up the badge and tracks the men who killed her lawman husband by

ambush. No less intriguing in her way is Nellie Dupray, convicted of rustling in *The Glory Trail* (1978). One of his most popular books, dealing with an earlier period in the West with Kit Carson as its protagonist, is *Soldier in Buckskin* (Five Star Westerns, 1996). Above all, what is most impressive about Hogan's Western novels is the consistent quality with which each is crafted, the compelling depth of his characters, and his ability to juxtapose the complexities of human conflict into narratives always as intensely interesting as they are emotionally involving. *Valley of the Wandering River* will be his next **Five Star Western**.